Other Works by the Author

Books

The Anzio Death Trap
Flower Power
Shaft
Absolute Zero
Shaft Among the Jews
Shaft's Big Score
Shaft Has a Ball
Shaft's Carnival of Killers
Goodbye Mr. Shaft
The Last Shaft
Dummy

Films

The French Connection
Shaft
High Plains Drifter
Shaft's Big Score

Line of Duty

Line of Duty

a novel by

Ernest Tidyman

Little, Brown and Company

Boston - Toronto

FIRST EDITION

T 10/74

LIBRARY OF CONGRESS CATALOGING IN PUBLICATION DATA

Tidyman, Ernest.
  Line of duty.

  I. Title.
PZ4.T5588Li   [PS3570.I3]   813'.5'4   74-8940
ISBN 0-316-845116

Published simultaneously in Canada
by Little, Brown & Company (Canada) Limited

PRINTED IN THE UNITED STATES OF AMERICA

For Ben R. Tidyman

Sometimes we walked the halls of Cleveland's Central
Police Station together late at night. Passing policemen
nodded respectfully to this thin, angular man with vest
pockets bulging pencils, brown felt hat cocked over gold-
rimmed spectacles and soft parchment skin wrinkled in
smiles of sardonic amusement or frowns of bitter cyni-
cism. He looked the way a newspaperman should — a
strong man. a wise man. an interesting man. He was a
reporter's reporter who had trained scores of young jour-
nalists — including his sons Robert and Ernest — and
his hazel cat's eyes had seen it all.

"Ernest," he said one night. "there is only one reason
this burg Cleveland exists. It's a place to stop between
New York and Chicago and piss in the river."

Spoken like the honest gentleman he was.

Line of Duty

chapter one

THE BUILDING SMELLED like an old bum. Dempsey's nose wrinkled in a slight sniff of distaste. A tall man, slender in a dark gray suit, he moved down the hallway with quiet control. A single bulb cut the gloom. If any of the doors had opened on their worn hinges, Dempsey would have appeared to be just another shadow drifting in the darkness. Until his face came close — blue-black eyes set deep beneath a strong brow the dark hair curled tightly back around his skull and behind his ears. At forty-three, Dempsey's hair was in retreat and it had the effect of bringing his face to a point at the sharp nose and the long, narrow chin. It made him look hard and ruthless — like an insurance premium collector among the poor.

He stopped at the dark panel of a wooden door hidden under a decade's layer of cheap enamel.

"Yeah?" The voice behind the door sounded worried. Dempsey could hear it. Everybody on the other side of the doors in his life sounded worried.

"Dempsey," he said to the door. "Open up."

There was a hesitation before the turning of the key. Then the bolt knob turned and the door cracked slightly open on a three-inch section of guard chain that cut across the face of Max Godansky. Worried Max Godansky, with circles under his eyes. Dempsey thought he looked like the descendant of a circus monkey who had escaped his cage in Warsaw, the nose flat, the cheekbones broad and high, the eyes too small and vaguely oriental in a flat, broad face. And the forehead a kind of white cupcake with short, cropped hair on it instead of frosting.

"Come on, Polack, open the goddamned door."

It closed quickly, the chain slipped away, and then it opened again.

Godansky was walking away from him on short, bowed legs as it swung open, the muscles of his back rippling under the white cotton T-shirt as he raised a can of Carling's and pulled at it. He put the black and red container down on the porcelain-topped table in the middle of the room. The long barrel of the .38 Smith & Wesson service revolver in his right hand threw a longer shadow on the table as he turned around and held it on a line with Dempsey's left kneecap.

"What do you want?"

Dempsey ignored the gun. And Godansky. He looked around the barren wasteland of a room, the daybed sagging against the floor like a lumpy rectangle of brown clay, the linoleum fading from unswept corners to the center of the room where all its pattern disappeared, the rickety spindleback chairs so long without paint that the raw wood showed through, the oilcloth shades at half-mast on the curtainless windows.

"I hope you get this place in shape before the *House Beautiful* people come to take pictures," Dempsey said. "Do something about the smell, too." He looked directly at the small, dark eyes. "Maybe take a bath."

"What do you want?"

Dempsey nodded at him.

"I want you to put a shirt on and come downtown with me."

The line of the gun rose from his kneecap to the thigh. He ignored it. Ignoring the gun was very important.

"The usual bullshit," he said, looking around the room again in the other direction. "You'll be asked a bunch of questions."

"About what?"

"About *what*?" Sometimes it was hard to believe how dumb these Polacks could be. "What difference does it make what the questions are about? You just say 'no' every goddamned time. You keep saying 'no' until your asshole turns to emeralds. . . ." He took a deep breath, the sigh of a resigned educator. "And then you come back here and sit in your own stink."

Dempsey shook his head at the room. There was a fly-speck tattoo on the wall over the three-hundred-year-old refrigerator where Godansky probably kept the rest of his beer. He had never met a Polack in his life who wasn't within three feet of a beer, hot, cold or half-consumed.

"Put on a shirt and let's go. And give me the gun. They don't let civilians carry them in the station since the nigger came in and shot Lieutenant Czerny in the balls. Come on."

It was time to show impatience with Godansky. Dempsey put his hands on his hips and stared at the smaller man. He had been in the room five minutes. He only had about five more. Now the gun was pointing at his belt buckle. How did it feel to take one there? Like somebody was trying to drive a bread truck through your liver and out your spine. No good.

Godansky was sweating. "Listen, goddamnit. I ain't taking no bust. You got that? If I'm goin' down there,

I'm comin' out clean, same way as I'm goin' in. You got that?"

It was all right. Godansky had decided that he was going. There wouldn't be one in the belt buckle.

"Oh, come on. Stop the goddamned games. Give me the gun before my partner sticks his big red nose in the door and blows your head off." The little eyes flickered nervously at the door. "I go off duty in thirty-five minutes and I ain't going to screw up the evening over you." Sternly now taking charge. "Stop screwing around."

Dempsey pointed a finger at the gun in Godansky's bloodless white hand. When they got scared, all the blood drained to their feet. That's why they could run so fast when you caught them stealing.

Something in Godansky's eyes relaxed. He flipped the pistol around and extended the butt to Dempsey. What was that small shade of light? Fear? No, besides that it was the crushed look of a man asking for charity a break. Dempsey had seen it before. Now he remembered what it was. Mercy. Sure Max. Merciful justice.

"Get dressed," he said.

Godansky turned with a slight shudder and picked up the blue cotton shirt he had hung over the back of one of the chairs. He pulled it on and made his stubby blunt fingers punch the buttons through the holes. Monkey hands, Dempsey thought. The plaid work jacket was hanging from a hook screwed into the wall and Godansky got it in silence, holding the cuffs of his shirt as he wormed into it.

Dempsey was looking at the Smith & Wesson while Godansky found the groove of the zipper and pulled it up tight. As near as he could tell, all six chambers were loaded. One chamber was in line with the barrel and he couldn't see that. Or the one at the bottom of the cylinder in line with the frame. But the four chambers visible on either side of the barrel brimmed with fat little pig noses of lead. He held it in his left hand.

"Okay," Godansky said. "Let's go."

Dempsey took his own Colt .38 Python from its holster under his arm, raised it, and shot him through the heart. The first bullet smashed dying Max Godansky back against the table and splattered a tablespoon of blood among the other crimes that had been committed against its surface. The second bullet got him in the right wall of the chest and lifted him in a slow arc upward and around toward the floor on the other side of the collapsing table. There, the third slug ripped into his chest just below his throat, smashing the yoke of his collarbone into fragments. It was excellent shooting. Godansky had been a moving target for the last two.

Dempsey put his revolver away and switched Godansky's weapon to his right hand. He reached for his handkerchief even as he walked the few steps across the faded. squeaking linoleum to squat beside Max Godansky's corpse.

The midnight-to-eight shift turned Gorman's head around. It had for the last sixteen years. Once every month, the shifts changed. Once every three months, he was on midnight to eight. And for that entire month he did not like the way he felt when the dying buzz of the little white Westclox alarm drove him out of bed and heckled him through the dark house toward the bathroom and an attempt — no, a forced achievement — of wakefulness.

His eyes were cold blue and looked alert in the mirror over the yellow porcelain sink. The eyes and the brushing he had flashed through the silver-gray hair gave the square and slightly florid face the look of alertness. He always looked alert — even in his sleep, Annie said. It was one basis of his progress in the department: he always looked like an alert cop and it was assumed that he was one.

Gorman's thick right hand moved across his neck and chin with the razor while the other stretched the hide and pulled the whiskers into accessibility. Twelve minutes out of bed, he was showered and shaved. One and a half minutes later, he was moving out of the bathroom, his face still tingling with the razor burn's reaction to the Bay Rum he used as an astringent. A fresh white shirt, almost crackling with starch, was on a wire hanger on the knob of the bedroom door and he hooked it off the way speeding trains used to hook mail pouches from station platforms in the rumbling night.

He had buttoned the cuffs and was starting on the front of it when he got to the kitchen.

"Good morning — or what the hell ever it is," he said.

Annie Gorman turned away from the counter at the sink and smiled at him. She was ready for bed, the ash blond–to–brown hair pinned back in two or three places and her body — a good body, still firm as she came close to forty — was hidden away in a long, dark blue housecoat. She did not like the cold, even though the nights were only cool now, and the housecoat went all the way down past her ankles. He couldn't see if she was wearing slippers or going barefoot, a habit that amused him and, he often thought, defeated her purpose.

"How did you sleep?" she asked.

"I sleep the sleep of the innocent because my heart is pure," he said, reaching for the coffeepot and the mug that had been set out beside it on the yellow GE stove. She liked the golden, creamy color — as close to the sun as she could get. He teased her that so many objects in the house were yellow that he expected to wake up one morning and find that he, too, had been painted to color coordinate.

8

"Good," she said, turning back to the counter. She was preparing the next day's meal — a pork roast out of the freezer, sprinkled with lemon pepper and then wrapped in foil for a slow defrosting. There would be roast potatoes with it and homemade applesauce. He noticed the big red McIntosh apples in a bowl on the sideboard. There was one large one on top of the pile. He thought that it was just about the size of one of her breasts and he wished with a moment's desire that he was not going to work — or that he had just a little more time before he did. Perhaps in the morning. She was wonderful about that. He had always worked a schedule that could have created an agony of frustration. She had coped. She would not rush off into a morning of chores, but would come back to bed and curl up with him in a golden warmth if that was what they wanted. They always seemed to be reaching for each other, whatever the hour. The time was always right.

Gorman finished the first cup of coffee quickly and started on another. He put it down a moment to slip the black wool tie beneath the hard collar and tied it in a simple four-in-hand knot, then finished the coffee. She put the brown paper bag in the refrigerator — they still called it the icebox, as their parents had — and turned to him. Their son's lunch was ready. So was Gorman's good-bye.

She was very warm against him as they embraced and kissed softly.

"Come home to me safely, Michael."

"I will," he promised. A final squeeze.

She did not follow him to the front door. She said it was too much like a good-bye. After all, he was just going to work. He stopped at the hall closet and reached up to the inside wall above the doorframe. Long familiarity sent his hand directly to the .38-caliber Colt automatic hanging by its trigger guard on a nail he had screwed into the plaster years ago. It was the place he checked his gun when he came into the house. There were others, of course, locked away in various secret places. The .38 service revolver he had been issued as a rookie patrolman the lightweight, snub-nosed Detective Special he had purchased when he went onto plainclothes detail as a sergeant, first in burglary, then in the gambling squad. Then this gun, nickel-plated and pearl-handled, a small shield worked in gold inlay along the barrel casing. It was very flashy and it was the only gift he had ever accepted in his years as a policeman. A gift from an automobile dealers' association for directing the detection and arrest of a very large and very smooth group of thieves who were jumping wires and driving new cars right off the lots where the dealers had them on display.

He slipped the gun into the holster on his left hip. He was right-handed and would draw across his belly if he needed it quickly. It was faster and simpler while he was sitting in the car — and easier when he was crouching or running. The gun was covered by the flap of the uniform blouse, the big gold and enamel shield settling heavily over his left breast, over the area that supposedly represented his heart. Then he was ready. He had an overcoat at the office if he needed it.

Then he turned, went quickly out the door and across the lawn to the beige Ford sitting there with its whiplash aerial quivering in the night breeze. He could feel the night was misty, verging on snow. The seat was cold against the small of his back as he turned the key and brought the engine to life. The car was still in good shape, one of the few that hadn't been overworked into premature mechanical arthritis, and he let it idle a minute before he switched on the two-way radio, lighting his face and the interior of the car with the little red light that said he could now communicate with his headquarters. He listened to the crackle of static and the routine calls that were passing back and forth between the station house and the vehicles on the streets.

"101 to Central," he said.

"Go ahead, 101," the dispatcher responded quickly. Either they were awake down there or anticipating his call.

"101 in the Second District and coming downtown."

"Okay, 101. In the Second District. coming downtown." There was a brief pause before the voice continued. "Good morning, Inspector. It's been a busy night."

He did not reply. If it had been a disaster, he would have been called out of bed. Short of that, he'd find out soon enough. He replaced the small, black microphone in its bracket, backed out of the driveway into the street and drove north toward Lake Shore Drive. He was careful not to gun the engine and disturb his neighbors as the car rolled past the large, white frame houses, most of their windows closed and dark with sleep.

He wondered who in his city had chosen this night to commit mayhem upon his neighbor, friend or passing stranger. There was no anxiety about his speculation. The tragedies would be there waiting for him when he got to work.

Independence and Cuyahoga Heights. Newburgh and then the Cleveland line. The wheels of the big Dodge whined against the surface of the Willow Freeway and the sound was a Lorelei to the ears of Harry Prochak. The vibration of the engine flowed up the steering column to his arms and shoulders. It made him one with the machine, an extension of its power. Truckers are born, his old man used to say. That was a fact that Harry Prochak would not deny. He was born to the road, he thought; but he was also a very basic human being. He was a trucker. Glancing at the side mirror, he caught a Volkswagen on his tail, its driver trying to squeeze more juice from the lawnmower engine. Prochak grinned and gave the truck more gas as he saw the small, white car make its move.

"Work for it, bastard," he muttered. "Sweat it out."

The little car struggled past, uphill all the way.

Prochak braked slightly, watching the speedometer needle slip down from 65 to 50. He was running ahead of time. Eleven-thirty, the man had said. Clark Avenue cutoff at 11:30. If he kept screwing around, he would be too early.

It was a good spot, over the municipal line so that the State Police wouldn't bother, and yet far enough out to be almost beyond the concern of the city cops. Prochak touched the air brakes with a tender foot and guided the rig onto the shoulder of the road. He climbed down from the cab and walked to the rear of the truck, taking a flashlight with him. It was cold and a thin, powdery snow drifted across the road like lost scraps of lace. He moved slowly from wheel to wheel, shining the flashlight on the tires as though inspecting them for signs of damage. He could hear the other truck coming, but he did not glance at it. When he reached the rear of his truck, he turned his back to the approaching beams, hearing the truck brake with a scratch of gravel, hearing the doors open, hearing the crunch of footsteps. He gritted his teeth and waited, closing his eyes in anticipation. A hand gripped his shoulder and turned him, almost gently. Then a million flashes of light stabbed his eyeballs and shot through his brain. He did not feel himself falling. He seemed to be floating off into an immensity of space, drifting into dark banks of cloud. He stretched out his hands to touch the stars and felt only the icy hardness of the embankment.

He looked upwards. The two trucks were above him, looming against the night sky like great square buildings. Men moved between them. Prochak shut his eyes and pressed the side of his face against the cold earth. It eased the throb in his temple where a blow had laid open a five-inch gash. Blood flowed in a warm sheet across his forehead and down over the bridge of his nose. It was not an unpleasant sensation. He struggled against the urge to sleep. There were things to be done. He wasn't out of it yet. He forced himself to his knees and reached into his back pocket. The steel handcuffs were jammed sideways and he lost his balance twice in his effort to pull them out, falling farther down the embankment, tearing his pants at the knees as he slid over the hard soil. Finally, the cuffs were free and he held his hands behind his back and snapped them onto his wrists, wincing as one of the steel jaws pinched his flesh.

It was over. It was done. The wind was clearing his head and the blood was stiff across his face, gluing his left eye closed. It took him twenty minutes to make it up the embankment to the road. Where it was steep, he sat down, his back to the road, and dug in his heels. He pushed, five or ten inches at a time, until he rolled over the top and got to his feet. It was clumsy work, his balance difficult with the shackles behind him. The other truck was gone and the back doors of his truck were wide open. He stood, swaying slightly, by the side of the truck. Three cars passed him without slowing down, ignoring his shouts. There was no market for blood-stained hitchhikers. Finally, a panel truck swerved to the side and pulled up beside him. The driver leaned over and rolled down the window on the passenger side. He was a young man, his features taut with fear and concern.

"Jesus! What the hell happened to you?"

"Help me," Prochak gasped. "Call the police . . . I've been hijacked."

The disembodied voice of the police radio dispatchers stayed with Gorman all the way downtown. They were his disc jockeys, his news reporters. An early March spring fever was in the air despite the cold wind whipping in off Lake Erie and the snow that still annoyed the more distant suburbs after the bitterest winter in memory. The whores were back on the streets and being rounded up. Some garage gamblers had been caught and were being brought in. Not willingly. The gambling detail had called for assistance. There was a hit-and-run at Euclid and East Seventy-fifth Street, a liquor store holdup at Forty-seventh and Hough, a brawl in Scranton Road down in the flats. The hard-core base of the city's crime statistics. There would be more during the night. More brawls as the bars closed . . . a shooting or two . . . several knifings for sure . . . a brick through a store window . . . a few muggings . . . maybe a rape. Gorman barely listened to the flat monotone coming over the receiver. Nothing that he heard was, at the moment, of any concern to him. It was not his responsibility. He didn't go on duty for another ten minutes.

chapter two

INSPECTOR CHARLES GRUEBNER LOOKED sourly at the stack of papers on his desk and then glanced at the clock. Midnight. The red second hand swept on past the 12 and was down to 6 when Gorman came into the office.

"You're late," Gruebner said. "Thirty-three seconds." He eased his bulk out of the chair and stretched his large, beefy hands toward the ceiling. "Jesus, has this been a night. The shit hit the fan about six o'clock and it hasn't stopped flying."

Gorman glanced at the hefty stack of reports. "Tell me your troubles, Dutch."

Gruebner shook his head. "All that crap's self-explanatory. Vice Squad went on a tear. We must have every whore in Ohio upstairs."

Gorman smiled. "It might be a fun night. Stick around."

"Yeah," Gruebner said. "Fun. You should see 'em. They're fighting each other like starving cats." He belched loudly, a gunshot of a belch. "Excuse me. Don't eat at that new place over on Walnut. They've got a cook who hates cops."

"What'd you have?" Gorman asked, taking off his jacket, hanging it in his locker beside the door.

Gruebner belched again. "Who knows? Something under tomato sauce." He opened the top drawer of the desk and took out a gun in a worn, black leather clip holster. He hooked it on his belt, just under the pouch of his ample waist. The pistol in no way altered Gruebner's appearance. He looked like a stolid brewmeister with an inordinate fondness for his own product. The gun seemed out of place.

It was deceptive. Gruebner was old in the job at sixty-one, a commander whose life bridged the old and the new. He had a grandson in a beat car in the Fifth District of the East Side, and he had been tough enough, wise enough and flexible enough to survive. He could quit anytime he wanted with a thirty-year pension. But not yet. Survival became the game after thirty years. The goal was simply to find another day of life waiting each morning.

"They've got Jimmy Dempsey and Carl Rich up in Homicide making statements. Jimmy dropped a guy he was picking up."

It all comes together: the small talk, the reports on street solicitation, the bitching. Gorman thought, at least he let me get my coat off.

"Who?"

Gruebner got the still-smokable remains of a cigar from the ashtray on the desk and then dumped half a dozen ground-out butts into the wastebasket. The office stank of them.

"A part-time truck driver named Godansky. The clown pulled a gun on Jimmy."

"Max Godansky?"

Gruebner nodded, his big, blunt fingers moving with surprising tenderness over the cigar, smoothing it, wiping off flecks of ash. "Yeah. Max Godansky. You know him?"

"I know *of* him."

"Kiss him good-bye. Three in the chest. Dempsey's having trouble with his ears. All that noise in a small room — but he's okay. Irish luck that close."

"That's what they say." Gorman was troubled, but it wasn't obvious. His wife would have noticed the slight flush in his cheeks, the tenseness of his jaw, and his deliberate effort to be casual. "Might be something in it. Irish luck."

Gruebner made a low sound deep in his throat. It could have been a growl or a belch. "Some luck. Your cousins in Belfast are killing each other off like a bunch of goddamn hillbillies. What does that make for Dempsey? Four?"

"Five."

Gruebner looked at him from under his heavy brows. "Five. The rookies probably wonder if he notches his gun."

"He's a good cop," Gorman said.

"Sure . . . sure. A hell of a cop. Anyway, I don't have a report on this one yet. You'll be getting the statements as soon as Welch can type them up . . . which might be in July."

Gorman smiled. Sergeant Earl Welch was a tall, whip-thin, black homicide detective who could do everything fast except work a typewriter.

"Anything else I should know?"

Gruebner studied the end of his cigar the way a jeweler might look at a watch. "I saved the best for last. There's been another hijacking . . . out on 21. Right on the god-damn freeway! They're sewing up the driver now. Somebody slapped him with a tire iron."

Gorman chewed his bottom lip and walked over to the desk that would be his until eight o'clock in the morning.

"Chief know about it?"

"Oh, hell, yes. He's sputtering like a pressure cooker. You get to call him at home after the driver makes a statement."

17

Gruebner opened his own locker and put on a jacket that was identical to Gorman's. only four sizes larger. The gold braid gave an august dignity to the great bulk.

"This Godansky character " he said doing up the buttons. "How do you know of him?"

Thirty-one years of professional suspicion lay behind the question. The memory became a reflex. Always ask — and ask again until the answers provide a conclusion. Why are you here what have you done, why did you do it? And who is Max Godansky to you?

Gorman sat down behind the desk and rearranged everything slightly shifting the telephone altering the position of the pencil cup to accommodate his reach. "He was a Robbery Squad pigeon. Daley and Winshaw had him on the string. I m supposed to be the only one who knew about it. I cleared it for them."

Gruebner's scowl corrugated his face. "If he was a pigeon, why would he pull a gun on Dempsey?"

Gorman toyed with the pencils in the holder. "Dutch, I just got here three minutes ago — remember?"

"Okay, but you're the night chief and you get paid to know everything." He shrugged into his overcoat and moved through the doorway into the hall, walking slowly as though he were reluctant to leave. It was strictly an illusion.

"See you at the funeral."

"Sure," Gorman said not looking up. He listened to Gruebner's heavy footsteps going down the hall then leaned back in his chair and stared at the ceiling for a moment. He was in command now, as alone with his duty as a ship's captain in the middle of the sea. The streetwalkers had been booked so they were of no concern to him. His immediate priorities were the Dempsey shooting and the hijacking. Leaning forward, he flipped the intercom switch that connected him with Communications.

18

"Gorman," he said briskly. "I want to see Daley and Winshaw."

"They're both on day watch, Inspector," Sergeant Kelmo replied blandly. "They're off duty now."

Gorman did his best to disguise his irritation. Kelmo hated everybody above the rank of sergeant for passing the promotion examinations he failed with stolid, stupid regularity. The president of Harvard and all his men couldn't have tutored Kelmo through an examination. Thank God. He was a bad sergeant; he would have been a rotten lieutenant.

"I don't care if they're on vacation. I want to see them. Get 'em in here as soon as you can."

"Okay, Inspector."

It was ten minutes past twelve o'clock and already his stomach was feeling the strain. He lit a Camel and coughed. Godansky. One million people in the city of Cleveland and James Dempsey had to shoot Max Godansky. He took a deep drag on the cigarette and then snuffed it out in the ashtray that would contain the butts of exactly one package when his shift was through. He picked up the phone and called Homicide. Welch answered, his voice distorted as he cradled the phone in the hollow of his right shoulder.

"Homicide. Welch."

"Gorman. Is Dempsey there?"

There was a slight pause. Then. "You might try the lab, Inspector."

"Do you have his statements?"

"No, sir. I'm working on Carl Rich's now."

"I want to see them as soon as you're finished. And when Dempsey gets back from the lab, tell him to come to my office."

"Yes, sir."

Detective Sergeant Earl Welch hung up and then stared morosely at the paper in his typewriter. There was nothing in God's world that he hated more than typing up reports, and this one seemed to be going on forever. He felt like he was typing a goddamn novel.

"Okay," he sighed. "Then what did you do?"

Carl Rich shifted uneasily on his chair. The palms of both hands were wet with sweat and he kept them pressed to the side of his pants. His thin, almost fragile face had lost what little color it normally had and his pale blue eyes seemed startlingly dark in contrast to the gray paste of his skin. He looked every second of his fifty-two years.

Welch stared at him dispassionately, waiting for him to speak. He had never given much thought to Carl Rich in the past, just another detective on the wrong side of fifty. One of the lifers putting in his time, waiting for the pension check. Carl Rich had been wearing the badge when Earl Welch was a kid in knickers. He had been around a long, long time, but he had never been pointed out to Welch as a man to emulate. There were no great "cop" stories about Carl Rich. He was a zero. Just one of the crowd. Welch wondered idly what supreme act of faith made it possible for Carl Rich to get up in the morning and face another long day.

"Well?" he asked softly.

Rich ran the tip of his tongue over his top lip and cleared his throat. A very delicate cough.

"Where was I?"

Welch suppressed a groan. "You were in the hallway of number 357 East Twenty-third Street."

Carl shifted again on the hard chair, crossed and then uncrossed his legs, and leaned forward, staring at the dirt-streaked linoleum floor.

"I . . . uh . . . remained in the hallway of premises to

back up Detective Dempsey as he entered room of suspect Godansky . . ."

"Slow down," Welch hissed between his teeth. "I'm not a tape recorder, man." The rigid, black shafts of his index fingers jabbed the worn keys of the old Remington. "Okay," he muttered. "Room of suspect Godansky . . . Go on, but slow, man, slow."

"Uh, there was an exchange of words with the suspect Godansky that was not clear to me. Uh, better make that 'was indistinct' to me. This exchange of words was followed by the sound of gunfire. A total of six reports were heard by me. Three of the bullets discharged struck interior of . . . make that 'interior surfaces' . . ."

"Christ," Welch muttered in exasperation as he made a series of Xs. "Make up your mind."

"I'm sorry," Rich said. He was starting to sweat badly and nausea was gripping him, rising up his throat like mercury up a tube. It was hot in the small, desk-cluttered room and he thought longingly of the cold, wind-swept street outside. He yearned to be on that street, running with his face to the mist, breathing the crisp, clean air.

"Don't leave me in suspense," Welch said with exaggerated enthusiasm.

Rich took a deep breath. It sounded like a gasp and Welch eyed him with concern.

"You okay, Carl?"

"Sure . . . sure. I'm fine."

"You look a little green. Can I get you something? A glass of water? A Coke?"

Rich shook his head. He was holding himself together with his fingernails. Another minute or so and it would be all over. He had to hold on.

"Read the last part back to me," he said thickly.

"Interior *surfaces* . . ."

"Yes. Interior surfaces of the room . . . and emerged in hallway . . . near position I had taken. These bullets lodged in woodwork and plaster of hallway . . . and were subsequently recovered for ballistics examination.'

His body felt icy. A thin ribbon of sweat coursed down his back and collected in the hollow of his spine. Each tap of the typewriter keys was a tiny hammer slapping a nail into his skull.

Welch typed a period with an extra punch. "That it?" Rich jerked his head in what Welch took to be a nod. "You weren't hit with anything? Plaster? Fragments of wood?"

'No.' Rich said, a little too quickly. 'I was bent over. I was almost on my hands and knees . . . that is, after the first bullet came through the wall . . . way down in a crouch.'

Welch sucked air through his teeth. "To hell with it. We don't need that. The goddamn thing's too long anyhow." He whipped the document out of the typewriter and thrust it in front of the detective. "Read it and sign it."

"I don't have to read it."

"Yes, you do. Don't you know the regulations? Read it."

Rich read it, or rather, pretended to read it. Without his glasses the single-spaced copy was merely a blur of black lines on white paper. He could have taken his glasses out of his coat pocket, but it wasn't vanity that prevented him from doing so. The truth was that he didn't want to read it. He didn't want to see the lies.

"It's fine," he said quietly. "Give me a pen."

Welch handed him one with a flourish. "Been nice doing business with you, Mr. Rich, and I hope you enjoy the car. I'll fill in the blank spaces later."

A smartass, thought Rich moodily. Well, he could afford to be. He was young. Life hadn't kicked his teeth in yet. Every day was a cakewalk. He stood up, his nausea becoming more critical. He gritted his teeth and prayed that he wouldn't hurl everything all over Sergeant Welch's desk.

"Can I . . . go now? I'm . . . bushed."

Welch waved a hand airily. "The night is young. Enjoy! Enjoy!"

Rich turned away sharply and walked stiffly out of the room and into the hall. He made it to the restroom and vomited into one of the urinals, resting his clammy forehead against the wall.

The gun made a dull, barking sound and the smell of burnt powder filled the room — almost, but not quite masking the odor of Otto Mengus's pipe. The pipe was not merely a piece of carved briar, it was an extension of Mengus's face, jutting out from the side of his jaw like a dark, brown tusk. Pungent smoke drifted from the caked bowl. To find Otto Mengus in the building, follow the trail of his tobacco.

"And one for good measure, Jimmy," Mengus said out of the side of his mouth. He pointed Max Godansky's Smith & Wesson into a steel barrel filled with cotton waste and pulled the trigger. The big gun bucked in his small hand, the report muffled by the barrel and the thick wads of cotton.

Dempsey straddled a chair, watching him, a look of bored indifference on his face. He glanced around at the long, narrow room with its cluttered tables and profusion of instruments.

"This place looks like a garage sale."

Mengus grinned. The crime lab had been his domain for as long as anyone could remember and he took pride in its capacity to function in utter chaos.

"We get things done," he said blandly. He placed the gun on a table between an electric coffeepot and a microscope

23

and then went fishing in the cotton batting, pawing through the long fibers as a bum might scrounge through a garbage can. He made little clucking sounds as he found the two slugs. He placed them in an envelope and stapled a tag to it.

"Okay, Jimmy. Just sign the statement that these are bullets from Godansky's gun and you can get out of here."

"About time." He stood up and walked over to the table. "What'd you make on the gun?"

Mengus shrugged. "Just an old revolver with Godansky's prints all over it. A few hair strands and some dried blood under the grips. Somebody got slapped silly with it a long, long time ago."

"If guns could speak," Dempsey said quietly.

Mengus handed him the envelope and a ball-point pen. He scrawled his name across the bottom of the tag while Mengus blew a blue-gray coil of smoke toward his face.

"What do you smoke in that thing, Otto — dead mice?"

"Quarter of a cup of Old Crow to a pound of Cavendish. One orange peel . . . a lemon peel . . . stir lightly and seal for a month."

"You could make a fortune on it as a roach spray," Dempsey said.

Mengus mulled over the insult as he followed Dempsey to the door. "My old man was a chewer. Mail Pouch soaked in rum. My mother wouldn't let him chew in the house. He used to sit out in the garage and spit in a bucket."

"You had some old man."

"There are worse things you can do with your life than just sit and spit." He held the door open. "You going to the Rinzo funeral?"

"It's the social event of the season," he said.

Mengus looked at him through the top half of his bifocals. "Don't be disrespectful of the dead, Jimmy."

"We're all dead, Otto," he said.

Gorman stepped out of his office on the way to the water cooler and spotted Harry Prochak. He was in the corridor flanked by two uniformed officers. Dried blood still caked his cheek and the bandage around his head was dotted with scarlet. His hands were still handcuffed behind his back.

"What's that prisoner doing here?" Gorman snapped.

Prochak grinned weakly at him. "Hell, I ain't no prisoner, I'm a goddamn *victim*."

One of the cops came to a semblance of attention. "He was hijacked out on 21 . . . sir."

Gorman glared at him. "Why is he handcuffed?"

The cop shrugged. "That's how we found him."

"Well, get those cuffs off."

"Would if we had a key."

There were times, Gorman thought, when he wished he was a turn-of-the-century precinct commander, one of those salt-to-the-bone Irishmen who weren't above kicking a patrolman in the ass, very squarely and very firmly with the tip of a heavy, knob-toed shoe.

"We have a shop," he said, articulating slowly, doing his best to keep any trace of anger out of his voice. "It's down in the basement. There are all kinds of things down there. Hacksaws . . . bolt cutters. Now, I want you to go down there, and I want you to go down there quick because I want those cuffs off that man, and I want them off in five goddamn seconds."

Prochak was grinning like an ape. It was beautiful to watch a six-foot cop jump like a kid bawled out by his scoutmaster. He was still grinning five minutes later when he was ushered into Gorman's office.

Gorman motioned the truck driver to a chair.

Prochak sat down gratefully, still massaging his chafed wrists. "Yes, sir . . . out on 21. I thought a tire was going flat so I pulled over to the side."

"Where on 21?"

"Near the Clark turnoff. I got out to look at the wheels . . . you know. shining a light on 'em . . . when I heard a truck pull up behind me. I didn't pay no attention . . . you know, figured it was a buddy stoppin' to lend a hand. Anyway, next thing I knew I was down in the bottom of a ditch with my hands cuffed and a crack in my skull."

Gorman eyed him silently. Then:

"You didn't see the man who hit you?"

"No, sir. I didn't see a goddamn thing."

"Who do you drive for?"

"The Dondero Lines."

"What was taken?"

"About two hundred cases of booze . . . Bourbon whiskey . . . all bonded."

Gorman whistled softly. Fifteen major hijackings in five months. Four teams of detectives working around the clock and they hadn't come up with one solid lead. Nothing. The hijackings were like some mysterious virus that eluded all scientific efforts to isolate and destroy it.

"Where the hell are the detectives on this?" Gorman asked the young cop he'd chewed on.

"Upstairs, sir, waiting for him," he said. "We were just told to bring him over from the hospital."

Prochak smiled wanly. "As soon as my head stops ringin' like a bell."

"We'll find a place for you to lie down. But we'll have to ask questions."

"Okay," Prochak said. "Thanks."

The man's gratitude was evident and it gave Gorman a feeling of satisfaction. He was unabashedly playing the role of the Good Cop. It might do no more than make this truck driver express a grudging respect for the police department the next time he had a drink in some Division Road beer joint. But they needed all they could get.

He let them go upstairs. The shifts were still changing and the hour from midnight to one in the morning was a period of relative calm, a tiny lull as the transition of duty from one group of men to another took place. The night squads would be on the streets soon and then the phones would start ringing. He shuffled through the arrest reports. Everything seemed to be in order just a bunch of girls picked up for offering their bodies on a rental basis. Average age, twenty-five. One woman of fifty. One of nineteen with a notation that she might be much younger. Send her over to Juvenile. He was absorbed in the reports and didn't see Dempsey come into the office.

"You look like a math teacher grading exams," Dempsey said.

Gorman snorted in disgust. "I just flunked the bunch."

Dempsey stifled a yawn. "That's the spirit. Give 'em hell."

"They've already got it." He pushed the reports into a neat pile, taking his time about it as he studied the tall man leaning against the door. Dempsey looked tired, but no more than usual. His face bore only the strain of normal fatigue.

"You had a bad night," Gorman said.

Dempsey nodded and took a crumpled pack of cigarettes from the breast pocket of his coat. "A bummer, as they say."

"How and why, Jim?"

Dempsey smoothed a cigarette between his fingers and stuck it in the corner of his mouth. He made no attempt to light it.

"I know how it happened, but I'm goddamned if I know why. I knocked on this character's door. He told me to come in, that the door was unlocked. I went in and the joker just opened up at me."

"What was Godansky to you?"

"A nothing. Just a lead, and a slim one. Carl and I have

27

three cases open. That Higbee pilferage case being number two on the list. Everybody in the goddamn department has been on it. I got a tip that a part-time trucker by the name of Godansky worked for Higbee's from time to time and he might just know something . . . for a price. I decided to follow it."

"You ever run across him before?"

Dempsey wrinkled his brow in thought, then shook his head. "The name had a familiar ring, but I've never seen him around."

"And he just started shooting the moment you came into the room?"

"No. He gave me time to close the door."

The unlit cigarette dangling from Dempsey's mouth bothered Gorman like an untied shoelace. He held up a book of matches.

"You want to light that thing?"

Dempsey grimaced. He took the cigarette from his mouth and rolled it to shreds between his fingers. "My mouth feels like an old sweat sock. Maybe I'll kick the habit."

"Sure," Gorman said. He stood up and walked over to the door as Dempsey watched him with tired eyes.

"Get out of here. Detectives in this division have to be bright-eyed and busy. That's number one in Gorman's law."

Dempsey's grin barely cracked the tight lines of his lips. "Fire me."

"I'll do that. Get out of this bughouse for forty-eight hours . . . and that's an order."

"I appreciate it," Dempsey said.

"Carl, too." It was a redundancy. Dempsey and Carl Rich were a team and you kept a team together, in sickness or in health.

"But make the funeral tomorrow morning," Gorman added. "The Chief wants as many there as possible."

Dempsey's face was stone. "I saw the particulars on the bulletin board. Sixteen cavalry, twelve motorcycles, bugler, rifle squad, honor guard and every office of command rank. An inspector's funeral for a twenty-seven-year-old kid from Mayfield Road."

"It's the least we can do for him," Gorman said lamely.

Dempsey snorted in disgust. "He put in six years at a hundred and fifty bucks a week. If he wanted target practice, he had to pay for his own bullets. That's something to think about when you got a wife and three kids. Maybe if he'd had practice. . ."

"The priest takes care of the sermon, Jim."

"I'm right and you know it. This funeral isn't for Eddy Rinzo, it's for the papers."

"Go home and get some sleep."

Gorman didn't want to argue with Dempsey. He felt pretty much the same way about it. A young patrolman gets killed in a gunfight with a drunk. Sad, but just one of those things. The killer hadn't even remembered doing it after they sobered him up. It was an accident, like a car crash. The man should have been decently buried by his family with a small contingent of his fellow officers as pallbearers and his watch commander as official representative of the department. But no. They were burying him like a martyr to the cause of law and order. There would be full newspaper and television coverage. Eddy Rinzo was being used to personify the embattled cop in the trenches of the city. His funeral might give some people thought. It might give them understanding. A young man, a husband and a father, an ordinary he-lives-next-door kind of man, had met bloody death in an alley. Gorman understood. The funeral was a blatant appeal. The police needed it as they had never needed it before.

The intercom stopped him — short, angry buzzes. Gorman stepped over to the desk and answered it.

"Gorman."

"Good evening, Mike."

Captain Ralph Henderson's voice. Polite but detached. Twenty years in the Communications room had left its mark on his personality. Twenty years of listening to the hysteria of a city and responding to that hysteria calmly and rationally had turned him into the most imperturbable of men. Had he been told that the earth was due to explode in five minutes, he would have relayed that information with no more emotion than his report of a traffic accident.

"What is it, Ralph?"

"Sixty-sixth Street may need assistance. They request all units on standby."

Gorman held the phone a little tighter. "Why?"

"Someone in a passing car threw a firebomb through the window of the Save-More market at Seventy-third and Hough. It failed to explode. Just luck. It was a well-made device."

He cursed softly to himself as his mind raced, digesting the information. In the past, his reaction to the bomb call would have been simple. He would have sent every available cruiser to the scene. But time and bitter experience had taught them all the folly of overreaction. The bomb could have been thrown just for that reason — to have a lot of police cars congregated in one area, stirring up the neighborhood, adding fuel to the fire of rumor and mistrust. There were many people in the city, both black and white, who wanted incidents to happen. Then again, someone who was pissed off at the high cost of food could have thrown that bomb — or a gang of kids hell-bent on burning down the entire northeast side of Cleveland. There was nothing to do but sweat out developments. Dave Blackman at the Sixty-sixth Street station would be sweating it out, too.

"Have Blackman call me if anything else happens."

"Will do, Inspector."

Gorman hung up the phone and stared at it. It was now 12:45 A.M. and his shift had really begun. Another day, another dollar.

chapter three

THERE WAS A SMALL ROOM about the size of an old-fashioned pantry in the back of the club. Nikki Davis used it as a dressing room. She had managed to persuade Dondero to improve it. But not much. He agreed to take the laundry bags out and put them in the basement. Now the waitresses and the busboys tossed their soiled jackets and napkins down a dark flight of stairs where a porter stuffed them into the big canvas bags for the laundry pickup. That was the improvement she had got. The laundry was gone, but the odor of it remained. It was the smell of cooked food, spilled whiskey, and dead cigars. It would be part of the room until the building fell down. She might be part of it, too. But she hoped not. She had determined that she would not.

She was thirty-one years old, claimed only twenty-six or twenty-seven on the calendar, and suspected that the lines around her eyes said thirty-five or possibly even forty. Those lines. The surface marks of experience. The road map of a girl who had been around. She worked at them, paying very careful attention to herself in the small mirror that she had leaned against the wall on the top of the table. Looking at the lines depressed her. She glanced at the pictures of the cats. Around the mirror, attached to the smudgy, yellow wall with Scotch tape, were pictures of kittens and cats she had cut out of magazines. Angoras, all fluffy and white; blue-eyed Siamese, so cool and self-contained; strange and solemn Abyssinians, more regal and dignified than the sculptors of ancient Egypt had made them; tiger-striped and brown-spotted alley cats. Just looking at them made her feel better. They looked so warm and loving, so unthreatening and gentle. She had not had her own cat since she was a child in Charleston, West Virginia, when she had also had the name Nelda Courts and a father who drove a truck and a mother who worked behind the counter in a service station diner. The cat had been named Nicolette. Something she got out of a magazine, as she now got the illustrations. Nicolette had become Nikki to her father, when he was there. And some time later, when she needed a name that didn't sound as stupid as Nelda, she took it.

Sam Dondero did not bother to knock when he came into the room. It never occurred to him to knock on any door in the club. He owned it. He felt that, in one way or another, he owned whatever and whoever happened to be behind the doors. He was wearing a shiny, black mohair suit that even the best alteration tailor in the city couldn't transform. He still looked like a farmworker who should be walking up and down the rows of tomato plants with a hoe in his hand. The gray silk shirt with its extremely long collar was stretched tight across his chest and the cuffs fell out over his hairy hands about three inches from the cuffs of the jacket. A swarthy man, dark and strong. An ugly man.

But in many ways, that's what she liked.

He flipped the door shut behind him. He banged it a little too loudly. It wasn't irritation. He did things that way. There was no thought. No notice that it might have been an offensive or inconsiderate act. It was simply an act. He came up behind her and looked down at her in the mirror.

"How 'bout you get your ass out there, huh?"

She continued to work with the mascara. He put his hand on her chest and worked it down into the yoke of her sequined, black dress to her left breast. He cupped it in the stubby fingers that even a manicure every other morning could not retrieve. He found the nipple with a rough thumb and forefinger and rolled it between them. She felt a twinge of reaction, but it was a chill, not an arousal.

"Don't . . . screw . . . up . . . my . . . mascara," she said, "or I'll have to start all over again."

He continued to roll the nipple and cupped his genitals with his left hand, the diamonds around the sapphire ring flashing in the mirror.

"How about a little oil on the tonsils before you go out?"

"A good blowjob would put you in the hospital for a week, Sam," she said. "Don't tear my dress unless you want me to do the next set topless."

He laughed, removed his hand, and turned away moving toward the door. "Maybe that's a good idea," he said. "But get it out there."

"Sure, Sam, sure."

He probably hadn't heard her reassurance. He was in a good mood. She wondered what had happened to make him happy. For six or seven days, more than a week, he had been tense and silent. He had spent little time around the club. When he was there, his anger and tension were obvious. He threatened to kill the chef for a minor oversight, knocked down a porter with a vicious slap for allegedly failing to keep the bar supplies in neat order, and

34

accused the cashier of cheating at the register. Now he was in a good mood again.

Nikki finished with the mascara, dabbed at her eyes with a folded Kleenex, and got up from the small stool, pushing down the tight gown with care not to break or snag the sequins. She could handle him in his bad moods or good. It didn't matter with any of them. All you had to do was pay attention to how they felt, what was going on inside them. You went the same way. She didn't have any trouble with Dondero when he was being a miserable bastard, and she didn't have any trouble with him when he was riding high. And she got what she wanted.

Going out the door, into the corridor and past the toilets and the kitchen entrance that led to the bar, she wondered how much further along she would be if she had learned that before the lines began to show up around her eyes. She wouldn't be playing the piano and singing in this goddamned dump, that's for sure.

Carl Rich was going to say something. Dempsey could feel it coming. He always could. Rich was driving the beat-up Plymouth up Nineteenth Street to Chester. He would take a right turn, head downtown, and drop him off. The big, weather-stained Central Police Station on Payne Avenue between Eighteenth and Nineteenth streets could be forgotten. A green, white and black patrol car, obvious with its siren and municipal paint job, passed them in the opposite direction. Rich looked to see if it was anyone he knew and raised a hand in the fraternal gesture of police passing in the night. Dempsey ignored the other car. He felt no fraternity. He felt only a desire to avoid listening to Carl Rich break the silence. That was the trouble with them when they got old. They assume that the years have given them both the authority and the freedom to say what they thought. Rich had nothing to say that interested him. He knew what happened to Carl's mind. When circumstances became too unpleasant and frightening to face, his imagination searched for an escape. A lot of cops did that. They wanted to get as far away from the ugliness as they could. Rich did it in fantasy. He called it thinking.

Dempsey was thinking about Max Godansky. It had been very simple. He had raised Godansky's lifeless hand and put it around the butt of the Smith & Wesson. Squatting beside the body, careful not to get blood on his suit or shoes, he squeezed the dead man's finger on the trigger. He fired three shots that way. That put the marks of the powder on Godansky's dead flesh. First, of course, he had wiped off all of his own fingerprints from that area of the gun. And when he was done fixing the final part of it, making it look for sure that Godansky had been shooting at him, he let the gun fall to the floor beside the body.

"You know something," Rich started.

"What?"

When he had finished firing the three shots from Godansky's gun with the dead man's hand, he went back to the door to wait for Carl. He had come up the stairs as fast as he could. Dempsey had told him to wait while he went upstairs. There was no point in both of them going up into the tenement, was there? It was a simple business, wasn't it? He might as well sit there and listen to the radio, save his strength. Rich let him do that. It helped a great deal. In fact, it made it all possible.

"In five or ten years," Rich said, "there's going to be broads riding in these cars. I won't see it, but you will."

He could always leave Rich in the car when he had to. Carl was frightened. Carl was old. Carl had Della out there in bed, able to move around only if someone lifted her into a wheelchair. Carl had to be there to take care of her, didn't he? A man with that kind of responsibility had to be

36

scared. He couldn't get himself killed. He couldn't even get himself hurt.

"Bullshit," Dempsey said.

"No, I mean it," Rich insisted. "Maybe you'll even have a broad as a partner after I turn it in."

"I hope it's a big, strong Polack," Dempsey said. "She can get out and push when we get stuck in the snow."

It was typical of the crazy fantasies that came out of Carl when he didn't want to think. Last time, it had been a scheme to organize all the retired policemen who had little chicken farms in the country into a cooperative to supply supermarkets. Dempsey could not remember what it had been the time before that.

"You think it's a joke," Rich went on, "but you'll see. Look at where cops came from."

"Most of the new ones came out of some sewer," Dempsey said.

"No, they came from the lower classes. Cops always came from the lower class that was trying to do something better. You look back. What do you see? You see cops who were all Irish first. How come? They came over here because there was a potato famine in Ireland. They didn't want to dig ditches, so they became cops."

"My relatives dug the ditches," Dempsey said.

At least this bullshit conversation was killing time. Rich took a left off Chester onto Walnut and the car moved slowly toward Ninth Street.

"Then it was the Dutchmen, the Krauts, and the Guineas. Maybe with a little sprinkling of Polacks and Bohunks. But it was always the lower classes. There was security, a pension, and a chance to do something for the community. You got respect out of it."

"That's more than you get these days," Dempsey said. "Let me out on the corner there. At Ninth."

"I'll take you."

"No, just let me out there on the corner. So what you're saying is that women are the lower class and they're all gonna become cops so they can get some security and respect."

"That's it," Rich concluded. There was a note of triumph in his voice. "Not all of them, naturally. But a lot of them are going to want to go this way. You'll see."

"And the rest of them are gonna go dig ditches," Dempsey laughed. "Boy, are you full of shit."

"You'll see."

"In a pig's ass. Give Della a hug for me. How is she?"

He was opening the door, getting out on the bleak corner, feeling the pull of the wind that barreled up Ninth Street off the lake.

"Okay. The same. She asks about you. The other night, she was praying and she said, 'I don't see Jimmy anymore. But I always pray for him.' She thinks about you. If you get a chance, come out and see her."

He felt sorry for Rich, as sorry as he could feel for anyone.

"I'll talk to you in the next day or so."

The cold, north wind rolled off the lake and down the breach of Ninth Street like a cannonball. Dempsey liked it, even as it made his eyes sting and water and penetrated his clothes and made him cold. A policeman liked the wind and the cold, a fireman hated it. For the cop, it kept the bastards off the streets. They stayed in their little rooms, trying to keep warm, hoping for a break, thinking of ways to get what they wanted. But thieves were lazy and mostly cowards. They didn't like to be uncomfortable while they worked. So they stayed home, out of the cold wind. But it was bad for fires. Any little spark, any little mistake could be caught by the wind and whipped into roaring conflagration in a matter of minutes.

38

This place had changed a lot in his lifetime. He was forty-three and he had been looking at the city, paying attention to it, sensing its change and movement for nearly twenty-five years. More than any of the other large communities he had seen, this one had become less a city than any. Where had it come from and why did it continue to exist? Dempsey had grown up with the same disdain and general loathing for it that he supposed most people felt. He had once asked his father about it and that large, red-haired man seemed surprised that anyone should care. Dempsey's father had been a printer and had worked on Linotype machines in one of the publishing houses and two of the newspapers.

"I don't know," he said after a moment of thought. "I suppose somebody traveling between New York and Chicago stopped to take a piss in the river and a crowd gathered."

That was it. It had been more of course. This is where John D. Rockefeller had begun stacking up the first of his innumerable collections of dollars. When the cry went up for steel just before the turn of the century, somebody discovered that the crowd had gathered around the man pissing in the river halfway between the Mesabi range and its rich, red ore and the coal that could be gutted from the hills of Pennsylvania, southern Ohio, Kentucky and West Virginia. They lighted the hearths in Cleveland and half the population of middle Europe seemed to gather around the fires to warm their hard, stubby hands.

What had happened to the city they had built? Where were they all? The East Side was almost totally black. The West was almost completely white but without much ethnic identity. It was just there.

Dempsey turned into Short Vincent, a small street where a nightclub or two have always hidden. The Lake Lounge was about a quarter of the way down the street, just past the small, dark coffee shop that turned out thin sandwiches on paper bread for the girls who worked in the office buildings, and a shoe repair shop that put paper soles and heels on their shoes while they waited.

She was at the piano for her first set on the platform above the bar when he came in. The crowd wasn't paying much attention. There was a good crowd, full of whiskey and conversation, and little taste for music, but her voice came through. It was low, husky, burned by booze and cigarettes. She was doing a Cole Porter thing and the voice was very good for that. He watched her move with the rhythm, her body pushing tight against the sequins. The voice and the movement made him want her. Right there. Now. He would have liked to have taken her off the piano bench and into the back of the club. Up against the wall. Or across a table. Or even on the floor. But now.

Nikki saw him and let herself smile over the lyrics. He got up to the bar behind a man who was talking about a baseball player and Perry made him a drink without asking. They knew him there. Through the refraction of the bottles on the island in the middle of the large horseshoe bar, he could see Dondero talking to the cashier. The greasy little bastard looked pleased with himself.

Dempsey looked back at the girl at the piano. Dondero saw him. Like an insect or a rodent, he always knew, saw or sensed when someone or something came into a room. Even a crowded room full of noise, like this. It was the second sight God had given thieves. Dempsey watched the girl until she looked at him again. He raised the glass and drank. It was a toast, a message that he was there for her. Her smile was even brighter and her melody stronger as she acknowledged it. Dempsey wiggled the empty glass at Perry and put it down on the circular cardboard coaster.

It would be filled when he got back. He turned and moved away from the bar toward the rear of the club. Forty tables were clustered in the rear of the place with the bar protruding into them like the prow of a ship. Dempsey's passage through them was quiet and casual as he headed toward the men's room. In the back corridor, there were eight or ten familiar faces. He made a point not to look at them, but he knew who they were. Two or three gamblers, a hulking linebacker from the Rams with a girl about one-eighth his size, two quiet, dark men from Mayfield Road with napkins tucked under their blue chins into the collars of their white shirts — "businessmen" in the same commerce that attracted Sam Dondero — a jockey who'd won two races at Thistledown that afternoon, a moneylender and at least two burglars. All professional. They would not have been frightened or upset if Dempsey had noticed them and made a point of having them notice him, but they would have thought about him and given some special significance to his presence there. He didn't need it. A cop came into a place like this for work or play. If he were playing, then it was his business and nobody cared. You couldn't draw lines and keep a man from crossing over them when he wasn't on duty. But in certain circumstances he might also come into this place looking for any one of those eight or ten faces that he recognized and arrange to take them outside. As far as they were concerned, he was playing tonight.

The men's room attendant, a short, twisted, almost dwarflike man in a white coat, was sitting on a bootblack stool reading a copy of *Male Magazine*, its idiot's collection of neurotic fantasies spraying violet, red and yellow ink across his lap as he traced the words with a finger and mumbled them to himself. Dempsey washed his hands at the black marble basin and then stepped to the urinal.

"Hey, Sam." Dempsey heard Dondero come into the lavatory. "Go get yourself a cup of coffee, all right?"

"Okay, Sam." the men's room attendant said.

It amused Dondero that the man who swept up the cigarette butts, put out the towels, and checked the soap and toilet paper was also named Sam.

Dondero stood at the neighboring sink. He urinated in a strong, splashing stream to a sigh of relief and satisfaction.

"Two best things in the world,' he said to Dempsey, glancing over his shoulder to watch the other Sam leave the room, "is a good steak and taking a piss when you have to go."

Dempsey was silent. He had nothing to say to Dondero now. He waited. It was the way he had Dondero figured. Never give him so much as a centimeter of personal association. To Dondero, that would be weakness, and he would use weakness in any form it came for whatever purpose he might have. Let him wonder. Let him speculate. Never give him anything more than what he bought and paid for. Dempsey waited.

Dondero sighed again. "What did Max have to say?" he asked.

"He said good-bye."

Dondero laughed. If a dog could laugh, it would sound like that.

"Good," he said. He reached inside his suit coat for the brown manila envelope and handed it to Dempsey. Dempsey put it inside his own jacket.

He zipped up, walked back to the wash basin, and washed his hands again. Dondero didn't bother. A swamp guinea, Dempsey thought. He stood a little behind and to the left of Dempsey, watching him in the mirror.

"You gonna have somethin' to eat? We got a great steak. I finally got the fucking kitchen straightened around. You ought to have something."

42

"No."

"When you get hungry . . ." It was a standing offer. They only had one business. Dempsey wanted him to know it.

"Yeah," he said.

Dondero didn't want to let it go tonight. "How you gettin' on with Nikki?" he asked.

"How am I supposed to be getting on with her?" Dempsey asked, turning around with a towel in his hands. He looked into Dondero's small eyes. Dondero was afraid of him. He probably wasn't afraid of much of anything, but he was afraid of Dempsey. It showed. Just a tiny glimmer of it. But that was all he needed to tell.

"She treating you right?"

"Just fine," Dempsey said. "I'll see you around."

"Sure," Dondero said. "God bless."

Dempsey left him standing there. Whether God did or not, Sam Dondero's invocation was the least likely he had ever had.

Michael Gorman, the night chief of police, left his small drab office at 1 A.M. to make what he considered a necessary show of authority. Ishmael Elliot, a thirty-three-year-old unemployed laborer, left his even smaller, even drabber room in a tenement near East Sixty-sixth Street and Hough Avenue at the same time for the same reason. Gorman wore his authority in the large gold shield, the look of doubt and question, the pearl-handled automatic on his hip. Ishmael Elliot wore faded cotton work pants, a white shirt and an old-fashioned 44.40 lever-action carbine stuck down the inside of his trousers' right pants leg, forcing him to walk with a pronounced limp. Gorman believed that the show of authority was necessary for the efficiency and responsibility of the small community he commanded. Ishmael Elliot believed this of himself even more fiercely,

43

for he had become God early in the afternoon, reaching the secondary stage of incipient paresis while he was being harassed by a clerk at the Unemployment Compensation Office for failing to show up at job interviews and for being unable to keep track of the small pink card that was the documentation of his incompetence.

But beyond this, each of them had other reasons for his movements which were not immediately apparent.

Gorman's movements seemed to be casual. He stopped first at the lieutenant's desk, where a white-haired Irishman in old-fashioned gold-rimmed spectacles dealt with as much of the public as was permitted into the station by the armed guards at the three entrances to the building. He had nothing to report to Gorman. There was a woman at the counter, pleading with one of the patrolmen who worked as a night clerk — a man assigned to a desk job because he had been injured or fallen ill and wasn't ready to go back to the street — pleading for permission to see her husband. The patrolman was explaining, as politely and kindly as he could, that she would have to come back during the daytime. Across the tiled hallway, Gorman found the Auto Squad making tea on a hot plate in their own small locker room. He declined a cup and asked if anything new had come along in the investigation of a hit-and-run accident in which two children were injured two days earlier. The sergeant in charge said that the continuing canvass of garages had failed to turn up a vehicle with unexplained damage and that the neighborhood was still being worked for possible witnesses who might have gotten a description of the car or even a fragment of a license number. They would think about it, knowing that he was thinking about them and their efforts. The chances of finding the driver would be multiplied. He went out to the corridor and the elevator.

Ishmael Elliot limped through the dark deserted streets of the East Side ghetto. His fantasy Apostles walked with him. They were singing. It was a hymn Ishmael had heard as a child. What else did the Apostles sing? They roared the glory of Ishmael Elliot's ascension. He was made deaf and blind by the golden glory of their voices. Consequently, he did not see the three or four hurrying figures who moved past him down the street. His blindness saved their lives.

Gorman had been briefly in the Communications center, the squad room of the Detective Bureau and the jail by the time he reached the small third floor office occupied by the Burglary and Holdup Squad. He stepped in, closed the door behind him, and felt the waves of gloom that surrounded the two men waiting there for him.

"Inspector," acknowledged Sergeant Robert Daley, a relaxed and casual-looking man built wide and strong like a plank farm fence. James Winshaw, ten years younger than Daley's forty, a lean and tall collection of sharp angles, was staring out the window, one foot up on the radiator, looking out into the darkness of Payne Avenue. He turned but he had nothing to say. His face was filled with bitterness.

"Well," Gorman began, "what happened?"

"We had a little bad luck," said Daley.

Winshaw whirled off his one-legged perch on the radiator. An angry stork, an enraged flamingo.

"Bad luck? We had nine months tied up in that poor bastard. We did everything but wash his socks and cook his meals. He was setting it up for us. And that trigger-happy baboon comes along and blows it to hell in three minutes. Bad luck?"

"That's enough," Gorman said. "I want an explanation, not an argument. I cleared this pigeon for you and now he's dead. Why?"

45

"Because Dempsey likes to shoot people," Winshaw snapped.

"Hey . . ." Daley began. "You're getting way off the track . . ."

"I am like hell. Everybody on the job knows enough to stay behind Dempsey."

"Can it," Gorman said. The tone was sharp and direct. It slapped Winshaw back into the awareness that he was a subordinate. "Did you know that Godansky had a gun?"

Daley's green-gray eyes flickered with an awareness of what was coming.

"We knew," he said.

"But we couldn't take it . . ." Winshaw began.

"Shut up," Daley said. "He started carrying the gun a month after we started talking with him. I figured he was paranoid then, going to get a lot worse by the time we led him into a situation. I decided to let him keep it." He emphasized the decision. He was the sergeant.

"All right," Gorman said. He would have let Max Godansky keep the gun, too. As informer, Godansky would have been in constant danger from his own growing fears of discovery and retaliation, as much as he was from the physical act of revenge. Men are not like steel. They're like glass and they go brittle and shatter under pressure. "Are you going to sit here on your ass blaming another cop for blowing it? Or are you going to get out and make it work? Who knew Godansky? Where was he taking you? He talked to you, then he talked to somebody else. Who, goddamnit, who?"

Ishmael Elliot was talking to Jesus. Ishmael said Jesus looked tired. Jesus said the cross was heavy. Ishmael told Him to put it down on the sidewalk and leave it there, promised that they would get another bigger and better one later. Maybe it would be made of neon. Jesus smiled but did not answer and trailed behind Ishmael as he came to the deserted yellow-brick building at the corner of Sixty-sixth Street and Hough. It had been empty for years, the blind sockets of its windows filled with darkness. Ishmael ripped away two of the planks that had been nailed over an entrance. They came off easily and fell to the trash-covered ground with a muffled clatter. Ishmael stepped into the dark chamber to look for the stairway. He paused a moment to remove the rifle from the trouser leg. It was heavy with the fat pug-nosed bullets he had put into its chamber in his room. His pockets were heavy with the others that had come in the box. But he felt weightless and strong. He moved toward the shattered staircase.

He paused for a moment on the stairs and looked at the rifle. He puzzled at its soft gleam in the lights that came through the tattered sides of the building. He had forgotten something. What was it? Why was he carrying the rifle? Then he remembered. It was his terrible swift sword.

Gorman left Daley and Winshaw to think about it. Maybe that was his job. Making them think. If they did that and followed the rules, the rest of it would fall into place. It was a routine, a discipline. Most of it dealt with the shattering of lives. There was a way, a technique of gathering the pieces and putting them back together. You didn't get the perfect life when you did, but you usually found out who had smashed it. Gorman believed very strongly that this was so. He dealt entirely in effect. He was constantly seeking the cause along a direct route.

Ishmael Elliot ascended the broken crumbling staircase of the building until he reached what had been the sixth floor. He would have gone on to the roof, but the stairs ended there. He was breathing heavily, unaware of it. He felt, instead, that the moment was approaching for which he had prepared. The one true moment. He was surrounded now, in this world, by false prophets and the practitioners of evil. They had risen under the bright sun of his charity, his mercy. It was now time to be a just and wrathful God. It was time to root out the evil that had infested his creations. He picked his way across splintered floorboards to the window opening. Below, the traffic light swayed on cables above the center of the intersection, changing red to amber to green and back again. He watched the light for a few moments, then began to notice the pedestrians moving through the cold morning. There were two of them, a man and a woman, and they moved quickly around the corner, east on Hough Avenue, suddenly hidden by the store building. Then the streets were empty. They should be filled with the joyous believers who had come to praise his decision and his action. Perhaps the light frightened them. It was a false idol. He raised the heavy rifle to his shoulder and leaned against the bare frame of the window. He aimed for the amber, the center of the light, and pulled the trigger. The explosion of the rifle echoed through the old building. The traffic light dissolved in a jangle of sparks and smoke. And it went dark. Now Ishmael Elliot's ears were filled with the ringing of great bells. He worked the lever of the rifle, casting out the spent cartridge while another moved up into the firing chamber. It felt very good to have acted, to have declared himself. He knew that the streets would soon be full. Here came the first chariot. Its lights were apparent on the pavement even before the vehicle itself appeared, moving slowly north toward the intersection on Sixty-sixth Street. But was it the vanguard of the faithful? Or the soldiers coming to crucify His Son? He raised the rifle as the car, a 1972 Oldsmobile, containing a young man named Leonard Foster and his common-law wife, Ruby Anderson, slowed tentatively, looking for a signal light that was no longer there. Leonard put his foot to the accelerator. He could go ahead. The light was out. There was no traffic. The bullet came through the windshield and tore away the right side of his chest just above the spleen. In the spasm his foot drove the accelerator to the floor. As Ruby screamed the car rocketed across the intersection and through the plate-glass window of a dry cleaning establishment, where it set off the burglar alarm, then plowed up the counter and cash register before stopping. The motor continued to roar while the tires screamed helplessly against splintering wood and glass. Ruby, her head shattered against the windshield, was unaware of the ringing of the alarm or the beginning of the fire as gasoline trickled out of the automobile tank. She had the forgiveness of Ishmael Elliot as she died.

Gorman stopped once again at the radio room on his way back to his office. A gleaming, blinking, clicking and buzzing collection of electronic equipment, it still bore the antique name of the days when it was first decided that the modern policeman could be dispatched and controlled through wireless communication. A thousand changes had been made in its style, technique, and equipment. But the basic commodity remained exactly the same. This was the first place where crime was reported. And this was still the first place to get a decent cup of coffee on the night shift in Central Police Station. The men of the radio room, most of them with some technical training in communication, sat at consoles taking calls from every point and corner of the city, writing out the emergency in a technical shorthand on small order sheets. The orders could range anywhere from one to a dozen or a hundred policemen. The radio men passed the slips along to the dispatchers, each working a specific area of the city with its assigned number of patrol cars tuned to a particular wavelength. They were a very efficient group. Henderson, the captain in charge for this shift, a slender man with a slow and studious manner — looking as if he felt himself to be in charge of a laboratory rather than a police operation — was proud of his group. He was also proud of his coffee. It came out of an electric percolator that the captain operated himself on a small table to one side of his desk. He put his steel-rimmed glasses on the table and poured for Gorman.

"What's on?" Gorman asked.

"Quiet," Henderson said.

Gorman raised the cup to his lips for a first scalding sip. Coffee came out of electric coffeepots so hot it would take the first layer of sensitivity off your tongue. But after that it was good.

One of the men at the telephone stood up with a white slip of paper in his hand. When a man stood up it meant he had something hot. Henderson moved with surprising speed and grace to the phone man's side. He took the slip, looked to Gorman.

"Sniper," he said. "Sixty-sixth and Hough. Fire in a nearby building and one auto is a wreck."

"Where's the armored truck?" Gorman asked.

"Sixteenth Precinct," one of the dispatchers said.

"Get it there," Gorman ordered.

"Is Blackman on?" Dave Blackman was the deputy inspector commanding the district.

"I have him," another dispatcher said.

"Tell him," Gorman said. "Get a fire department unit there. Ask them for a pumper. Do we have sound equipment in the area?"

"I got it," the first dispatcher said.

Gorman's mind was considering both possibilities in the problem. He had a sniper in the middle of the black ghetto. They had to react swiftly. But if they overreacted or reacted in the wrong way, it could turn into a riot. The decisions and commands he had to make were governed by a discipline and routine for the community's good. But there was also the community's sensitivity to be considered. He was pleased it had happened under the geographical command of Dave Blackman. He was a tough, strict strong commander, a man who moved decisively but not a jealous commander who would mind that Gorman had taken these first steps in dealing with the situation. And he was not an old-timer who would attempt to tear apart the neighborhood as a response. It might be a kid, it might be a nut, it might be somebody's imagination after a backfiring auto had disturbed his sleep.

"Get about six cars there," Gorman said. "Seal off the neighborhood four blocks in each direction and tell them to be careful. Stay the hell out of sight 'til we actually know what we have."

Henderson and his men did all this very quietly and quickly. The good Lord himself would have a difficult time being effective under the smothering blanket of police reaction they set about throwing over Ishmael Elliot. If he had known that, he might not have pulled the trigger.

"Where's your husband?"

They had taken her car. Dempsey didn't have one. He depended on Rich to pick him up when they were going to work; occasionally he grabbed a cab. Or he rode in Nikki's Mustang, vaguely uncomfortable with his long legs pushing against the floorboard, his knees barely clearing the dash.

"Working." She was a good driver. It took no special skill at two o'clock in the morning when the streets were as empty as bowling alley lanes, but her movements were efficient and her progress steady. It didn't take heavy traffic to show up bad drivers. They kept pushing down and letting up on the accelerator. After a while, your neck began to hurt with the nervous thrusts. Claire drove that way.

Johnny Davis. He was a punk. Nice enough looking in an open, pie-faced way and he worked as a dock boss on the pier of the small trucking company Sam Dondero operated in a desolate loading area along Rockwell Avenue. It was only about six or eight blocks from the police station. But Davis wasn't really the boss of anything. He was a punk who had to jump and smile to the snap of Dondero's hairy fingers. They both belonged to Dondero in one way or another. Dempsey had never asked her about it. She would probably lie if he did.

She had turned up at the piano in the bar and that's where Dempsey first saw her. He had stopped for a drink. And was watching her. She wasn't beautiful and she was four or five years from being pretty. But there was an open, frank and special sexuality about her. The word for it was ripe. A lot of women looked that way. Most of them turned out to be all look and no interest in or capability for dealing with the passions they provoked.

But Nikki was real. He knew it the moment he first saw her, standing at the bar in the club, listening to her sing, watching her play.

"She could stick a tit in each of your ears."

Dempsey had not turned to look at Dondero. His eyes remained on the girl at the piano.

"Without straining."

Dondero knew about this one, the same way he did. Maybe she was Dondero's woman. Dempsey didn't care. Nor if she was married and had eighteen children and a history of hemophilia.

He didn't have to answer Dondero. His attraction was obvious.

"She has another five, ten minutes up there. Give her five to get the shit off her face, and come on back. I'll tell her to expect you."

He had two more drinks by the time she finished and went backstage to her small dressing room. Dondero had spoken to her. He had given her to Dempsey. It was as simple as that.

"Light me a cigarette?" she asked.

He got them out of her purse, used the lighter on the dashboard, found the menthol taste only slightly annoying, and placed it in her mouth. He let his hand linger a moment on her chin and then traced the clean line of her neck. She had thrown him. The beige raincoat she had thrown over her shoulders as they were coming out of the back door of the club to the small parking lot had fallen away in a rumple on the seat. The skirt, already short, had ridden higher on her legs as she drove, moving from accelerator to brake. Dempsey put his left hand on her leg and moved it slowly back and forth, up and down the soft inner flesh of her thigh. She was silent for several moments but he could hear her breathing. She sucked at the cigarette. then put it out by leaning over the ashtray on the dashboard.

Her only acknowledgment of his hand was a tightening of her thigh. He fondled the soft flesh with gentle strokes. He looked at her face, but she kept her eyes on the road. Look at me, he thought. Show me something of what you feel. But she didn't. It was as if he had challenged her and she had accepted the challenge, locking them into a momentary sexual competition. He glanced at her hands on the wheel. They were firm but not tight in their grip of the plastic circle.

He moved his hand higher on her thigh and stopped,

53

fingers just barely touching the stretch of nylon there where her legs came together. Would she give a sign now of his violation?

Not a blink. His fingers began to move very lightly, delicately, as if he were touching the most fragile of flowers. They moved lightly over the nylon. He did not try to trace the outline of her, but he could feel the soft crinkly hairs brushing against the fabric.

Her face began to show that it was happening. Her eyes narrowed slightly and her tongue fluttered quickly at her lips, her mouth opening a fraction of an inch. It's happening, isn't it? he thought. Now he let his fingers be surer, more seeking. There was a dampness coming to the cloth as he massaged the soft lips beneath the floss. He eased his fingers into the elastic trimming of the panties and moved inside them. She was wet, even the soft spongy nub of her clitoris was wet as he closed two fingers on the delicate membrane and massaged it between them. Now her hands were clenched tightly onto the wheel. She began to move under and against the persistence of his fingers. With the nylon stretched against the back of his hand, he cupped her with the whole of his hand, letting his forefinger slide into the slick, moist folds of her inner flesh. He pressed the palm flat against her and began to rotate it slowly.

"Oh you sonofabitch. I'll wreck the car . . . I'll drive up a pole . . . Please I can't . . ."

She turned the wheel hard and cut sharply across the street to the curb and pulled up against it with a grating of wheel rims, just out of reach of the streetlamp on the corner. The car stopped with the same jerking spasms that were shaking her body. She managed to put the shift into Park and switch off the engine in one hurried gesture then slipped herself across the seat against him, her hands clutching and grasping, her mouth sucking hungrily at his

54

face in a rapid flurry of wet open kisses that finally found his mouth. She was tearing at her clothes and he was helping her. Between their hands, they rolled panties down and she ripped them with the small brass buckle on one shoe as she pulled up her knee to get free.

She climbed above him, knees apart, straddling him with her back to the windshield, bumping against the padded dashboard. Both her hands were at his groin.

"Goddamn that fucking thing," she screamed, grabbing at his waist. She had kneeled on the pistol. She snatched it out of the holster and hurled it into the back of the car. Then her hands were busy with him again, unzipping, unbuckling, unbuttoning.

He had opened the top of her dress and was fondling, nuzzling at her breasts. The nipples were rigid knots of flesh in his lips and teeth. He sucked as she grasped his penis with one hand, held her skirt with the other, and raised her hips. Her need for him was a fury. As soon as she inserted the tip of his flesh, she drove her hips down against him in a powerful surge, rose and drove again. She was soaring. His hands moved from her breasts, around her waist to the firm cheeks and flanks of her buttocks. He dug his fingers into the flesh and pulled her down again with a thrust that brought him to some fleshy bottom of the warm depth.

"Ah!" she gasped, pained. She twisted away and he tightened his fingers in her buttocks, pulling her down again as hard as he could, thrusting up from the seat.

She cried out again. But he would not let her pull away. He lunged again. As hard as he could each time. Her groans of shock became raspy, low shrieks. She was falling apart. He could feel the demand of his orgasm beginning to rise. He tried to forestall it. He postponed himself by thinking of the crazy situation, the strange scene they presented — two adults copulating in the front seat of an automobile on a generally busy street. Then she began to come.

"Hanh! . . . hanh! . . . hanh! . . ." she chanted. "Oh, Jesus! I'm coming."

She moved so rapidly he couldn't hold her. A pneumatic drill of love, riding him, driving him back against the seat. Dempsey could hear his own hard rasping breath and submerged himself in the great rolling waves of her orgasm. He came with a guttural cry between clenched teeth, a cry of so much furious release that she interrupted her spasms with a moment of fear, then fell down around him in a heap of spent flesh. He groaned into the fluff of her hair covering his eyes, nose and mouth.

She lay there breathing heavily. Limp. Then she nuzzled toward his ear and began chuckling very softly. She whispered, "You don't fuck like a cop."

He was surprised. He thought for a moment. He told himself he had underestimated her.

"How does a cop fuck?" he asked.

"Like a fireman," she said. "In and out of a burning building."

She thought it was very funny and she continued to shake with a small giggle as she raised herself away from him and fell back into her seat behind the wheel.

"Oh, God!" she said, pulling her skirt down. She reached down and disentangled the panties from the one foot to which they were attached. She held them up in the light and frowned at the torn shreds of stained and smudged fabric. She rolled down the window and tossed them into the street.

"That's littering," Dempsey said. "You get $200 or thirty days for that."

"Fuck it." She started the car. "Find everything?"

He was leaning over the back support, kneeling on the seat.

"The gun," he said. "Where did you throw it?"

"Back there someplace. I nearly broke my leg on it." He found it on the floor, reached the cold metal with a grunt, and settled back on the seat.

"Now that you've got your little toy, do you want me to drop you off at your apartment?"

"I don't think so," he said. He turned to look at her and her eyes were strong and bright. "Let's go to your place . . . and find a position where I can watch your ass move when you get going."

She said, "I think there's a way if we move the mirror."

A fifteen-year-old high school student used a Day-glo spray can to write "Cleveland sucks" in bright orange on her father's black Oldsmobile sedan, then left home with thirty-three dollars from her mother's purse. She was apparently traveling on foot, according to the report, because she did not know how to drive, had no boyfriends with vehicles (that anyone in her family knew about), and there was a definite shortage of public transportation in her neighborhood at one in the morning, when her absence and her vandalism were discovered. Her father happened to be a member of the City Council, and his outrage, as well as his influence, made the matter more important than the customary delinquent-runaway report.

A thirty-two-year-old lathe operator at the Fischer Body Plant on the eastern outskirts of the city had suffered a minor attack of nausea after eating three bologna sandwiches during his lunch break and returned home unexpectedly to discover his plump and decidedly unattractive wife of eight years committing adultery with a bartender named Steve Papko, who also played the accordion at weddings and small dances in the Lithuanian community around the West Sixties. The lathe operator, who was surprised that anyone who got around as much as Steve Papko did would want to screw with his wife, as ugly as she was, was still so offended by the invasion of his privacy, as well as the drinking of his beer and the soiling of his bed, that he broke Papko's nose and blackened both his wife's eyes. He then turned on the gas of the small space heater in the bathroom of the apartment, pushed both of them into the room and held the door shut. Steve Papko's bad taste and the wife's minor transgression would have suffered the ultimate punishment in approximately ten minutes if Steve had not decided to have one last Camel before joining that great polka band in the sky. The explosion shook the neighborhood as well as the apartment building. The most seriously injured of the three individuals taken to the hospital was the lathe operator, who had been carried by the door through the apartment and out a large hole in the wall — flying upside-down all the way.

An automobile containing a family named Davis — father, mother, two children and a nephew — returning to Cleveland from Akron, about thirty miles to the south, completed twenty-nine miles of the journey safely and was then spread over a portion of the final mile by a collision with a tractor-trailer moving van proceeding in the opposite direction at a speed sufficient to carry it across the highway divider and directly into the path of the Davis vehicle. Counting the truck driver who had been at the wheel almost eighteen hours, the ambulance crews counted six dead.

Each of these incidents had been logged during the few minutes it took Gorman to move from the Communications center to the police garage. None was important enough to delay or stop him. They happened every night, with one name or another. The system would enfold them, tabulate them, solve them to the extent that death and disaster can be solved, and divulge them to the media to be served at breakfast.

The sniper at Sixty-sixth Street was part of the future; for all Gorman knew, the worst was yet to come. With an extra driver, a sergeant named Jeremy Kilross, and a siren screeching and echoing against the darkened streets all the way, he made it to an observation area within a block of the sniper's lair in exactly seven and a half minutes. It was very good time. He told Kilross so as he ducked out the door of the car and scrambled in a crouch to an armored shield which had been set up ten feet behind the two huge arc spotlights. The beams were floating balloons of light across the face of the old building. The officers in the group acknowledged his arrival without words.

"What do we have?" he asked.

"Can't tell yet," said David Blackman, a tall, lean, forty-ish man, two years behind Gorman out of the police academy, now also a deputy inspector who commanded the Fifth District and the madman with the rifle. The officers of the Fifth District snapped to his brisk, cold commands; the madman, of course, ignored them. "There were two shots from the fifth floor ten minutes ago. We responded. There hasn't been anything since. But one of our marksmen says he saw movement on the roof at the parapet near the corner. Can we get a 'copter?"

"If you need it," Gorman said. "What about water?"

"The hydrant's on the corner. We can't get in there without an iron umbrella. A 'copter would do it in five minutes."

Always direct, always to the point. Blackman would drop bombs on the dilapidated building if he had them to drop. He would undermine it with explosives and blow it into the sky — the sniper with it — if he could. It was the best way, the most efficient and practical way. But it was also overkill.

"No," Gorman said, "not yet. We don't know he's up there. . ."

The rifle shot from the building interrupted him and contradicted his doubts. The bullet also shattered the heavy face of one of the spotlights and closed its searching eye. Fifty rifles and revolvers spoke in immediate. roaring answer.

"For Christ's sake." Gorman shouted, "tell them to cut it out. They'll shoot up the whole goddamn neighborhood."

"Hold your fire! Hold your fire!" the bullhorn roared above the guns. They settled into a few sporadic pops. "Hold your fire!" The shooting ceased.

"All right," Gorman said. "Tell them to put a couple of marksmen in a 'copter and come on in."

"Okay," Blackman said to a lieutenant at his side. There was more pleasure in his tone than Gorman expected. "Tell them to come in."

The lieutenant nodded and headed for the portable radio unit.

"I'll have that bastard for you in ten minutes," Blackman promised. Gorman was sure he would.

He hoped she was asleep. Or that she was pretending to sleep. Sometimes she did that for him. She knew how tired he had gotten, how close to the edge of fatigue his fear had driven him. She could not and would not ask any more of him then, but let him try to find what rest he could in the dark silence.

Fear was expensive, Carl Rich thought, as he found the bottle of Seagram's Seven Crown in the metal kitchen cupboard next to the stove. You had to pay with energy. Then your whiskey or your pills cost a lot and you wasted a fortune putting more locks on the doors, or more alarms on the windows. And it was all a waste. There was no way to burn it out, drown it, or prevent it with lock and bolt. He took a water glass from the kitchen sink, not caring if it was clean or used, and got an orange from the old-fashioned Coldspot refrigerator, holding the whiskey bottle in the crook of his arm. By inching the door of the refrigerator against the latch very slowly, he could close it silently, without the slightest snap. Then he moved out of the kitchen and down the faded hallway carpeting past the oak fence-rail staircase to the front of the house. Almost all of the old houses were built the same way, the dining room and the living room were on the right and the left of the front entrance. The long corridor to the rear of the house separated them. Part of the corridor was the stairway rising to the second floor and the bedrooms. But in this one, the dining room was a bedroom. The doors were always open. He stopped in the shadows outside them to look in. Her face was calm and slack in the soft illumination of the night light beside her bed. The rings hanging from a bar bolted into the ceiling cast the shadow of the double noose against the wall. She could pull herself out of the bed with them and slip into the wheelchair — when she was strong and her hands were not clenched with the pain of the rheumatoid arthritis that crushed and twisted her body like a sheet of paper being wadded for disposal. He stood there a moment, regretting each twinge of her pain, sorry for his inadequacy to deal with it, but also fearing that it would end and he would be alone. That was one of the fears. Another was that something might prevent him from coming there to stand over her. He turned away to the dark living room, found the controls of the Sears, Roebuck eighteen-inch television by memory, and turned it on. The earphone was a tangle of cord on top of the set and he trailed it out along the blue hazy path of the picture tube to a Naugahyde armchair set directly in front of it about six feet away — exactly the length of the earphone.

He put the tiny plastic receiver in his ear, settled slowly

into the chair, and held the orange in his lap as he unscrewed the cap of the bottle to pour the whiskey. It was purple-gold in the blue light. Grainy, raw, violent, the aroma of it singed the membranes of his palate. The soft gray eyes watered and the images in the television set became fuzzy and furred. He became aware of the voices echoing in his ear. They would paint his automobile in twenty minutes for thirty-nine dollars and guarantee the finish for five years. He didn't have thirty-nine dollars. He doubted if the Plymouth would go another five years anyhow.

That fear tried to find a place in his mind. But the whiskey took care of it. His stomach burned and grumbled. He poured another drink and put the bottle on the floor beside the chair as he raised the glass. Dempsey knew he was afraid. But it didn't matter, did it? He was strong enough for both of them. It was a movie. Betty Grable and Alice Faye were dancing in a Broadway show. They were both in love with Dan Dailey. Carl Rich pretended sometimes that they had children, that they were sleeping upstairs, that they would be there in the morning, take care of her when he was gone. Make sure everything was safe and secure. He pushed the robot station-control button and the pictures folded over and over on top of themselves to another channel. A car racing through the night in flight or pursuit. He reached for the bottle, reminding himself to peel the orange after this one.

God died at 2:17 A.M. The helicopter sputtered across the slums of the near northeast side, the spotlight rigged to its fuselage poking a finger of light into the alleys and streets below as it moved toward the besieged building. Four expert marksmen were also mounted on it, two with machineguns, two with rifles. But God couldn't wait.

Ishmael Elliot sensed the dissatisfaction among his children in the street below. He forgave them, regretting that they were unworthy of the new providence of his judgment. He sat on the stained tar-and-cinder roof, leaning against a brick wall. He removed his shoe, placed the muzzle of the rifle in his mouth, and pushed the trigger with a long brown toe.

She had been in the bathroom about ten minutes. Dempsey wondered if she had fallen asleep in there. He lay in his own quiet languor with three pillows between his back and the tufted blue satin headboard and smoked, dropping ashes in the brown faceted-glass ashtray set on the flat of his stomach. It was a good view. The apartment was on the eleventh floor of a new red-brick building near the lakefront. The lights of the city hooked out in a half-moon from this point to what he guessed was Euclid, forming the harbor on the dead sea of oil refinery and steel mill waste. It was ugly and it stank when you went down and became part of it, but it was very pretty here. He thought of a picture he had seen of the harbor at Rio, a great glistening stretch of sand on a beautiful blue sea with high buildings rising ineffectually toward the mountains. He supposed parts were ugly and stench-ridden there too when you got up close. All the big cities on the sea had the same problems. But it was a nice mirage.

There was a sound of water running, the metallic click of the medicine cabinet door. She flicked off the light before she emerged from the bathroom and her body was a soft shadow in the mellow gloom. A good body, as good as any. She might have done more with it and with herself than end up singing through the smoke clouds in a steak joint in Cleveland, Ohio, in the middle of the country in the middle of nowhere. She found the edge of the bed with her knee and came toward him across the mattress on hands and knees.

"Hi," she said. She put her hands on his knee. "Warm?"

"I was," he said.

She lay her head on his thigh, facing away from him, looking out the window. The muscles in his leg twitched involuntarily with the brush of her hair.

"Tickle?" she murmured. "I'm sorry . . ."

She started to raise her head. He put a hand out to stop her, found the soft smoothness of her face and neck and touched her ear.

"Don't move," he said. She grunted and wriggled closer. The weight on his leg was comforting and especially intimate. They had been that way from the start, both seeking and giving with a complete physical freedom and intimacy. It sometimes made him think of his wife because of the contrast. He had been married to Claire for eleven years and there were always barriers between them. Not all of them in bed, in sex, but he thought the most important ones began there. You keep secrets, you never really talk to me, she had screamed at him. If you can't fuck freely how can you talk freely? He had wanted to rage it into her porcelain head. This is where the frustration, the secrecy begins, this is where the anger starts between people.

"Ouch!" Nikki protested. He shook off his fantasy of bitter Claire, tight-assed Claire, frozen Claire. "You're choking me."

His hand had tightened on her neck. It was a spasmodic clenching. He wished his mind would stop going away like that. He needed to think. He must never stop thinking.

"Sorry," he said, not feeling it, just saying it.

"That's all right, baby. If you decide to strangle me, do it when I'm sleeping. I don't want to know about it."

She was rubbing her neck where his long, strong fingers

had tightened into the pillow of flesh. As she did, she moved her head back and forth, as if to ease a strained muscle or ligament her lips and hair brushing his leg. He reached for another cigarette.

"Just relax, baby," she said. The movement of her face against his thigh became rhythmic, patterned; her hand moved in unison on his other leg. Then he felt the touch of her tongue, the whisper of her warm breathing. She began to accompany the small kisses and wet touches of her tongue with the muted murmurs of arousal. She reached with her other hand to move the ashtray from his stomach and then rose slowly to her knees, sliding between his legs.

He smoked and watched her in the half-darkness. It wasn't true that she wanted to die in her sleep, she wanted to see it and be close to it, this life-and-death force that was part of him. She wanted him to kill her — as often as he could. He snubbed out the cigarette and put his hand on the back of her neck, pulled her head forward and down. She went willingly with a quiet cry.

Otto Mengus began by weighing the lead fragments that had been dug from Max Godansky's body by the deputy coroner, then he subjected flakes of them to chemical analysis. Eventually he placed them on a spectrograph, a kind of microscopic slide camera that could project pictures of the bullets onto a screen against the wall — there were really two pictures. One was of a fatal bullet from Godansky. The second was a test slug fired from Dempsey's gun. The marks that remained on the side of the slugs that had torn life from Godansky's frail grasp of it were twisted and imperfect. But sufficient of them remained to match the marks on the test slug. And they were similar in size and weight as well as content. This was the routine of ballistics in which Otto Mengus excelled. He noted each hairline of detail that the microscope found. He followed to the infinite purity of his science the routine that declared that James Dempsey had shot and killed Max Godansky with three bullets from a .38-caliber Colt revolver. Then he tucked the bullets, both fatal and sample into separate small boxes about half the size of penny matchboxes each lined with cotton, then labeled them and put them aside. They would eventually go into shallow file drawers in alphabetical order and remain there until a grand jury had reviewed the circumstances of the shooting and declared it justifiable homicide. He had to repeat the process with the revolver that had once been in Godansky's lifeless hand and with the three bent slugs that had been dug out of the woodwork and plaster of the roominghouse where the shooting occurred.

Procedure, routine. But he did not approach it unprepared. Mengus, whose hair was dark and full at sixty-two, whose face was lined with the furrows of concentration rather than age, got out the collection of reports that had come to him from the homicide bureau, the coroner's office, Dempsey and Rich, and set them out in chronological order — beginning with Dempsey's telling how the shooting had happened, concluding with the coroner's telling what the bullets had done to Godansky's vital organs. Then he made a cup of tea on the laboratory Bunsen burner and got a Muenster cheese sandwich from the refrigerator used for perishable laboratory specimens and sat down to read. He did not enjoy his lunch which was interrupted by a sergeant from the Fifth District turning in an old-fashioned .44-.40 Winchester carbine.

Gorman combined his return to the station with a ground tour of the East Side and the downtown area. Kilross embroidered a nameless pattern back and forth across

66

main streets where there might be problems or action. There was very little of either. When they passed a squad car, Gorman would look and nod and exchange salutes with the men. Letting them know he was out there with them if they needed him. Up Seventy-ninth Street all the way to Broadway then west to Fifty-fifth and back north again to Euclid, then west again.

He was thinking about Ishmael Elliot most of the time. After fourteen years of seeing it happen so often, he still felt sorry for the man as well as the driver he had killed. How many of them were there in a city of one million? Lost and frightened, screwed around by circumstance and chance from birth to death, they had no hope, they had no place except in madness. Everything would have to be changed — not just one agency, one city or one system, but everything — before there would be a hope of salvaging even one Ishmael Elliot from the turmoil. It wouldn't be done with helicopters and machineguns or with the sloppy, old-fashioned alternative of containing and forgetting. He recognized the feeling in himself of something like relief that the sniper had killed himself before the police marksmen had to do it. He questioned himself for a moment, slightly shocked that he should feel this way. Was he so resentful of Blackman's overwhelming and authoritarian lust for blood that he enjoyed seeing him cheated of the goal? Or was he simply relieved that Ishmael Elliot had solved the problem of his own madness? There is very little to explain about a gunman who takes his own life; it is the proof of his psychosis and universally accepted. When he survives you have the dual problem of accounting for the aberration as well as proving its consequences upon the dignity of a more lawful and less violent society.

"You gonna take lunch, chief?" Kilross asked.

Gorman glanced at his watch. 3:40.

"I guess so."

"Foster's?"

"Okay," he said. Kilross stayed on Euclid, pointing toward the chasm of Public Square, an amphitheater in which buses from various points of the city danced circles around stained, forgotten monuments before turning back out to their destinations. The center of the city was empty. Only one cab sitting at the stand in front of the terminal tower entrance and there was no driver in it. He had probably gone inside and down one of the sweeping granite ramps to use the restroom. There were no fares at this hour anyway, not even a wandering drunk who couldn't find his car and needed transportation home.

Gorman tried to think of the city in a total sense. He had trouble with the thought. It had changed too radically in his lifetime and was continuing to change. When he first went on the job it was a collection of neighborhoods. The blacks covered a part of the southeast. Central Avenue, Cedar Road, Woodland Avenue and Scovill Avenue. Those were black streets. It was the ghetto, he supposed, but it was more like a black neighborhood. Around it were other neighborhoods. Just a little farther south, the Polacks, Hunkies, Slovaks, Lithuanians, the Germans — all of Middle Europe — congregated in the separate streets off Kinsman Road, Broadway, Miles Avenue. The Irish, his family among them, were east and north of One hundred-fifth Street, around Collinwood and Five Points. They were all part of the working class, the lower class, and together then. They were neighbors with their own languages, even their own newspapers, their own shops, their own foods. The only ones who were really apart from them were the Italians who lived along the ravine that follows Mayfield Road to Cleveland Heights, where the Jew had his own enclave.

Kilross turned the car out of Public Square down into the flats toward the all-night restaurant that served cops and truckers and the rest of the night people. His generation had destroyed all that. They had fled the old neighborhoods just as they had fled the old family patterns. The families with the Anglicized versions of foreign-sounding names were in the suburbs now — Mayfield Heights, Garfield Heights, Solon, Berea, Parma, Olmsted Falls — or they lived over the bridge in the western half of the city because it managed to resist integration more implacably than any community in the South. The entire East Side of the city was black almost without exception, and it was a grim, gray shambles of a place that had lost its culture.

Where does a city go to die? Nowhere. It just sits there waiting to be buried. He supposed that he was one of the pallbearers.

The Cuyahoga River lay below them, its flat, oily surface gleaming under the moon. The Cuyahoga River, Cleveland's Seine. Had anyone ever written a song about the Cuyahoga, "Ooze on, ooze on, sludge and slime . . ."? Even in the moonlight the river looked evil, a thick black snake twisting through the city's main industrial section — a convenient sewer for a hundred years, its waters so saturated with oil waste it had burst into flames one night. A dead river oozing into a dead lake.

"I'll check us out," Kilross said. He parked in front of Foster's and reached for the radio mike. Gorman got out of the car and stretched. The air was cold, acrid with the smell of chemicals and oil, the odor of frying steak from the restaurant cutting through like something clean and fresh.

"All squared away, chief," Kilross said, joining Gorman on the curb. "It's deader than Kelsey's nuts."

It was 3:59 A.M. Four miles south and west of where

Gorman was standing, glancing over the line of police cars parked nearby, the fifteen-year-old daughter of a Cleveland city councilman was getting into a battered 1966 Volkswagen bus that had messages of youth's disappointment stenciled all over the side windows and a peeling LICK DICK IN '72 sticker on the rear bumper. A young man with a red beard was driving. Five other young men were in the back, curled up on a welter of old blankets and tattered sleeping bags. The interior of the bus was a chamber of rich aroma — sweat, pot and spilled wine. The girl was not repelled.

"How far you wanna go, baby?" the driver said.

"California."

"That's just where we're goin'."

She would get as far as Ridgeville, Ohio. A farmer would find her at 7 A.M. sitting naked and forlorn in a soybean field, her faith in mankind dented, but her sexual experience considerably polished.

Dondero finished counting the night's receipts, a ritual that he performed with complete indifference. Slim profits bored him. The club could have been a big moneymaker if Dondero had wanted it to be — he knew how to make things pay — but the club was his toy, his hobby and his listening post. There were not so many places in Cleveland that the Lake Lounge could be overlooked. Lunchtime and the late afternoon cocktail hour crowded the tables with the men who made the city tick. All you had to do was listen. Dondero listened. So did his bartenders and waiters.

Money bound them to him, both talkers and listeners. The keystone of their loyalty. He knew the power. It was stronger than love. Pay a man or a woman more money than they could possibly get anywhere else and you had a slave. That was Dondero's simple philosophy, his law, and he applied it to everyone, from Sam in the men's room to Nikki at the piano. Dondero's money was a velvet chain.

He shuffled a loose pile of worn bills together and fastened them with a rubber band. The packet made him think of Dempsey. He placed the money inside the wall safe and that also made him think of Dempsey. The safe accepted the money the way Dempsey accepted it, coldly and mutely. The safe wasn't grateful and neither was Dempsey.

"The sonofabitch," Dondero muttered as he closed the safe and spun the lock. It wasn't an expression of anger. He wasn't angry at Dempsey, merely puzzled by him. Dempsey was a cipher, a question mark. What the hell made the bastard tick? Dondero wondered. What the fuck did he really want out of life? There were no answers to be found in the tiny room that served Dondero as an office, no document on the paper-strewn desk that could explain why Dempsey killed people. Money was part of it, but when Dondero had hired men before, they had fallen over themselves to be pleasant and ingratiating, had accepted all gifts and favors with hot, eager hands. Dempsey just took the money and killed.

Nikki Davis looked down at him from the wall. She was smiling, her face tilted at a slight angle to give her a fey, ingenuous air, like a prom queen. An all-American honey blond, moist of lip and dewy of eye, the skin unblemished, the expression virginal. It was a dream face, created by darkroom alchemy and a soft focus lens. Dondero stared at the portrait for a moment before snapping off the light and leaving the office. Nikki. Dempsey had taken more than money, he had taken Nikki. She had been a gift, but Dempsey had never acknowledged it.

"Fuck him," Dondero said as he walked quickly down the narrow hallway that led to the front of the club.

The chairs were piled on the tabletops and the cleaning man was running the vacuum over the red pile carpet. The carpet, Dondero noted bitterly, looked a hundred years old and it had only been down six months. People were pigs. They dropped cigarette butts on the carpet and ground them into the nap with their heels. They spilled their drinks on it, puked on it, did everything but crap on it.

"Mornin', Mr. Dondero," the cleaning man called out over the whine of his machine. Dondero ignored the greeting as he crossed the room, scowling at the carpet, and went out through the side door into the alley.

He liked big cars — Eldorados, Continentals, Imperials — and he drove a new one every six months, leased from an agency in Shaker Heights. He was currently driving an Eldorado, arctic white with red leather seats and plush black carpeting, a car and color combination preferred by pimps. The car was parked in the alley next to the side door and Dondero got into it, sinking into the soft leather with a sigh of comfort. He switched on the engine, the heater and the radio. Lights glowed warmly on the dashboard, the engine hummed, and sweet music enveloped him from the stereo speakers. Dondero lit a cigar and leaned back contentedly, waiting for the windshield defroster to clear his view. This was the best part of any day for Sam Dondero, this moment of isolation in the luxury of his car. Other men might have this moment in the security of their homes, but Dondero had no home. There was no place where he hung his hat or laid his head. His vast wardrobe was scattered around the city in a dozen closets — in his office at the club, in his office at the Dondero Freight and Hauling Company, the S. Dondero Import Company on Lakeside Avenue, in the suite of his attorney in the Terminal Tower Building and in the apartments of various women. His arrival at any of these places was always unannounced, though not unexpected. He came and went without appointment or schedule and his business associates, employees, or women were always in a state of readiness to receive him.

Dondero touched a quarter-inch of fine white ash from the tip of his cigar into the ashtray and slipped the car into gear. As he pulled out of the alley and made a left turn into Short Vincent Street, a ragged, hollow-cheeked old man lurched out of the shadows and stood for a moment in the middle of the street, transfixed by the headlight beams. Dondero swore softly to himself as he touched the brakes. The old man stared unblinkingly at the light, then waved bony fingers in front of his face as though warding off an attack of bees.

Dondero hit the horn and the accelerator at the same time. The old man scurried out of the way, his tattered overcoat streaming behind him like moulting wings.

"Bum!" Dondero snarled out of the corner of his mouth. He could have touched the wheel a little to the left and slammed the man into the middle of next week. But that might have marred the jewelled surface of the fender.

He jammed his foot on the gas and the big car rocketed out of Short Vincent into the emptiness of East Ninth Street. He made a wide, tire-squealing turn and headed for Euclid. There was a patrol car parked at the intersection of Ninth and Euclid, its red light blinking. The driver and his partner were standing on the sidewalk talking to a tall black man who kept shaking his head vigorously, denying whatever the two cops were saying to him. Dondero slowed down as he turned east on Euclid, pressed the button that lowered the window on the passenger side, and leaned over.

"What ya doin' out so late?" One of the cops glanced at him and grinned. Everybody knew Sam Dondero.

It was 4 A.M. when Dondero parked in front of the restaurant on Mayfield Road, The Swell Guy from Italy pizza parlor, open twenty-four hours, food to go. This was the center of The Hill, Little Italy, Dago Town. They had come from Italy and Sicily and settled in this section early in the century, scorning the flatlands where the Polacks and Hunkies had built their ramshackle houses. They had hungered for the high ground, the hills of home, and they clung tenaciously to it. The inexorable tide of black encroachment had failed to uproot them. The district where Dondero now stood was the last enclave of the all-white and the all-Italian in the city, and there was an almost holy determination on the part of the residents to keep it that way.

Dondero hesitated in the doorway of the pizza house. The smell of pizza revolted him. How could anyone sink his teeth into a wedge of half-baked dough and scorched tomato sauce? It was an American invention, like chop suey. Dondero's taste in food ran to meat — steak, or, if he ate Italian, *osso bucco, agnello con piselli*, or *scaloppine con funghi* with a dish of *budino di mandorle* for dessert. He looked at the pizza eaters with contempt. There were eight of them, four young couples seated at a long table in the center of the room. All of the tables were draped with bright red-and-white-checked cloths; wicker-covered Chianti bottles hung on the walls like spiders and green plastic grape leaves were entwined through latticework partitions. The young couples were enjoying themselves in the Italian atmosphere as they sipped Cokes and munched the wilting remnants of their pizzas — the Special, anchovy, pepperoni, sausage, onions, shrimp and mushroom. Dondero watched a girl throw her head back and laugh. Her breasts moved heavy and braless under a pale green sweater. Dondero raped her with his eyes.

"He's in back."

74

Dondero turned his gray eyes away from the girl. Tony the clubfoot had come out from behind the counter with a tray of Cokes.

"Alone?"

"Yeah," the waiter said, as he limped past Dondero toward the center table. Dondero took one more look at the girl. She was licking a shred of mushroom from her sleeve. A nice tongue, moist and pink. A girl could go a long way with a tongue like that.

Guido Franchini sat at a table in the back room that was part office and part storage space. Guido owned the pizza parlor. It was the only business he listed on his income tax returns and it made money. A good little business. It was pointless to speculate how such a small enterprise could return such rich rewards. however. IRS agents went through the ritual every year of trying to determine how such a place could provide Guido Franchini with a hundred-thousand-dollar house in Shaker Heights and a small mansion in Palm Beach, Florida.

"I know how to stretch a dollar" was Franchini's retort to all questions. Go prove otherwise.

"Hello, Sam." Franchini pushed a dog-eared ledger to one side and reached for a dusty bottle of Barbera. "Get yourself a glass."

Dondero made a wry face. "I been havin' this trouble lately. I don't know, seems like everythin' I drink turns to acid. I been livin' on Rolaids." He pulled a chair to the table and straddled it, resting his folded arms on the back.

"You know how it is, Guido. That Max was a pain in the ass. He was givin' me gray hair — and ulcers."

"Was?"

"Yeah."

"Dempsey?"

Dondero nodded. "Neat as a pin. Never pull a gun on a cop."

Franchini said nothing. He filled a water glass with red wine and sipped it slowly. Franchini was sixty-three years old and could have passed for fifty. His tall frame was lean and straight, his thin, sensitive face unlined. He looked like a scholar or a priest, a man of quality. His forefathers had been nobles in Sicily, *barones*, impoverished but proud. The breeding showed and the heritage had asserted itself. Guido Franchini was an American baron, infinitely richer and more powerful than any of his ancestors.

"I got this call from Joey," Dondero said. "Things are easin' up. He'll be shippin' four bags on Monday, all pure."

"Good," Franchini said. He took another sip of wine and wiped the corner of his lips with the tip of a finger. "You know, Sam . . . this Dempsey worries me. The man's *matto*. I don't trust crazy people."

Dondero shifted uncomfortably. "The sonofabitch does a job. You know, he don't leave no loose ends."

The older man's lips parted slightly in what could have been a smile or a sneer.

"Lots of men can do a job. You need a soldier, I can get you a soldier. This Dempsey . . . this *cop* . . . what is it, Sam?"

Dondero fished a cigar from the inside pocket of his coat and began to toy with it.

"He uses *police* bullets, Guido. Remember Tedeschi? There would have been cops crawlin' up our ass if some soldier had burned that bastard. A man like Carlo Tedeschi dies with a bullet in the head the cops are goin' to ask *why*. They're goin' to start lookin' for *answers*. They're goin' to put two and two together and we wouldn't have liked one damn thing they came up with! You know that, Guido. So what happened? The greaseball dies, right? He pulls a gun in a dark alley and tries to shoot Officer Dempsey. Officer Dempsey is lucky the greaseball is a poor shot. What is Officer Dempsey supposed to do?

"Tedeschi dies with a gun in his hand. That's a closed case, Guido . . . that's a shooting in the line of duty. You can't send me a soldier who has a badge in his pocket."

The jukebox started to play in the other room, Dean Martin singing "That's Amore." Franchini drained his glass and set it carefully on the table in front of him.

"You didn't drive out here to tell me about Joey. Something is eating you up, Sam . . . inside. All that vinegar in the belly. What is it? Dempsey?"

Dondero crushed the cigar between his blunt fingers and tossed it into a corner.

"I can't figure the bastard. Like . . . I try to talk with him, you know. I try to kid around a little, put everything on a personal basis. I pay him big . . . I give him the best piece of tail in Cleveland. He could have the shirt off my back and he knows it, but it's like puttin' your arm around a snake. Know what I mean, Guido? The guy ain't a human being. He's got no blood in him."

"He's a cop," Franchini said softly. "He'll take your money and curse your guts at the same time. Maybe he curses his own, too. I don't know. Cops aren't like other people. They have their own world."

Dondero got to his feet. He felt shaky and very tired.

"Okay . . . maybe I made a mistake, but I'm stuck with him. If I could just reach the sonofabitch. You know, find the spot where he comes together."

"You never will. If you were smart ya'd make a contract."

"Yeah, sure, sure, a contract." Dondero rubbed his eyes with his knuckles. There wasn't a soldier in the country clever enough to take Dempsey. If the old Don didn't know that then he was getting senile. "Look, Guido, forget I said

77

anything about the bastard. Maybe he's peculiar . . . crazy, even. So what? It's a crazy world, right? We get along where it counts. I ask him to take care of something and he takes care of it. What the shit. I don't have to marry him."

"Do what you think best, Sam. How are other matters?"

"Fine . . . better than fine. *fenomenale*."

He was on top of the heap, in the center of a golden river. Everything was falling into place like well-oiled gears — the drugs, the girls, the numbers and the hijackings — all in his hands and under perfect control. So why did he feel so depressed?

"I better get some sleep," he said. "I got this fuckin' insomnia. I get maybe five hours every three days."

"Eat a pizza and you'll sleep like a baby."

Dondero grinned lewdly. "I got a little pizza that eats *me*. *Ciao*, Guido. I'll phone you sometime tomorrow."

"Do that. *Buona notte*."

Guido Franchini watched Dondero go out the door and then poured himself another glass of wine. Insomnia. He had that much in common with Sam Dondero. The thought amused him. They were poles apart generations apart. Dondero was an animal without breeding. A coarse and ugly little man. He was clever. Franchini had to admit that. He had done a fine job and they could find no fault with him. He paid his cut and never as far as was known, held back. The only thing that disturbed him about Dondero was the breach in tradition. Dondero had gone outside by bringing Dempsey into the fold. Dempsey! Don Franchini shook his head and drank some more wine. Times were changing. The world had turned. The old codes . . . the traditions — *finito*.

Sharon was in jail. Poor Sharon. She pressed her face against the cold bars, the cruel and ugly bars and wept. Indigo mascara flowed down her cheeks to make a mess of the scarlet rouge. Poor Sharon. She groaned in an agony of self-pity. If only she weren't alone; but Fern and Angel were in the next cell. They too were weeping, but at least they had each other to cling to. Sharon had nothing but the bars. She held the bars with her slim, beautiful hands and pressed her body against the cold steel.

"Cocksuckers!" she wailed. "Dirty bitch pigs!"

It was so unfair. It had been little Angel's birthday and Sharon had given her a beautiful party, a lovely party, plenty of wine and gin and amphetamines. There had been eight lovely, elegant guests — Fern and Sweet Willow, Barbie and Princess Pat, the stunning Dawn Glow and the terribly sexy Mama Do. Such wonderful girls . . . so much fun . . . everybody happy . . . everybody grooving on the drinks and the pills. The party had grown too big for Sharon's tiny apartment . . . the beauty of the night had beckoned through the open window . . . the moonlight had whispered to them and they had answered the call — dancing out onto Belvedere Road and then down to Hough where the pigs had been waiting for them.

"Cocksuckers!"

Officer Joe Murphy winced at the sound. He was four hours into his shift and he had hated every second of it. He detested working the prisoner detail. He was young and tough, an ex-Marine who had served two tours in Southeast Asia. He loved police work for the excitement his body needed. He had a reputation for being a good man to have with you. He had one commendation for bravery for stopping a knife-wielding madman with one careful shot in the leg. A cool young man. A good shot and a good learner. He would make detective soon. but right now he was still a rookie learning every facet of police work — radio cars, communications, beat patrol, tactical riot prevention — and the handling of prisoners.

"I'm going down there," he said tautly.

Officer Frank Robards looked up from his newspaper. He was older than Officer Murphy and was, technically speaking, his superior, having been on the force fourteen months longer.

"Forget it. Let 'em howl."

"PIGS . . . DIRTY BITCH PIGS!" Sharon's voice reached a new peak of fury.

Officer Murphy muttered something inaudible and reached for a cigarette. His mouth felt dry and little beads of sweat were popping out on his forehead. It was hot in the jail section of the old precinct house. There was no circulation and the place stank of vomit, urine and Lysol. He glanced at the big clock on the wall behind Officer Robards's desk. 4:15.

"Jesus," Murphy said. "Why don't they haul 'em downtown?"

"Because we can handle it." Robards folded his newspaper and jammed it into the wastebasket under the desk. "Saturday night guests. You should be used to 'em by now."

Murphy took a deep drag on his cigarette. The smoke made his throat ache. Christ, he wished that he could quit smoking. He wished his shift were over so he could get the hell out of there. His nerves felt like stretched wires and a muscle twitched in his jaw.

Frank Robards eyed him with some concern. "The trick is not to listen. You know, they try to get your goat. They just love it when you blow your cool."

"COCK-SUCK-ERS!"

"That does it," Murphy said. He dropped his cigarette on the floor and crushed it like a bug.

"PIGS . . . PIGS . . . PIGS . . . PIGS!"

Sharon felt laughter bubbling up inside her, driving away the tears. No more tears for Sharon. No more anguish. Nothing but blue skies . . . nothing but rainbows. Joy to the world, baby.

"SING, SISTERS! SING FOR THE FUCKING PIGS!"

"You tell 'em, Sharon. You go an' tell 'em, baby."

Fern's voice. Sweet and mellow Fern.

"Please, Sharon . . . PLEASE! They'll HURT you, Sharon. PLEASE, PLEASE, PLEASE."

"Don't you worry, baby," Sharon whispered to the bars. "Don't you worry none about Sharon, little Angel."

She heard footsteps coming down the passageway and stepped back from the bars, dabbing at her cheeks where the mascara had made a ruin of her makeup. She wished that she had her compact. She wished that her beautiful new wig, the luscious golden blond wig, hadn't been lost in the scuffle with the pig patrol on Hough. Her fingers flew to her head, hoping that by some act of magic the glorious blond tresses were still there. But the wig was gone . . . lost forever . . . kicked into the filthy gutter by a filthy pig boot.

"OH, SHIT."

"Shut your goddamn mouth!"

Officer Murphy stood in front of the cell. What he saw disgusted him. It was like looking at some strange and repulsive animal. That was what Chief Blackman had said one afternoon at a briefing. Officer Murphy and six other rookies had just been assigned to the precinct and the inspector had personally talked to the new men, to explain the problems they were likely to run into and what his own personal attitude was toward some of them.

Animals, he had said at one point in his speech. *That's the only word I can use to describe them. Unnatural, unhealthy animals that prey on the sick and debauch the innocent. I want these creatures off the streets. I want them to know that they will not be tolerated. Fortunately, there are laws that prohibit the practice of unnatural sexual acts and those laws will be enforced — to the letter. The rise in homosexuality in this country is an ominous sign. It strikes at the very heart of American values.*

The lesson had been clear to all the rookies — lean on the fags.

"SHIT SHIT SHIT," Sharon screamed.

"I said, shut your goddamn mouth," Murphy said, speaking slowly and ominously spelling it out, his hard eyes fixed on the contorted face behind the bars.

"That's no way to talk to a lady," Sharon hissed. "You're a rude and dirty pig."

There was a shriek of laughter from the adjoining cell. It was Fern. Sharon grinned. Fern was just like her, she didn't take no shit. Poor little Angel baby was another breed of cat. She was a pussy, she whimpered and cried. That was why Sharon loved little Angel.

"I want my little Angel baby. I want her right here . . . right in here with me . . . and my Angel needs her sweet mama."

Officer Murphy felt sick to his stomach. The liverwurst sandwich that he had eaten a half-hour before was rising up his throat in a hot, sour mass.

"Shut up," he said thickly. Holy Mary, what made them that way? How could a man sink into that pit?

Angel was an emaciated nineteen-year-old car wash worker by the name of Arthur Pierson. Fern was a hulking twenty-five-year-old day laborer named Fletcher T. Brown. Sharon was Owen Watkins, aged thirty years, unemployed. He was in a separate cell pending a report from the print identification section at Central. Owen Watkins fitted the general physical description of a man wanted in East Cleveland for a string of house robberies and at least fifteen vicious rapes.

Officer Murphy tried to calm his raging stomach by staring straight ahead. He fixed his eyes on Owen Watkins's Adam's apple. It was unusually large, jutting out from the slack throat like a shelf.

Look at the suspect's throat. If it's a real woman you will not detect an Adam's apple. Presence of such is a dead giveaway that the suspect is a male dressed in female clothing, a masquerade which is a clear violation of the statutes.

Lessons by vice squad officers had not prepared Officer Murphy for the realities. His knowledge of homosexuals had been limited to the few he had known while growing up on Cleveland's West Side — an aging man who had lived with, and doted on, his mother, and two mincing, lisping, limp-wristed men who owned a flower shop on Lorain Avenue. He had run into a few when he joined the Marines, had even been propositioned by one in a bar in Oceanside, California. But the approach had been low-key and Murphy had been more amused by the incident than outraged. He was too certain of his masculinity to feel threatened by gays, but the creatures he had been forced to deal with during the past year weren't gays, they weren't fags or fairies, they were macabre specters, distorted travesties of human beings, strong men, most of them, wrapped in female trappings. They were not easy to arrest. They resisted intrusion into their fantasies with any weapon at their disposal — razors or knives, broken bottles or six-inch hatpins. They clawed and bit, kneed and punched. Like women, they fought dirty, clawing for the eyes or the genitals. Officer Murphy hated them and feared them.

"Cute, ain't she?" Officer Robards said as he walked up beside his partner. "A real cutie."

Owen Watkins struck an exotic pose, pleased and flattered. "Do you think so? Do you *really* think so, pig?"

"Gorgeous," Robards said. "A gorgeous kid."

The man spread his legs and rotated his hips in a slow grind. White panties showed beneath the thin black dress.

"Eat your hearts out."

Robards laughed, but Murphy's face was a rigid mask.

Sharon was happy. She was rising up on waves of erotic delight. She wished she had more speed but she had taken plenty and the glow was still there.

"I'm flyin', Angel baby."

God, if only little Angel was in the cell to take care of her need.

"Love you, Angel baby . . . LOVE YOU LOVE YOU."

"Keep it down," Robards said sternly.

"EAT IT, PIG."

Sharon wanted to be naked. Her body was on fire and the clothes stifled her. She tore at the dress, ripping it away from her shoulders. The brassiere slipped up on her flat, hairless chest.

"I'M GETTIN' READY, ANGEL."

"That does it," Robards said. "Let's get the cuffs on him." He sorted quickly through the keys he carried on a large ring, found the right one, and unlocked the cell door. By the time the two men entered the cell the prisoner was naked except for high-heeled shoes and the dirty white bra. The dress and panties lay in torn strips all over the floor. Officer Murphy held a pair of handcuffs in his right hand and tried to move behind the prisoner and grab one of his arms.

"LOVE YOU, ANGEL."

Sharon was ready for love. Lovely Sharon. Wild and beautiful Sharon. She threw her arms around Officer Murphy's neck and pressed her hot, sour mouth against his mouth, her tongue seeking his tongue.

84

"BASTARD." Joe Murphy reeled back in horror, vomit scorching his throat. He acted without thinking, without plan. The face in front of him was something out of a nightmare and he swung at it, the steel handcuffs wrapped in his fists. Every ounce of his one hundred and eighty-five pounds went into the punch, the steel-shod blow catching Owen Watkins between the eyes, lifting him off his feet and sending him backward against the wall. He stayed there for a second, arms outstretched like a naked black Christ, before his knees buckled and he slumped to the floor. A few muscle spasms, the sharp uncontrollable kicks, accompanied his dying.

"Sharon?" The voice from the next cell was high-pitched, tottering on the edge of hysteria. "Sharon, honey? Sharon? SHARON? SHARON?"

The name bounced off the thick walls, became amplified by the narrow passageway, drifted to the front of the precinct house like the wail of a tortured soul — SHARON! SHARON! SHARON!

Deputy Inspector David Blackman stared fixedly out of the side window of the patrol car as his driver, Officer James Fallon, turned the car off Chester Avenue and drove north on Sixty-sixth Street. Blackman was in a bitter mood. His pride had been stung by Gorman's attitude. A sniper in a building was hardly a unique occurrence in Blackman's district and his men were well trained to deal with such a situation. They didn't need anyone from Central telling them what to do. Gorman had seemed concerned that Blackman would overreact, shoot up the entire neighborhood just to get one man. Blackman was aware that Gorman and the other inspectors at Central considered his methods a bit too direct, a bit too strong at times, but he didn't care what they thought. They didn't have his problems. The Fifth District was another country, a dangerous and hostile land, a battle zone in the urban wars.

"Sure a lot of people on the streets for four in the morning," Fallon remarked.

"Four-twenty," Blackman corrected.

Fallon smiled. But to himself. That was just like the chief — Mister Precise.

"Which way on Hough, sir?"

"Back to the station," Blackman said. There was no more to be seen. The population within a ten-block radius of the shooting site had been aroused by the gunfire, the bullhorns, the sirens and the low-flying chopper. Noise had wakened them and rumor had drawn them out of their beds and into the street. But it was not a movement, not the beginning of a riot situation. People stood on the sidewalks in small groups, talking quietly. One or two had even waved at the police car as it drove by, the inspector sitting tall and erect, showing the braid.

Blackman lived with the ghost of riot. It occupied his thoughts and molded his policies. It was his responsibility to maintain order in a district that looked on the police, even black police, as an occupying army. The most justifiable arrest could spark a riotous demonstration. A less dedicated man than Blackman might have weighed the question of upholding the law against the very real factor of civil disorder, but Dave Blackman was not a man who believed in compromise or expediency. He had the ultimate responsibility of upholding the law of the land and the State of Ohio, and there was nothing on God's earth that could deter him from doing his job.

His job — his life. The two words were interchangeable. His dedication was absolute and he demanded nothing less than perfection in every officer under his command. He thought of his division as an elite force which he had created in his own image. He had heard all the cracks that circulated in the other precincts — *Blackman's Raiders, The Fifth Legion, The Bible Brigade* — and he turned a deaf ear to them. His men were in the front line. When people in the comfortable, middle-class sections of the city read about a policeman getting killed in the line of duty, that policeman was usually from the Fifth District. Eddy Rinzo . . . dead of a bullet in the chest. Eddy Rinzo had been shot by a wino who had found a gun in an alley, but he could just as easily have been sniped at or had a fifty-pound carton of scrap iron dropped on his head from the roof of a six-story tenement. Such incidents had happened and would continue to happen, until they learned. It was guerrilla warfare even if the general public was reluctant to think of it as such. Blackman knew better, and he had a great pride in the men, his men, who faced the dangers of this war every time they pinned on the badge. He set a standard for them to follow and expected his qualities to be theirs — dedication, incorruptibility, bravery and faith. It was his habit to read a short passage from the Bible at the start of every shift and he encouraged his men to do likewise, not to increase their religious knowledge, but to arm them spiritually for the awesome task.

It was 4:25 when Fallon pulled up in front of the precinct and Dave Blackman stepped out of the car.

"Oh, Jesus," Sergeant Wolinsky muttered to himself as he spotted Blackman entering the building. Sergeant Wolinsky eased his two hundred and ten pounds from behind the desk and hurried to intercept his chief.

"A problem in the cells, sir," Wolinsky said. He felt like an idiot. *Problem*. Jesus, what a word to use.

Blackman removed his stiff-billed cap and ran a hand across his thinning gray hair. "What kind of a problem, Bert?"

Wolinsky shifted his awesome weight from one foot to the other, like a small boy about to explain how a window got broken.

"A . . . a prisoner was . . . hurt."

Blackman scanned the sergeant's face. His eyes were small and hard, like the eyes of a hawk. "Hurt? How?"

Wolinsky looked away and pointed a beefy hand in the general direction of the lockup.

"The doc's down there, now . . . with Robards and Murphy. I don't know how it happened, but I think . . ."

Blackman was no longer listening, he was half-running toward the rear of the station.

"What's up, Bert?" Fallon said as he came through the door.

"Jesus," Wolinsky said miserably, "don't ask."

Johnny Davis stared at the clock. The red second hand swept slowly up to twelve and the black minute hand jumped forward one notch. 4:26. In another minute it would be 4:27. That's how it went. That was life, one lousy minute after the other.

"You gonna sit in there all day, man?"

Johnny Davis snapped out of his reverie. Swiveling his chair slightly, he grinned at the tall black man who lounged in the office doorway.

"What's your beef, Charlie?"

Charlie Greene stretched the tired muscles of his back, his hands almost touching the ceiling.

"Shit, man, no beefs on *you*. What the fuck time is it?"

"Four twenty-six — and a half."

The young black man groaned. "Three and a half fuckin' hours to go. This motherin' shift is killin' me. I gotta go back on days, I mean it."

"You serious?"

"Damn right. You been to my house, man. You know what the fuck goes on there in the daytime. I can't tell them kids not to play, man. I gotta sleep, but they gotta play. That's how it goes. I just gotta live a more normal life, know what I mean?"

"Yeah," Davis said quietly. "I know."

"I mean, I gotta work days and sleep nights. I'm just wearin' myself down to the bone an' that's a livin' fact."

"I'll talk to Sam about it."

"Do that. Tell him I can get a day job at Interstate. I don't think he'd like to lose me."

"No," Davis said. "And neither would I."

"You lose me, you lose the league cup, man — and don't you forget it." His long right arm came down in a slow, graceful, underhand arc, the thick wrist turning sharply at the end of the movement. "Strike! Inside corner of the plate, right at the fuckin' knees."

"You've been high and outside lately. Don't give me that right-at-the-knees crap."

Charlie Greene went through the actions of the softball pitch again, only this time more slowly, a study in stop motion.

"I been savin' myself for the play-offs. It's goin' to be no-hitter-Greene from now on, man." He sighed deeply and fished tattered work gloves from the back pocket of his blue jeans. "Well, see ya later, man. Don't forget to ask Dondero."

"I won't forget."

Work days and sleep nights. That was normal. Millions of men did that. They put in their days on the job and then went home. They ate dinner with their families and they went to bed with their wives. Johnny Davis felt a sharp pang of anguish. He fumbled a cigarette from a crumpled pack of Camels on the desk and lit it with a shiny Ronson lighter. Nikki would be in bed by this time, curled up under the blankets, her hair a fan of gold on the pillow. Of course, if he worked days that would come into conflict with Nikki's hours. She'd be heading for the club when he got home. What he had to do was ask Dondero to let him work a special shift one that would get him off about two in the morning. That way he could meet Nikki at the club and they could go home together maybe get a bite to eat someplace first and then go home and go to bed — together — man and wife. That is what they needed, the normal conjugal rite of going to bed at the same time. He took a deep drag on the cigarette and stuffed it into an overflowing ashtray. He was kidding himself. Dondero wouldn't give him a special shift and Nikki wouldn't like the idea of his meeting her at the club every night. No way. He had married Nikki but she had set the rules, the conditions of the marriage.

Just don't crowd me, Johnny.

He never had. It was the price a guy had to pay for such a beautiful and talented woman. What the hell did she need him for? What could he give her? He was boss of a loading dock, a blue-collar man with a two-bit title and a plywood office.

He lit another cigarette and stood up. He was a big man and the bulky knit sweater that he wore under a bright green warm-up jacket made him look even bigger. He was only a shade over five feet ten, but the awesome thickness of his neck and the girth of his chest gave an illusion of greater height. Most people were surprised when he stood up, expecting to see a man six foot or over. He had the build of a good lineman or running back. He might have made it in pro ball if he'd gone to college, but he hadn't. He'd quit high school in his senior year and joined the Air Force. He'd thought of making the service his career, but

90

he'd met Nikki in Dondero's club one night, the first night of a two-week leave.

Johnny Davis sucked in his breath sharply. That one fragment of time was like a half-forgotten dream. Six years. It seemed like sixty . . . or six hundred. He couldn't remember a time when he hadn't been married to her. His life before that moment was a blank. Why she had married him was a mystery. He had never questioned her motive at the time; he'd been too overwhelmed by her acceptance of him. He'd tossed her a pass and she'd picked it up. He hadn't really expected that, it had been just an idle pass, but she had gone with him to a hotel early that morning and they'd made love until noon. She'd been crazy about his body and his baby face.

Marry me, he'd said impulsively.

Why not? she had replied. *What the hell, why not?*

It had been as simple as that. A great basis for a marriage. So they had married and he had moved into her apartment in Lakewood where the monthly rent was on a par with his monthly pay. He'd suggested, halfheartedly, that they move to a place he could afford. She had only laughed at the suggestion.

You need a decent place to live, lover . . . a nice address. You're going places, baby . . . after you shed that dumb uniform.

He'd had six more months on his enlistment. He spent those months at an air base in Florida, a dismal place on the edge of a swamp, not a fit spot to bring Nikki — not that she would have gone, anyway.

I've got my career, lover. Never forget that.

Her lovemaking the night before he departed for Florida had left him limp for a week. She'd given him something to remember her by, and when he wrangled his first three-day pass he'd hitched a ride on a transport plane that was taking some brass to the NASA flight propulsion lab at Cleveland's Hopkins Field. He had arrived home, unannounced, at 4:30 in the morning and let himself in, very quietly, not wanting to wake her until he had slipped into bed beside her. Someone had beaten him to it.

He should have killed the guy. He should have picked him up bodily and hurled him out of the window. He should have slapped Nikki silly and then raped her with his clothes on. He had done none of those things. He had become hysterical, and while he had been screaming and babbling the man had got out of bed, dressed slowly and calmly, and walked out the door.

Grow up! Nikki had said. *You're a big boy now. Face the facts of life. I don't expect you to jerk off every night down in the Everglades. People need people sometimes. It's got nothing to do with marriage.*

It had been a moment of crisis, a turning point, and he had taken the wrong path. There was nothing he could do about it now. He couldn't retrace one step. His life from that time on had been in her hands. When he had left the Air Force she had found him a job. That had been his fate: a weekly check from Sam Dondero — and Nikki.

The intercom screeched and the tinny voice of Fred Bolen entered the cubicle.

"Johnny? Somethin's gone haywire with the steam."

"Kick the pipes."

"I don't get paid to kick pipes."

"Okay, okay." Davis got up with an obscene finger gesture for the intercom and Bolen and walked out of the office onto the loading dock. A cold wind off the lake swept through the open dock, whistling on the steel roof. He thought of himself standing on a wharf, waiting for a big ocean liner to pull in. Where would that ship take him?

Manila? Fiji? Anywhere. It didn't matter so long as it took him away. But the ship wouldn't be any ship, just a trailer truck in from Akron at about five with a load of tires. And even if there had been a ship, he wouldn't have been able to board it. Not without Nikki and whatever need he had to be part of her life.

He waved at Charlie Greene, who was loading a trailer with a handcart, and walked into the dim cavern of Number 4 warehouse. There was barely room to walk. The warehouse was jammed with piles of crates, boxes, mounds of new tires wrapped in brown paper, coils of electric cable and pyramids of paint cans. It would all be moved out by noon to make room for another stockpile. The sight never ceased to surprise him. A portion of everything the city made or consumed passed through the Dondero warehouses or was hauled from one place to another by a Dondero truck. A dumdum could have run the business and gotten rich. There was no reason for all the other shit — the back room, the phony books and the phony invoices. No reason other than pure greed.

They called it the back room but it was actually another warehouse, separated from Number 4 by a wall of cinder-block. Davis unlocked a steel door and stepped inside, closing the door behind him.

"Here's . . . *Johnny!*" Al Summers called out, swinging an imaginary golf club. Al was the class clown thirty years later, the shop cutup. A good worker — when he was sober. What he was doing tonight must be hell for him, Davis thought. Nothing but booze, two hundred cases of Old Crow lying around. All that whiskey and not a drop to drink.

Fred Bolen was leaning against the commercial dishwasher that Davis had rigged up with a steam vent. Two dozen bottles at a time could be pushed through the machine and the live steam stripped the labels and tax stamps off like magic.

"Fix the sonofabitch, will ya? We still got twenty cases to do."

"What's the matter with it?" He walked over to the machine and felt the steam pipe that ran into the top. It was searing to the touch. "You got plenty of steam."

"Not where it counts," Bolen said.

"Then the jet's clogged. I told you. All that paper turns to mush. I told you before, all you gotta do is ream it out with a piece of wire."

Bolen spat on the floor. "The first I heard about it." He was an arrogant, stupid bastard.

Davis let it ride. There was no point in arguing with Fred Bolen. It was a lost cause. "Mary, have you got a hairpin you ain't using?"

"Sure, Johnny."

She rose from behind a sea of bottles that were lined up on a table, a short, muscular woman dressed in baggy blue overalls and a pink sweatshirt. Her iron gray hair was wound into a tight knot on top of her head. She waddled toward him, digging at the hair with thick fingers.

The night crew, Davis thought wryly, slaving away in a damp warehouse for Sam Dondero and the almighty dollar. Fred Bolen who had a strong back and a weak brain; Al Summers, his eyes floating in the alcohol of a thousand drunken days; and fat Mary who was just happy to have a job, any job. They would all make a nice bundle of change for this night's work — two hundred cases of bonded bourbon, unloaded from the cases, run through the steam machine, dried, fixed with bogus tax stamps and new labels, house brands mostly, for distribution by one of Dondero's companies to bars and clubs throughout Ohio and Indiana. One hundred percent profit per bottle.

"How are you, Mary?" Davis asked.

"I'm getting by," she said. She smiled. She was touched. He had given support to her false notion that somebody in the world actually gave a damn and a moment's thought about her and the people like her.

"Good," he said. He wouldn't ask Bolen if the sonofabitch lay dying on the wet concrete floor.

The steam vent was jammed with glue and papier-mâché and the bottom of the washer was clogged with the remains of Old Crow labels, a sodden mass of debris. He cleaned out the vent with the hairpin, working quickly and efficiently. As he worked he thought of Nikki. Maybe if he made enough money she'd go with him . . . to Yokohama . . . Singapore . . . Australia. First-class cabin on a first-class ship. Just the two of them.

"For God's sake, Doc, give him a shot! Give him a jolt . . . Christ, I hardly touched hi——"

"Shut up," Robards said sharply.

Murphy looked into Robards's furious eyes, then looked quickly away. Everything had happened so fast — the fag coming at him, kissing him, pressing his dirty body against him. Jesus. He'd pushed him away, hadn't he? Just pushed the freak off of him. That was all he'd done. A little push. *Watch it, fella, none of that.* Wasn't that what he'd done? He looked around, seeking an answer to the question. Everyone was looking down — Robards, Sergeant Grimaldi, two detectives from robbery that he didn't know. All looking down at Doc Wilson kneeling on the floor of the cell, his head bent over the black man's naked chest, a stethoscope in his hand. Doc Wilson. A city jail doctor. A quack — everyone joked about the old guy. He couldn't find the tick in a five-dollar alarm clock.

"Give him a shot . . ."

Carter Wilson, M.D., thirty years a police surgeon, plucked the stethoscope from his ears and stuffed it into his coat pocket.

"They haven't invented a shot to cure corpses."

"He can't be dead," Murphy said fiercely. He made a move toward the body but Sergeant Grimaldi held him back.

"Take it easy."

Murphy had always liked Sergeant Grimaldi. He had been to his house, had played catch with his ten-year-old kid while the dinner was cooking. He looked into Grimaldi's face, hoping to find understanding. He saw nothing that was of any comfort.

"It was an accident," he mumbled. "Wasn't it?"

No one said anything.

Blackman came striding down the corridor, his heels ringing on the concrete. The two detectives, grim and silent, backed out of the cell and stood to one side.

"What the hell is going on?" the inspector barked. He didn't expect an answer. He knew the moment he entered the cell. The two white-faced officers, the naked black man on the floor, blood oozing from his forehead.

"That man's been beaten."

"I . . . I had to hit him, sir, when he . . ." Murphy stammered to a halt, struck mute by his own words. *I had to hit him* . . . God Almighty, he'd killed a man.

Blackman drew in his breath, fighting the urge to slap Officer Murphy across the face. All hell would break loose in the next couple of hours. Newspaper reporters, FBI, civil rights lawyers. A prisoner beaten to death in his cell.

"Report to my office in fifteen minutes," Blackman said. "You too, Doc. I want a full report."

"Should I call the crime lab?" Grimaldi asked.

"The man's dead, isn't he?" Blackman replied icily.

"You handle this one by the book, Sergeant." He turned sharply on his heels and walked out. As he went down the corridor someone shouted "Murderers!" from one of the cells. Blackman neither slowed nor flinched, but he was quietly glad the first of all the shouts and cries had come so quickly. He would not — and could not — be taken off-guard by any of it.

Gorman sucked at a back tooth. He would have to see a dentist. He couldn't chew meat without particles of it getting wedged in the tooth. As he paid his bill, he dialed a toothpick from the little wooden dispenser next to the cash register.

"How were the chops, Inspector?" Eddy Foster asked as he punched the register keys.

"Great." Gorman smiled to himself. Grilled pork chops, apple rings and hash browns at four in the morning. The late shift turned everything upside down. He would never get used to it. When he retired, he would live nine to five, and never vary it. He wondered if all the other night people who had lunch at Foster's felt that way.

"How do you like the toothpicks?"

Gorman's face was blank. "What?"

"The toothpicks. They're new . . . mint-flavored. Pick your teeth and clean your breath at the same time."

"Wonderful," Gorman said, poking at his back tooth. He picked up his change without counting it and stepped out into the night.

Kilross had preceded him by twenty minutes. He was fighting his weight and had limited his lunch to a rare hamburger patty and a scoop of cottage cheese. The sight of Gorman's sizzling pork chops and crusty brown potatoes had been intolerable and he had excused himself and gone out to the car to monitor the calls.

97

"What's happening?" Gorman asked as he got into the car.

"Nothing much. 604 broke up a Sterno party on Davenport. Two of the bums were already dead. There's been a couple of prowler calls from the second district, and that's about it. How were the chops?"

"Terrible," he lied. "Greasy."

"I feel better," Kilross said.

The radio crackled softly, the background music of their night.

"702 to Central . . . leaving Thirty-sixth and Prospect . . . negative call."

"Okay, 702 . . ."

"Central, this is 604 . . . still waiting for that ambulance at Davenport and Twenty-second — in the alley."

"604 . . . ambulance is on the way . . ."

Gorman was oblivious to the sound. Nothing that was being transmitted at the moment was of any immediate concern to him. Only the rookies listened to every call, fearful that they might miss their own in the general static. The ear became attuned to it, over the years. You didn't hear what didn't concern you. As you rose in rank, there was less and less to become involved in.

"It's being married to a Hunky," Kilross said, starting the car. "I should have married an Irish girl, like my mother. We ate good when I was a kid, but nobody got fat. I gotta pick a Hungarian. Sour cream on everything."

"609 . . . see the woman . . . 928 Grandview . . . code 3."

"The hell of it is, I love it. That woman is a *cook*. Take liver. She slices it with a razor, browns it in butter with onions, and then mixes in the sour cream and serves it with — "

"Central to 101 . . . phone Inspector Blackman. Please acknowledge, 101."

Gorman plucked the mike off its rest beneath the radio. "This is Inspector Gorman. We're just leaving Foster's."

"Inspector Blackman wants you to call him immediately, sir. He's in his office."

"Okay, will do."

"There's a call box on Fourth Street," Kilross said.

Gorman shook his head. "I don't feel like standing in the cold — back up to Foster's. I'll use the pay phone."

There was nothing unusual in being asked to use the telephone rather than the radio. No confidential conversation could be sent out over the airwaves where anyone with a short-wave radio could listen to the call. But Gorman felt a light uneasiness as he slipped a dime into the wall phone at the back of the restaurant. The sense of foreboding was confirmed the moment Blackman came on the line.

"A terrible thing's happened, Mike. A prisoner was beaten to death in his cell. I'm charging two of my men."

Gorman whistled softly through his teeth. "How did it happen?"

"I don't have all the facts yet, but how it happened is unimportant at the moment. The point is that a male Negro was arrested at midnight along with two of his friends — three transvestites. drunk, disturbing the peace and possession of drugs. One of them is now dead."

"Is the story out yet?"

Blackman laughed hollowly. "I'm not worried about the press, Mike. What I'm worried about is *now*. The district is like a coiled spring. I don't know how rumors leak out of this place, but they do."

Gorman felt a chill on his spine. "I'm on my way back to Central now. I'll put every unit on the East Side on the alert including the Fire Department, but I don't think we should jump the gun on this."

"But be ready for anything, Mike."

"Did you call the Chief?"

"No . . . not yet. There's no point in waking him unless a situation develops."

"Okay, Dave . . . keep me up to the minute."

"Of course," Blackman said, and hung up.

There would be a ruckus. Gorman did not think it would come as a full riot right now, but it would come. Thank God it was cold; they were off the streets. The death of a black homosexual in a jail cell would not be a direct cause of bringing them out, but merely a contributing factor, one reason among many others. The storm was rising. When and how it would break was a guess, because you could only make guesses about mobs and their movements. He could make one of his own. It would be a summer evening in the middle of the week — a Tuesday or Wednesday. A protracted heat wave would have driven people out of their rooms and apartments to sit on the front steps or wander up and down the streets. Nerves would be frayed. Men would have nothing to look forward to except a sleepless night and a day of toil to follow. Couldn't even get drunk. Might lose their jobs if they came in late or with a hangover. Nothing to do but hear the inescapable cries of uncomfortable children. Then something would happen. It needn't be anything as dramatic as a man being beaten to death by a couple of jail cell cops. The cops might shut off a fire hydrant that was being used as a sprinkler. They might arrest a liquor store owner for selling beer to juveniles. Anything that would attract a crowd. That's how Watts exploded — an argument over a traffic ticket. Some nameless black man was going to spit on the sidewalk one hot summer night, a white cop was going to get uptight about it, and one quarter of the city of Cleveland would go off like a firebomb.

He helped himself to three mint-flavored toothpicks on the way back to the car. The palest streak of green tinged the eastern sky and Gorman shuddered in the predawn chill. There would be no riot tonight.

"Anything cooking?" Kilross asked.

Gorman shook his head. There was no point in telling him. Kilross would find out soon enough on his own. The news was probably spreading through the precinct houses now. One cop told another cop who told his buddy who told someone else. Keeping it in the family, of course. Firemen would have to read about it in the papers, but all the cops on this shift would have the grim details, each teller of the tale adding his own bit of graphic fiction. That was how rumors leaked out of Blackman's precinct. Poor Dave. He thought he was General Patton sometimes. He thought he was commanding the Foreign Legion, but all that he had under his command were overworked, underpaid civil servants who enjoyed their office gossip just as much as any overworked, underpaid file clerk in city hall.

"Let's get back to the barn, Jeremy." He lit a Camel and blew smoke through his nose like a dragon. Jesus, what the hell was the answer? If you stopped a black man in the Fifth District and asked him what his real, most important complaint was, the chances were ten to one he'd say the police.

They always leanin' on me, man . . . always pushin'.

It was a fact. They were always suspect, and the police could justify the roust of a black man simply because he was a black man. The cop was the enemy, the storm trooper in the ghetto. The belief was unfair, a stereotyped image. But that was the beef on the streets. You didn't hear from the black middle-class because they were inside hiding, like everybody else. They hated the scum of their community even more than the whites because they had to live with it, raise their children with it. Gorman had once talked with a black juror who was outraged at the whites on the jury for their mushy attitude toward a black burglary defendant.

"That animal is coming through *my* window first if we let him out of here," the man had told the jury. "If we could hang the sonofabitch, I'd be the first to vote for it."

The jury tempered justice with mercy. The man was furious. Didn't anybody understand the good and bad of the whole racial situation?

And there were plenty of good cops, too, fair, compassionate men who were oblivious to the color of a man's skin. Maybe there just weren't enough of them, or the old image was too ingrained in the black consciousness. Gorman had no answer to this problem. The police were an extension of white policy and a reflection of white attitudes, even when the city had a black mayor. As society changed so the police would change. It was as simple as that. The tensions would exist as long as the whites moved in one direction and the blacks in another. If they ever found a single, unified direction, it could be so good and simple — the community would become its own law.

Gorman had sat in on many sessions during the past couple of years where representatives of the black community, ranging from silver-haired ministers to Afrostyled young militants, could talk over their gripes and fears. The talk had always been angry, impassioned, bitter . . .

If a black girl gets raped you cops just wink at each other and you don't do nothin' about it.

You always bust the black pusher. Now, the black pusher is probably a junkie too, right? He's been hooked. He's a sick man. He's pushin' the shit just to live, man. But I don't see you bustin' the man who sells the stuff to the pusher. No. He's some fat white cat livin' out in Shaker Heights with connections.

There is no communication between us, sir . . . no meaningful dialogue. We both pray to the same God, but you do not believe that we will go to the same heaven since we do not come from the same neighborhood.

He rolled the window down a fraction and flipped his cigarette into the empty street. So much of what they said was true. So the police tried to be fairer . . . they really tried . . . but something always seemed to happen and the tarnish went right back on the badge. A black fag in a jail cell, beaten to death by a white cop. Another horror story to add to the pile, another reason for hatred and mistrust.

"706 to Central. Coming downtown . . ."

"Okay, 706 . . . 904, 511 in progress, 427 Decker, code 2. All units vicinity Chester and Sixty-third, officer needs assistance . . ."

There was a new breed of cop out there answering those calls. Young men like Eddy Rinzo who willingly put their lives on the line, without promise of a special heaven.

Kilross turned onto Rockwell and crossed Public Square. Windows on the fifty-second story of the Terminal Tower building turned pink with the rising sun, but the rest of the city lay in darkness. An old man ran in erratic circles around a monument to the Civil War dead.

"I'm runnin' with Jesus!" the man screamed, waving his fingers at the headlight beams. "I'm runnin' with the Lord!"

Kilross grinned as he touched the brake. "Want to call a wagon for him, Inspector?"

"No," Gorman said. "If I had time, I'd get out and jog with him."

chapter four

H<small>E WAS DROWNING</small> in a perfumed sea, sinking into silky depths of coral and green. He brushed tangled strands of hair away from his eyes and rolled away from her to face a rose-colored room.

"You moved," Nikki murmured sleepily.

"It's getting late," Dempsey said. A bedside clock whirred gently. Ten after six. He had fallen asleep for half an hour, something he had never done before in her bed. His movement had pulled a tangle of sheets away from her body, and he looked down at her breasts, the nipples soft now, specks of brown in rings of coral.

"I was dreaming about you," he said. "You were pulling me under for the third time."

"Four," she said, opening her eyes and smiling at him. "Four times. I counted!"

"Go to sleep." He pulled the sheets and the blanket up to her chin and she turned onto her side, snuggling into a ball, knees drawn up to her chest, curling up for sleep like a child or a satisfied cat. She looked very small and vulnerable. Dempsey was reluctant to leave her.

"I'll let myself out."

"Damn right." Her voice was barely audible under the covers.

He walked the five blocks from her apartment to Euclid and then took a cab to his own place on Kinsman near Woodland Hills Park, one room and tiny kitchen on the fourth floor of a five-story red-brick apartment house that still bore a few graces of a more elegant past. He could have afforded a better place if he'd wanted to, a smartly furnished apartment in one of the new lakeside high-rises, but he was oblivious to his surroundings. There was no one he wished to impress or entertain. All he needed was a bed, a shower and a closet to hang his clothes in.

There was a small elevator that creaked upward on rickety tracks and rusting cables. Dempsey never used it. There was always an odor in the elevator, the musty smell of decay. He took the stairs, making no sound on the worn carpeting, passing dark, empty landings and silent halls.

The room offered no clues to the man who lived there. It was as barren of adornments as a monk's cell. When Dempsey had moved in there had been a cheaply framed reproduction of van Gogh's *Sunflowers* hanging above the daybed, but he had taken it down and stuck it in the back of the closet. There had been something pathetic about the picture, as though the previous occupant had tried to turn the little room into a home. All Dempsey had been seeking was shelter; four walls and a roof with nothing to remind him of the home he had just left. It would have been easy to fix the place up. Nikki would have done it for him, or the tall redhead who sold cosmetics at Higbee's. He knew half a dozen women who would have sewed slipcovers or hung drapes, papered the bathroom or even painted the walls if he had asked them to. But he hadn't wanted the slightest touch. His only concession was a woman who came in twice a week to clean the place and take care of his laundry. It was clean now, smelling of lemon oil and ammonia. The bed was made and there was a box of shirts from the laundry on the coffee table along with change from the ten-dollar bill he had left under the sugar bowl in the kitchen.

Dempsey stripped off his clothes, tossing his shirt and undershorts into a corner and draping his suit over a chair. He walked naked into the bathroom and stepped into a tiled shower stall that no amount of bleach, scouring powder or scraping would ever rid of its grime. He turned the hot water on full force and moved without flinching into a cascade of steam. Some of Nikki's scent rose from him in the steam, some of the aroma of their sex with it. He soaped his chest and genitals with rapid movements, then shampooed his hair and washed his face, closing his eyes to the scalding spray. When the soap film was gone from his body he reached out blindly with both hands, turning off the hot water and turning on the cold. The shock made him gasp for breath, but he luxuriated in the icy stream. It drove blood to his head and made him feel vibrantly alive. He was new, reborn, when he stepped out of the shower. He whistled softly to himself as he shaved and combed his hair. It was only eight hours since he had killed Max Godansky, but the incident seemed lost in time, an event that had occurred in the life of someone else. As he splashed after-shave lotion on his face and under his arms he thought about Max Godansky and the man who had killed him — a police officer named James Dempsey, a tired, overworked, nerveless man who had been forced to shoot in self-defense. A policeman's lot was a hard one. Constant danger for little pay. Public servitude. Support your local police — they need your help. He pitied Officer James Dempsey.

"You're a poor sonofabitch," he said to the mirror. The mirror was not a true one. The face staring back at him was distorted, like a face in a funhouse.

He put on a heavy brown terrycloth robe and went into the kitchen. There was nothing in the refrigerator but a pint of milk, a stick of sweet butter and half a loaf of wheat bread. A jar of instant coffee was on a shelf above the sink. He made toast, two slices at a time, in the shiny chrome toaster that Carl Rich had given him. Carl had come by one morning to pick him up and had seen him holding a piece of bread over the stove burner with a fork.

What the hell do you think you're doing?

What the hell does it look like? I'm making toast.

Nobody makes toast that way anymore.

It beats my Zippo.

Carl had said nothing, but when he came by the next morning he brought the toaster with him in a box.

Call it a housewarming gift.

For Christ's sake, Carl, you can't afford that.

Take it. I couldn't sleep last night thinking of you setting fire to yourself for a lousy piece of toast.

He appreciated the toaster, not because it made toast with automatic General Electric efficiency — bread singed over a gas flame had a unique flavor that he found pleasant — but because Carl had given it to him. With Carl, the gift had to be a sacrifice. Rich was a good man; he was Officer James Dempsey's partner and his best, maybe his only, friend.

The toast was buttered by the time the water boiled. He scooped three teaspoonfuls of instant coffee into a china pot and poured in the water, then carried the pot, toast and a cup to a table in the other room. Before sitting down to eat he took the brown envelope from the inside pocket of his suit coat and placed it on the table, propping it against the pot. The envelope contained fifteen thousand dollars in fifty- and one-hundred-dollar bills. Max Godansky would have been flattered to know how much he had been worth.

When the toast was gone and the pot drained, Dempsey opened the envelope and counted the money. It was all there. Fifteen thousand. Sam Dondero was a man of his word. He counted out three thousand dollars into a separate pile, hesitated a moment, and then added to it. Five would be better. Claire wouldn't expect that much; that would be the wedge. She couldn't refuse when she had all that money in her hand. Or could she? Dempsey wasn't sure. Claire's rigidity defied analysis. She clung to the letter of the court order where the children were concerned. The judge had given Dempsey two weekends a month as his visitation rights. The ruling had been unfair. It hadn't taken into consideration the nature of his job. There were many weekends when he had to work. He should have the right to see his kids anytime he had a day off. If Claire had been reasonable, they could have worked this out between them. But no, she stuck to the words of the judge — every other weekend — period.

Thinking about Claire and the kids was bad. The thought pressed his mind and he felt pain coming into it. He had forty-eight hours off. It was Easter vacation and the kids were out of school. If Claire said it was okay he could rent a car and take them on a little trip. Maybe they could drive to Canton and visit the Football Hall of Fame, or just meander through the back roads and see the farm country, maybe stay overnight in one of those little towns in Clark County where the Amish lived. Cathy would get a big kick out of that — and the white gingerbread frame houses, the Amish farmers coming into town on their horse-drawn wagons, green fields and red silos. Maybe she could ride a pony or hold a baby pig. It was a pipe dream and he knew it. The most he could expect from Claire would be permission to take them out for the day, maybe see a movie or have a picnic in Wade Park. That was better than nothing. He counted the five thousand dollars again and smoothed the bills into a neat pile.

He dressed slowly, choosing his clothes with care. Claire hated sport coats. She hated so much. He put on a dark gray mohair with a faint white stripe, a pale blue shirt with a button-down collar and a dark maroon tie. He was dressed and ready to go by 7:30. It was too early. The rapid transit would get him out to Warrensville in twenty minutes. If he left at 8:15 he would be at Claire's before she left for the nine o'clock mass at St. Timothy's. Forty-five minutes to kill.

The gun was on the chair where he had hung his suit, the Colt .38 Python that he had carried for ten years. The grips were worn and dull streaks of metal showed through the bluing. He pulled the gun out of its holster and sniffed at the barrel. It stank with burnt cordite. A dirty gun. Fired four times that night, three of the slugs tearing into Max Godansky for five thousand dollars a bullet, one into Otto Mengus's barrel for nothing. A good gun. A Colt moneymaker. He placed it carefully on the table and gazed at it. A good-looking weapon, the blade of the front sight rising up like a shark's fin. So efficient. So perfect. Officer James Dempsey's tool of the trade.

There was a gun-cleaning kit and a box of bullets in the top drawer of his bureau, under his socks. He took them out and sat down at the table to strip and oil the revolver. He worked quickly and efficiently, performing a ritual. He swung out the cylinder and ejected the bullet. The gun carried six slugs, but he had always heeded the advice of the shooting instructor at the police academy about keeping the hammer on an empty chamber or a blank round.

But it would hold six. Six bullets — six men. Dempsey raised the gun slowly and peered down the barrel. He used his thumbnail to reflect light into it. He could see tiny grains of matter — garbage from the slugs or powder. He reamed the barrel out with a wire brush.

Six bullets — six men.

Joseph Crespi. From the sewers of Duluth. "Fat Joey" Crespi with a sheet as long as a whore's dream. He trailed him into every club and gin mill in the city. He trailed him into a small club that Dondero owned on the far South Side. Carl had remained in the car.

Dondero had been there, seated at a table in the back, talking with Crespi, no drinks in front of them, not a social call. Crespi had left and he had been ready to follow, but something in Dondero's eyes had drawn him to the little table near the men's room door.

Hello, Dempsey.

Sam.

You're tailin' that fink. Good. He's bad news. You know, that bastard wants a slice of the liquor action. An' he'll get it.

Dempsey put a drop of oil on a patch and pushed it slowly through the barrel with a rod. It made a tiny sucking sound as it came out the end.

You'll work it out, Sam.

A man like that just walks with trouble, you know. He's a loner but, like, he's got the family. If a guy gets sore about bein' pushed around he might dump Fat Joey in the river an' then he's in all kinds of shit with the family. They may all hate Fat Joey's guts but they wouldn't let nobody get away with puttin' a hole in him.

Sam, it's very sad.

The gun needed bluing, new grips and a general overhaul by a gunsmith. There was no point in doing it now. In a few weeks he would be ready to go and he would toss the gun into the Cuyahoga on the way to the airport. He couldn't take it to Mexico with him. He couldn't take Sean and Cathy, either. All that he could take to Mexico was himself — and the money.

A man like Joey . . . hot-headed, you know. Does lots of crazy things. A real Neapolitan. He might do somethin' stupid if he knew he was bein' tailed.

He might.

It's happened before. Some meathead tries to burn a cop and lands up in the morgue.

Yeah.

If such a thing should happen to Fat Joey Crespi, God rest his soul, I would personally give five . . . six thou to my favorite charity.

Would you give ten, Sam?

It had been more than the money. He could have taken it in a thousand ways over the years if it had just been money. He had reached a point in time where something had to happen, some infusion of strength, some tangible proof of himself. He had been drained, sucked dry. He had been a shell, starting the long, slow drift into middle age.

Fat Joey kneeling in an alley behind a Woodland Avenue motel. Three-thirty on a Tuesday morning. Praying.

Holy Mother . . .

Dempsey shot him twice in the chest and once in the great roll of fat that rested on top of his thighs as he knelt there, trembling and sweating. He fell slowly onto his back, staring upward to the heaven he hoped to enter.

Maiale . . . !

He had been called pig before. It didn't bother him. He pulled a little ivory-handled .32 from the inside left pocket of Fat Joey's suit and pressed the gun into a waxen hand.

Arivederci, Joey.

He felt a tautness in the groin as he held his .38 toward the light from the window. The barrel was clean. It shimmered. The trigger guard bulged against his palm and he slipped his finger gently around the spur of the trigger, pressing it backward, feeling the power of the spring. He swung the gun inward and the cylinder flipped back into place. He squeezed gently, the hammer inching back . . . spring and claw turning the cylinder where the fat slugs would go.

Joseph Crespi. Karl Neale. Benjamin Adolph Myers. Carlo Tedeschi. Albert Jacoby. Max Godansky.

They had seen the finger curl and tighten, watched the hammer slap against the brass shells.

CHRIST! NO!

His hand tightened on the grips and he pulled the trigger sharply — click click click click — slamming ghost bullets into nothingness. He shuddered and lowered the gun slowly to the table. His body felt limp. It would have been so easy to slump forward into sleep. He fought back the urge. It was getting late and he had to see Claire.

The chief was late with his morning call. It was nearly seven o'clock before the phone rang. Gorman made himself comfortable before picking up the receiver, tilting his chair back and swinging his feet onto the desk.

"Good morning, Chief."

"What the hell's good about it?"

Gorman had known Martin Keeley for fourteen years and time had not mellowed him. He was a banty Irishman who had come through the ranks — patrolman to inspector to chief of police. A long road full of pitfalls and challenges. Keeley had survived, grown tougher and crustier every step.

"I've had Dave Blackman on the phone for an hour,"

Keeley growled. "I'll tell you, Mike, there are times when I hate to get up in the morning. How does it look to you?"

"About the same. A rotten thing to have happen. A rookie panics and a prisoner dies. A terrible thing, but not police brutality."

"The papers will turn themselves inside out," Keeley said bitterly. "Well . . . we'll ride that out, I suppose. What's happening on the street? Dave was vague about it. He couldn't take the time to look out the window."

"It's tense up there, but not exploding."

"No riot today, then?"

"Not *this* weekend."

Keeley sighed deeply. "Okay, let's talk about something we can handle, or *should* be able to handle, goddamnit. I couldn't sleep last night thinking about this hijacking business. It's got to stop, Mike. It's got everybody spittin' nails at me — the Teamsters, the insurance companies, Chamber of Commerce. They're starting to raise hell with the mayor. Now, I want something to happen."

"I have some thoughts."

"Shoot."

Gorman braced the receiver under his chin and reached onto his desk for a cigarette. "Such as ask the major truck line operators to come down here and talk it over. They could make it a lot tougher for the hijackers if they would take precautions — better locking devices on the doors, change their routes — that sort of thing."

"Okay . . . that's a start, anyway."

"I have another plan in mind but I'd like to talk it over with Gruebner and Dave first."

"Sure, Mike. Maybe we can get together after the funeral and kick some ideas around."

"Yes, sir."

The phone clicked in his ear. Chief Keeley was not a man

who believed in the formality of "good-bye." Gorman hung up and turned his chair to face the window. Pale sunlight streamed through the dirty panes, the hard sun of morning that revealed every speck of dust in the room and every line on the man's face. Gorman lit his cigarette and watched the smoke curl in the sunbeams. He felt numb to the bone. His shift was almost over but there was no going home except to shower, shave and put on a dress uniform for the funeral. That was the least he could do for young Rinzo, lose a little sleep.

"Inspector?"

Gorman swung his chair around. Sergeant Ronald Vale of the print identification section stood in the doorway.

"Come in, Ronny. You look like you had a long night."

The young sergeant smiled. "It was worth it. I got a positive ident on those prints Blackman sent over . . . Owen Watkins, the prisoner who . . . who got killed."

"What did you make him on?"

"Seven robberies and four rapes. A very careless guy with his fingerprints. He's the one who was doing all those jobs in East Cleveland and Bratenahl Village. No doubt about it at all. We got a lot of smudged prints from most of those places, but the MO is the same — a little robbery and a lot of rape — man, woman or child. He wasn't too particular."

"That washes. They picked him up in a dress."

The sergeant yawned, covering his mouth with the back of his hand. "A jock fag. Good riddance."

"Yes but I wish a homeowner had shot him coming through a window. Did you tell Inspector Blackman yet?"

"Oh, sure. Soon as I matched the first print." He checked his watch. "One hour to go. I've got some coffee brewing if you'd like a cup."

"No, thanks. I think I'll take off a little early."

Vale grinned. "What? And leave us leaderless?"

"I think you'll survive."

Some of the day men were drifting in, mostly detectives trying to get a head start on their paperwork. They grunted their good-mornings as Gorman strode down the hall. He stopped at the Communications room before going to the garage to get his car. Captain Henderson looked as cool and immaculate as he had at the beginning of his shift, but the radio operators were bleary-eyed and groggy.

"I'm going home, Ralph."

Henderson made a slight bow and waved a hand toward the great outdoors. "Give my regards to fresh air."

"Anything happening?"

"A couple of accidents on 21. Nothing serious."

"Okay."

He continued on, having a last look around, like a captain departing his ship. A dozen pimps stood chatting with the desk sergeant. They were all tall black men, gaudy as flamingos. One of them raised a languid hand as Gorman passed by.

"Top of the morning, Inspector."

"Same to you, Willie." He knew every one of them. Whenever their girls were run in they'd be down at the station bright and early with the bail. It was just a game to them — book 'em and bail 'em. What a waste of time.

Johnny Davis parked his yellow Vega in the subterranean garage, easing it carefully between a Cadillac and a Mercedes. The parking routine was usually a pain in the ass. Everyone going out when he was coming in. Also, it embarrassed him, something he had tried to explain to Nikki. This apartment house was even fancier than the one in Lakewood. The men he ran into at 8:30 during the week were businessmen or professional men. They wore two-hundred-dollar suits and carried briefcases. He felt out of place walking into the elevator in his Windbreaker and Levi's, his hands and face dirty after a long night at the warehouse.

I feel like some slob who's come to fix the furnace.

What the hell do you care? We pay our rent.

It was okay for Nikki. She waltzed in and out of the building like a movie star.

He thought about her all the way up in the elevator.

She would be asleep, of course, and he wouldn't wake her as he came in. She hated that. He would be very quiet, closing the door softly behind him, taking off his shoes before going into the bedroom. He would even take a shower quietly, not turning on the water full force. Then he would get into bed — also quietly, gently — and lie very still next to her with the fingers of his right hand barely touching her back. She would sense him next to her and respond to his touch — if she wanted him.

If *she* wanted *him*. He never pressed her, never started things going, never forced her.

He opened the door and closed it quietly behind him. He could sense that someone had been in the apartment. Maybe Dondero. But *someone*. He could always tell, even when they didn't leave dirty glasses or overflowing ash-trays. He could smell it. He took off his shoes and walked slowly into the bedroom. She was alone, curled up in a tangle of blankets and sheets. The bed looked as though two strong men had wrestled on it. He choked back bitter stomach juices. His teeth hurt and he gagged. Why did he take this shit? He was married to a fucking whore. No. Whores took money. Nikki did it for the fun. He peeled off his clothes and dropped them on the floor, then stood naked by the side of the bed, looking down at her, hoping that she'd wake up and see him. She didn't stir and he was afraid to make any sound.

What's sauce for the goose . . .

Only it hadn't worked out that way for him. He couldn't make it with other women. He'd tried. Nikki had been throwing it in his face one day, the I-am-a-free-woman crap. He'd stormed out and picked up a broad. Not great but fuckable, usable. They went to her place, drank a little — and nothing. He couldn't get it up . . .

What's the matter, honey?

He should have killed the bitch for asking. He had just dressed and walked out.

That was the story of his life with Nikki, walking out — but never walking far enough. The only real problem he had in the world was in the bed in front of him. It was a problem he didn't understand and would never be able to solve.

"Nikki?"

She opened one eye and peered at him through a gap in the sheet.

"What do you want?"

"Nikki," he murmured. "Nikki . . ." He knelt close to the bed and slipped a hand under the blanket, groping for her hip. "Nikki . . ."

Her reaction was intense. She slapped his hand away and turned convulsively onto her stomach.

"Go away! The night shift's over, goddamnit!"

He lurched to his feet. "Bitch!"

"That's right," she mumbled, her mouth against the mattress.

His robe was hanging in the closet and he threw it over his shoulders. Nikki wasn't angry at him. He could tell by the slow, rhythmic rise and fall of the blanket-shrouded body that her breathing was slow and normal. Not angry, just a little annoyed that he had wakened her. She would be okay later in the afternoon. They would have supper together before she left for the club. A cold crab salad, French bread and a glass of Chablis. Cold crab. That was her favorite.

He wandered into the living room and stood in front of the windows. It was a clear, bright morning, the lake stretching away to a sharp, clean horizon. He watched a ketch glide through the breakwater channel, past the lighthouse and on into the vast, wind-rippled green of Lake Erie.

They'd have a boat one day. They'd have that kind of money. Not too big a boat, one they could handle between them, but large enough for two good bunks and a nice galley. They'd sail for the horizon and it would never come any closer. Just sail on and on and on.

She could be so rotten to him sometimes . . . and then . . . right out of the blue . . . so fantastically wonderful. So *giving*.

The ketch was well out past the breakwater, the sun glinting off its white hull. It made a sharp tack into the wind and rolled far over on its beam end. He watched until it righted itself and then he turned away and walked over to the little bar in the far corner of the room. He poured half a glass of Jack Daniels and downed it in three quick swallows. They had nothing but the best — Chivas Regal . . . Tanqueray . . . cognacs and champagne. Painkiller for Johnny. He poured out another drink and carried the bottle with him into the bedroom.

He sat on the edge of the king-sized bed, far over on his side so that his weight wouldn't disturb her. The sheets were all screwed up and the pillow, his pillow, had been wadded into a ball and jammed between the mattress and the headboard. The pillow would stink with hair oil and sweat. The sheets would be sticky. He shuddered and took a drink, almost gagging on the whiskey. Bad to drink that way, he thought dully, too much booze on an empty stomach. His ears were ringing and his lips felt numb. He filled the glass, some of the whiskey slopping into his lap, and let the bottle fall to the carpet between his bare feet.

"Jesus," he said thickly. "Gotta stop this shit . . . gotta stop it."

He had to talk with her, make her understand what she was doing to him. She was killing him with this shit . . . cutting his heart out. If they could only sit down and talk it over . . . just talk . . .

"Look, baby . . . look, baby . . ."

The words wouldn't come. It didn't matter. She wasn't listening.

A wave of self-pity overwhelmed him and he tried to choke back the tears by drinking more whiskey. It didn't help. He could see the future and there was nothing in it for either of them. Not a damn thing . . . gray days . . . endless nights. He tried to put the glass on the nightstand and missed. It fell soundlessly onto the carpet, the whiskey making a dark stain on the golden fibers. He groped blindly for the pillow and buried his face in it.

George Fisher was fifty-one years old and a bachelor. A graduate of Western Reserve and holder of two degrees in forensic science, he shared with Otto Mengus the diverse responsibilities of the crime lab and the supervision of its technicians, almost all of whom worked the day shift.

George Fisher arrived punctually at eight. His punctuality was his pride, as was his sense of order — two qualities that, in his opinion, Otto Mengus lacked. They were the only faults he found in Otto, except for the pipe — George

Fisher detested the aroma of Otto's tobacco. And though he wished Mengus would pay more attention to time schedules and cleaning up after himself, he had never once voiced his feelings. He had too great a respect for Otto to carp about such minor failings.

"Good morning, Otto."

"George," Mengus acknowledged, not looking up from the swamp of papers on his desk.

George Fisher clucked his tongue at the mess as he hung his topcoat in the closet and placed his hat neatly on a shelf.

"Busy night, Otto?"

Mengus grunted, sifting through a handful of loose papers interspersed with 8 x 10 photographs of Max Godansky's body before it was taken to the morgue. Fisher walked to his own desk, the only uncluttered surface in the entire room, and removed a clean white smock from the bottom drawer.

"Anything you want me to follow through on?"

Mengus looked up for the first time. "There's a Winchester carbine over there someplace. You might run a ballistics test on it. Sniper shot himself with it."

"All right," Fisher said. He had known Otto Mengus for many years and he could tell that something was disturbing him. "Can I give you a hand with what you're doing?"

"You can answer one question for me. Does two and two still add up to four?"

Fisher removed his eyeglasses and breathed on the lenses before wiping them with a clean handkerchief. "If we're not into synergistic reaction, in which case two and two make five."

"I've been thinking about it half the night," Mengus said. "Certain laws of mathematics, including the theory

120

of probability, are going to pot. Either that or I'm getting senile."

"I wouldn't doubt it."

"No. Neither would I." He shoved the papers onto his desk and stood up. "George, you're a cool, rational man . . . a logical man. I'm going to fix myself a cup of tea and eat a stale donut. While I'm doing that, I'd like you to sit down at my desk and read some papers — very slowly and carefully — and then tell me what you think."

"Certainly — but if it's all the same to you, I'll sit at *my* desk."

Mengus gazed at his desk gloomily. "I don't know how it gets that way, George."

"I do. You have the only wastebasket in the building that's never been used."

"I can think of one thing I'd like to throw out — and you'll feel the same way." He gathered up the papers — the official statements of Carl Rich and James Dempsey, the photos of Max Godansky, his own diagrams and ballistic reports — and dropped them on George Fisher's desk.

Otto Mengus had time for two cups of tea and to stare out the barred windows at a dozen motorcycle policemen riding down Payne Avenue, one after the other, all in dress blues, the bikes glittering with polished chrome. They would be heading out for the Rinzo boy's funeral, he thought sadly. It was too beautiful a day to be buried.

George Fisher cleared his throat. "Well," he said. "Well, now."

Mengus did not turn around. "Finished?"

"Yes," Fisher said quietly. "Yes, I have."

"And?"

"Something is terribly wrong here."

"With my calculations?"

Fisher was silent for a moment. "I wish I could say that, Otto."

Mengus set the cup down on the window ledge and reached into his pocket for his pipe. "I wish you could, too."

There was a moment of bliss, a tiny oasis in the desert of her agony. It happened only in the morning. She would open her eyes and think, *I have no pain. Dear God, I'm well again.* It was a cruel joke. The pain was there, it had simply been drugged by sleep. It came the moment she turned her head on the pillow, or moved a hand. The pain was rooted deeply in her twisted joints and it would never go away.

"Carl?"

She called his name softly, almost apologetically. She hated to wake him if he was still sleeping, but she had no choice.

"Carl."

She turned her head and looked at the other bed. It was empty, the cover still on.

"Carl!"

The sight of the smooth bedspread panicked her. What if he hadn't come home? What if something had happened?

"*Carl . . . !*"

The cry slapped him out of a deep sleep and he came out of the chair in a cold sweat, his heart slamming against the walls of his chest.

"Della?"

"Where are you, Carl?"

"Here, honey . . . here." He felt disoriented, and he had to hold onto the back of the chair for a moment to recover his bearings. He was in the living room of his own house, early in the morning. The TV set was still on, a lopsided test pattern. Rich slapped the off button in disgust. What a waste of electricity.

"What are you doing, Carl?"

"Nothing, honey, nothing . . . be right in." He was slurring his words. Too little sleep, too much bourbon. He would have slept half the day if she hadn't called out for him, but there was no one else she could call. He combed his hair with his fingers and walked a trifle unsteadily down the hall and into the bedroom. She was straining to raise herself by pulling the metal rings that dangled from the ceiling directly above the bed. He leaned against the door frame and watched her.

"You're getting better than Tarzan."

She forced a smile. "I feel more like the monkey."

He waited until she was sitting upright before coming into the room.

"That helps the arms."

"I think so,' she lied. "It builds a little strength."

It was a game they played. It was called "Getting Better." Every new drug that her doctor prescribed or any suggestion that he made to help rehabilitate her wasted frame was greeted with enthusiasm. When it became obvious that neither medication nor therapy was doing much good, they refused to admit it. They kept the hope alive.

"Do you want your pills?"

"After I eat. They make me queasy on an empty stomach."

"I forgot."

"They're really a godsend, though."

"Yeah, they sure are."

She was moving her legs painfully to the edge of the bed, the legs that were now so thin, like flesh-colored sticks. Rich looked away. He got the wheelchair out of the corner. By the time he brought it around to the side of the bed, Della had covered her legs with her robe.

"What do you want for breakfast?" he asked, helping her into the chair.

"Nothing much. Coffee and toast."

"That's not enough. You won't get strong on coffee and toast. What you need are six eggs, a stack of flapjacks and a pound of bacon."

She smiled a little.

"You'd have to rob banks if I ate like that."

"Why not? Give me something to do when I quit the job."

He pushed the chair out of the bedroom and down the hall toward the living room. She would have her breakfast on a tray and watch television. She could wheel herself, but he enjoyed doing it. Before her illness had worsened, when only her knees had been affected and it had been difficult but not impossible to walk, he used to fold up the chair and put it in the back of the car and take her to Wade Park for the day. He'd push her all through the park, up and down the paths, watching the kids playing on the sweeping lawns and all the young couples going through the rituals of romance. That had been one of their great pleasures, the park and the museums, getting out in the sun, but that was all behind them now. They never went out anymore.

He wheeled her into a patch of sun that streamed through the front windows, then pulled the TV to face her.

"What would you like to see?"

"Anything you'd like."

"Okay, we'll find something. Let me get the coffee first . . . I just gotta have some coffee."

"You look — tired."

"I feel fine."

"You haven't been to bed."

"No . . . but I slept like a rock. Got halfway into the late show and went out like a light."

He turned away from her, trying to avoid her eyes. They had no secrets from each other. There was nothing they could hide. He felt her pain and she knew his fear.

"You need a drink now and then, Carl."

It was a simple statement of fact. There was no bitterness in her voice, or outrage. He had his back to her and he stared down at the bottle. It was on the floor next to his chair, along with a half-eaten orange and a scattering of peel.

"I had a couple of highballs . . . just getting the edge off a tough week."

"Carl . . ."

He could sense her agony. He knelt beside her and she drew away from him, pressing her thin hands to her face.

"Baby . . ." He touched her shoulder gently. "Baby . . . I got forty-eight hours off on account of a bust Jimmy and me made. We got a couple of days and . . ."

She shook her head. "Oh, God . . . why don't you just go — and keep going some night when I'm asleep — and just live like a human being while you still can. You could get a woman, Carl, have a decent life."

He held onto her with both arms. Her sobs frightened him. She was falling apart. He could feel her strength slipping through his fingers and he struggled to hold onto it.

"Baby, baby . . . don't talk like that, please — baby, it ain't you. I was kinda celebrating, baby — letting the spring run down — just unwinding, Della . . ."

Her sobs became moans. She didn't have the strength for weeping.

"You're all I have, Carl — I'm sorry, so sorry. Please

don't hate me for needing you so much — please don't hate me . . ."

He clutched her fiercely, pressing her face against his chest. Whatever had been there within him twenty-five years ago, when they first held each other, still flowed through him and gave him strength.

"Hate you? You're all I live for — you're all I think about."

His tears came and he could not stop them. Half a bottle of whiskey had failed to touch his fear and tension, but Della's anguish broke it down. He clung to her and she became a woman again, the stronger of them in some ways. She ran a hand across his shoulder and caressed the back of his neck.

"Carl, honey — Carl — don't cry . . . don't cry. Everything's going to be all right, honey. We can make it right."

The last note of taps hung in the still air a clean, brass sound followed by the sharp crack of rifles. Gorman flinched at the first volley, but the white-gloved hand that he held in knife-edged salute did not waver. Another sharp volley — and another. Twenty-one shots over the open grave of Eddy Rinzo.

Gorman let his eyes drift across the scene in critical appraisal. The police were burying one of their own, paying homage to the man and respect to his family. It was being done properly — the square of blue-clad men flanking the grave, the mounted police guard holding their horses in tight check, the gleaming phalanx of motorcycles parked in front of the hearse. The sun glinted from gold braid, brass buttons, polished saddles and gleaming chrome.

"A lot of crap," Inspector Gruebner said out of the side of his mouth. "You're just ruining a good man, Dave."

Gorman sighed and stared stiffly ahead. He stood between Gruebner and Dave Blackman, five paces behind Police Chief Keeley and the black figure of Patrolman Rinzo's young widow. Gruebner and Blackman had been sniping at each other since they arrived.

"If he killed a prisoner, he'll go to jail."

"Horseshit. A psycho fag rapist."

"A prisoner under arrest."

"Balls. He did the city a favor. This isn't Scout Troop 9."

"Fuck you."

"Knock it off," Gorman whispered. "Both of you."

A priest intoned a few words in Latin and the funeral was over, television cameramen recording the event for the evening news, panning the silent ranks of the police, the pale-faced widow, her bewildered children clinging to their grandparents' hands. A cop was being buried and a million people would see it. Would they sympathize or cheer? It was a funeral for the papers and the media, a good piece of public relations. That was what Dempsey had said and Gorman knew he was right. It was a funeral that would honor the police without offending anyone. Eddy Rinzo had died at the hands of a white drunk. If the killer had been black, it would be no night to be on the streets in the ghetto — for white or black. He looked for Dempsey in the ranks of detectives and other plainclothesmen who formed one side of the square. He would have been surprised to see him there. Chief Keeley escorted the widow and her family toward the black limousine and the motorcycle cops swung into their seats and kicked their bikes into life.

Gruebner plucked a long cigar from his pocket and peeled off the wrapper.

"A nice funeral."

"If there is such a thing," Gorman said.

"Well, you got to have one — it might as well be pleasant."

Blackman glared at him. "When we have yours, I'll bring out all the incompetents you want to protect. We'll have a wake!"

Gruebner bit the tip off his cigar and spat it into the grass.

"That's okay with me, Dave. Some of my best friends and fellow officers are incompetent."

"What did you mean by that, you fat sonofabitch?" Blackman took a step forward, but Gorman was between them to calm the storm.

"Come on, let's get out of here. I need some sleep. Can I give you a lift, Dave?"

"Thank you," Blackman said.

"Watch your speed, Mike," Gruebner said, grinning. "He'd give his mother a ticket."

Blackman walked in tight, angry silence until they reached the car.

"That goddamned Dutchman is exactly what's wrong with the police department."

"Oh, come on Dave. He's just as frustrated as you are."

"What in the name of God does he expect me to do? Pin a rose on the kid and tell him not to do it again?"

"Of course not, and you know it. If it had happened at Central, he would have done the same thing."

"I doubt it."

There was no point in arguing. It hadn't happened at Central. Gorman thanked heaven for that — and he was sure that Gruebner did, too. The death of a prisoner could not be brushed under the carpet, even when they hanged themselves. Blackman was stuck with the nightmare every cop lived with — having to prosecute obvious and fatal police brutality.

Gorman started the car and inched down the narrow cemetery road. The mounted police moved past, threading their way between the cars, hooves clattering on the paving.

"The Chief's in a sweat about the hijackings."

"I know," Blackman said morosely. "He's starting to get heat from City Hall."

"I told him I'd talk to you about it, work something out."

"Fine."

"He wants us to get together with the major truckers first. Give them a few lessons on cargo safety."

Blackman's smile was thin. "Very funny. We'll be lecturing somebody who's into it up to his ears. Only a trucker could handle the logistics of the job and the disposal of the merchandise."

"Probably."

"What are we supposed to do? Tip them off on how we're going to handle the problem?"

"You're not thinking, your head is still arguing with Dutch. We could tell them one thing and do another."

"Whoever these people are, they're smart, Mike, very smart. Whatever we do we're going to have to do fast, and do it like we mean it. No half-measures."

Gorman nodded in agreement. Two horses walked in front of the car. Gorman touched the brake.

"Speaking of horseshit," Blackman said dryly, "Gruebner has a plan that could be adapted. That cab-heisting thing a few years back."

"That was a tip from a pissed-off girlfriend."

"That's the one. But Gruebner had a decoy scheme that looked pretty good on paper."

"Ask him to dust it off — if you can stop insulting each other."

A rare smile graced Blackman's face. "I have to speak

to him. We're partners in a pinochle game every Thursday night."

They had reached the cemetery gates and the horse troop moved to one side to form an honor guard for the parade of cars. Gorman turned out of the line and headed along Mayfield Road toward Euclid, driving fast, eager to get home. There was very little traffic. If there had been, he would have flipped on the howler. A vision of crisp sheets and a soft pillow dangled before him like a mirage.

"Do you know Lewandowski?" Blackman asked.

"Big patrolman from the Eleventh Precinct?"

"That's the guy. He called me before I went off duty. He's been down at the morgue all night."

"Why?"

"The man Dempsey shot. They brought his mother out to the morgue to identify him. She doesn't speak a word of English so they got Lewandowski to interpret for her."

"So?"

"She won't go home. She's been sitting in the morgue since midnight, counting her beads — and waiting."

"What for? Where's the undertaker?"

"Lewandowski told me that she refuses to take the body — until she talks to the man who murdered her son."

Gorman felt coldly awake. He slowed the car down and drifted toward the side of the highway. Blackman was staring straight ahead, his face impassive.

"What does she mean . . . *murdered*?"

"How would I know?"

"Wasn't she told how her son died?"

"I'm sure. I guess she just won't believe it until she talks to the man who shot him."

"Oh, God! What do you suggest we do with her? Lock her up for loitering?"

"We? Not my problem, Mike. Dempsey's your boy."

"I gave him forty-eight off." He tapped the steering wheel with the palm of his hand. "I'm not going to ask him to face that."

"Well. she's going to be sitting in that morgue until he does or we carry her out of there."

"Oh, fuck!" Gorman growled. He was tired to the bone, to the marrow.

"If I were you, I'd go to the morgue and try to reason with her. She's got a right to be upset."

Gorman felt guilty. The woman who kept vigil at the morgue knew just as much sorrow as the widow of the cop they had buried. Fatigue was a funny thing. It tampered with your sense of values. The woman's son was dead; he, Gorman, was merely exhausted.

Gorman hit the gas pedal and cut out of the slow lane. Traffic was starting to pile up as he neared the junction of Mayfield and Euclid so he turned on the howler and drove everyone ahead of him to the side of the street. His vision of bed and sleep were erased.

The Cuyahoga County Morgue was new, big, bright and glossy. It reminded Gorman of a new supermarket in a suburban shopping center, waiting to be filled with groceries and wire carts. But it was functional. Here, though, he thought, the customers never complained. The guard at the front desk was startled to see an inspector of police in full dress uniform stride in, but he knew all about the crazy Polack lady who had spent the night seated on a bench in the hall. He pointed out the corridor for Gorman, then settled back with his Thermos of coffee and the fat collection of inaccuracies and middle-class pomposity in the newspaper.

She was old — seventy, Gorman estimated, although she could have been much younger. A lifetime of floor scrubbing could add ten years to any woman's looks. She sat stiffly on the edge of a bench in a corridor that was barren of any comforts or adornments other than a sand receptacle for cigarette butts. Her frail body was wrapped in a threadbare coat, a babushka of black cloth tied tightly around her head. A uniformed policeman sat beside her, bent forward, elbows resting on his knees. He looked up at the sound of Gorman's approach and got quickly to his feet.

"Charles Lewandowski, Eleventh Precinct."

"Good morning," Gorman said. "I understand you've been with Mrs. Godansky all night."

"That's right, sir. She . . . well, she just won't go home."

The old woman was staring at Gorman with small, feverish eyes. She said something in Polish that caused Lewandowski to squirm in embarrassment.

"What did she say?"

"She . . . asked me if . . . if you . . . ah . . . were the man who killed her son."

Gorman stared at him. "Is that *exactly* what she said?"

Lewandowski looked at his feet. "No, sir. She wanted to know if you're the dog's afterbirth who murdered her son."

"Okay. Now look, Charlie. I'm going to ask her a few questions and I don't want any of her answers changed in translation."

"She's very bitter, sir. Been scorching my ear all night about what a good boy Max was. She's got it in her head that the cops murdered him and that's just about all you'll get out of her. Nothing coherent."

"Tell her who I am first of all. She's staring at me like I was Jack the Ripper."

Lewandowski bent toward her and spoke softly. The woman continued to glare at Gorman until the young policeman had finished speaking, then she muttered something and turned her steady gaze toward the wall.

"She doesn't blame you, just your men."

Gorman sighed. "Ask her why she thinks he was murdered and why he carried a gun."

Lewandowski's softly uttered questions triggered an outburst of hysteria. The woman screamed her answer, pounding one bony, parchment-thin hand against the edge of the bench. The tirade ended in deep, gasping sobs but no tears.

"Did you get all that?" Gorman asked.

The policeman grimaced and scratched the long line of his jaw. "Most of it. She said that he was a good boy — hard-working. Always gave her money every week — not like her other children who are just bums. Max was her eldest and he looked out for her. She said that he carried the gun because he was afraid of a man. She said she met this man a couple of times. He came to her house when she was nursing Max through the chest sickness — I guess she means the flu or something. Everything got a little garbled after that, but the gist of it was that she'll sit here until hell freezes unless she gets to see the man who shot her Max. And she means it, Inspector. She's going to invoke a curse on him that will send him straight to hell."

"What do you think?"

"I don't know, Inspector. She's crazy with grief, but these old ones never lie. They know it's only a hop, skip and a jump from here to St. Peter. She has it in her mind we're trying to hide the man who killed her son — the way the *polizei* would do it in the old country."

Gorman felt like a man digging a well in the Sahara with a cake fork.

"I want this woman to go home, Charlie. Some hungry

reporter is going to get wind of this and blow it up like a balloon."

"The only way we'll get her out of here is to pick her up and throw her out. I mean it, Inspector. This is one determined old lady."

"I want you to tell her that I'm going to investigate. I'll be sending two detectives to her house tomorrow morning to get a full statement. Tell her that the police department will get the facts. Tell her that we seek justice just as much as she does. Tell her . . . that I promise her on the grave of my own mother."

Lewandowski was startled by the vehemence of Gorman's avowal. He was only a year out of the police academy and standing face to face with a gold-braided inspector was unnerving, but his conscience forced him to ask a painful question.

"Will I be leveling with her, Inspector? I mean, if nobody shows up tomorrow she'll be laying a good old Polish curse on me. And you."

Gorman suppressed a smile. He wondered what Blackman would have done if a rookie had doubted his word. Had him struck by lightning, he supposed, since they were now so involved in dark curses and invocations of the spirits.

"Do you know Sergeants Daley and Winshaw?"

"No . . . no, sir," Lewandowski stammered. "I've never met them, but I know of them."

"They were trying to deal with her son as an informer, so they have more than just a passing interest in what happened to him. They'll meet you at Mrs. Godansky's house, let's say, at ten tomorrow morning. Neither one of them speaks Polish so you'll work with them until this whole thing's settled. I'll clear it with your watch commander."

"Yes, sir."

"Now, get on with it — and be very, *very* sincere or you're going to be here for another twelve hours."

Gorman felt like having a cigarette but he knew it would be an unwise move to reach for one. The woman was listening intently to what Lewandowski was telling her, but her eyes were on Gorman's face, seeking the truth in his expression. Words were only words but a man's face never lied. He stood very still hands clasped behind his back, an imposing figure of authority and trust. When the woman lowered her eyes Gorman knew that she had agreed. He helped her up and gave her shoulder a comforting squeeze.

"See that she gets home all right, Charlie."

"Sure, Inspector sure. I'll take her to my house first and see that she eats something."

Gorman felt hunger himself. It seemed like days since he'd sliced into those pork chops at Foster's, and all he'd had time for when he went home to put on his dress uniform had been a cup of coffee. He willed the idea of food out of his head and concentrated on trying to remember Dempsey's telephone number. He couldn't recall one digit of it, so he went into one of the phone booths in the lobby and called Central. He got Dempsey's home number from Sergeant Rubel at the desk, then had him switch the call to either Daley or Winshaw. It was Daley who answered the phone and Gorman was grateful for that.

"Bob, this is Inspector Gorman."

"Hi, chief. What's new?"

"I just like to keep in touch."

The robbery detective chuckled softly. "You're getting more like Blackman every day. But I'll level with you, Chief. I'm sitting on my ass drinking a Coke and doing a crossword puzzle. But I got Winshaw out solving all the crimes in the world."

"With a hangover, no doubt."

There was a slight pause. Then: "We both hung one on last night. Nine fucking months right down the drain and we were *that* close."

Gorman shifted the receiver to his left hand and reached into his pocket for a pencil. He jotted Dempsey's number on the cover of a phone book before it slipped out of his mind again.

"Did you ever talk with Godansky's mother?"

"No," Daley said. "I didn't know he had one."

"I want her interviewed tomorrow morning. You'll meet an Officer Lewandowski, Charles Lewandowski, at her house. He'll translate for you."

There was a long silence. Gorman could hear the wheels going around in Sergeant Daley's head.

"Okay, chief, but what specifically am I to interview her *about*?"

"A man . . . a man who came to her house a couple of times. Max was afraid of him, she says. That's why he carried a .38."

Daley yawned loudly. "He had other reasons. Like slapping the shit out of people with the barrel — from time to time."

"I know, but she's his mother. Just let her talk. Take a tape machine. I want a record of everything she says."

"Is there anything else I should know?"

"No," Gorman snapped. If Daley was one thing he was a smart cop and all his antennae were up. "It's — just routine. Get the old lady's story and report directly to me. Is that clear?"

"Yeah," Daley said. "But it's not routine."

He hung up without waiting for an answer. Gorman dialed Dempsey's number. He hoped that he wasn't in.

What could he say to him? What could he — or should he — say about the old Polish lady?

Gorman held the instrument to his ear for a long minute and then placed it carefully, thankfully, on the hook.

The wheels of the electric train drummed the refrain into his head as it rattled out of the city toward the suburbs.

Clickity-clickity Claire . . . Clickity-clickity Claire . . .

Dempsey stared out the window. Drab streets and factory yards gave way to patches of grass. The shiny rapid transit train crossed the city limits and headed toward the green belts of Shaker Heights and Warrensville, Beachwood and the fringes of Woodmere Village. The homes of the middle-class rich came into view — brick and fieldstone, wood and glass. Well-clipped lawns sloped to pleasant streets lined with buckeye and elm. Dempsey saw nothing. He was listening to the wheels.

Clickity-clickity Claire . . . Clickity-clickity Claire . . .

She would say "yes" or she would say "no." She tossed the coin and she could call it either way. It was galling to be in that position, but that was how it was. The law was the law — and Claire was Claire.

Do you take this woman to be your lawfully wedded wife?

He wore a double-breasted blue suit and Claire wore a white dress. White for unplowed fields, white for little lies, white for tightly clamped thighs. An afternoon wedding at St. Boniface. Michael Gorman was there. A lot of smiling cops were there, half in the bag, full of bad jokes.

Honeymoon in New York City. Grant's Tomb, the Hayden Planetarium, top of the Empire State . . .

Look, you can see for miles. Is that New Jersey? . . . the Statue of Liberty, the Battery, Wall Street, Chinatown . . .

I feel silly — I can't use chopsticks.

A long day. Happy people. Like being on a date. Walking hand in hand through Central Park. No hippies, then. No muggers. Loving couples on the lawn, listening to the music. Gleaming towers of light beyond the dark trees.

Let's go back to the hotel, Claire.

That was part of marriage, but she could never accept it. It was the price a woman paid. A cross she had to bear. She wanted children, but why hadn't God in his great wisdom provided a better way? A cleaner way?

Don't hurt me!

I'm not going to hurt you, Claire.

It hurts! It hurts! Stop!

Her body had been ivory and just as unbending. A beautiful body, but worthless. He had kissed her nipples and she had turned her head quickly toward the window, wishing she was back in the park or in the restaurant. Dating was fun — but this? This was a nightmare . . .

What are you doing now? Oh, God, don't do that . . .

I have to, Claire . . . have to . . .

And it was done. She never forgave him for shedding her blood on the white sheets of a double bed fifteen stories above West Thirty-first Street in New York City on the night of July the twelfth, nineteen hundred and fifty-nine. His wedding night read like a police report. The rapist continued to violate the victim and to commit assault upon her person — from time to time. Victim continued to submit, sustained by visions of the Holy Mother weeping over her ordeal.

She conceived — twice. She bore children — twice. Her role as a woman was fulfilled and all further gross intimacies terminated. James Dempsey, the animal, could go straight to Hell.

Clickity-clickity Claire . . . Clickity-clickity Claire . . .

He got out at the end of the line and walked quickly

138

toward her street. He hoped she and the kids were home. It was a pleasant neighborhood to walk in, solid, well-cared-for houses, pruned bushes and budding trees, flower beds, lawn sprinklers. A man washed a new Oldsmobile in his driveway, running a chamois lovingly over the chrome.

Number 27 Thaxton Drive was a one-story ranch-style house with a white painted split-rail fence. A box elder spread its branches over the front of the house and neat beds of primrose flanked the curving brick path that led to the front door. A fine house, Dempsey thought. As fine as any on the block. He felt a sharp sense of loss that he had never lived in it.

The ten-speed bicycle that he had bought Sean for Christmas lay in the driveway. He picked it up and wheeled it toward the garage. The front wheel was bent and the rear brake handle needed tightening. Either the boy was hard on his things or he just didn't care. He'd have to give him a lecture on responsibility. A seventy-five-dollar bike, tossed around like a dime-store toy. He propped the bike against the side of the garage and walked to the front door. It opened as he was reaching for the bell.

"Hello, Claire."

She stepped back with a gasp of fear. "You . . . startled me."

"Sorry." He smiled at her. It was a warm smile and he meant it. She was a handsome woman, tall, red-haired. She was starting to get a matronly thickness in the waist and her chin had lost its firmness, but she was still attractive.

"What do you want?"

He raised one shoulder in a shrug. "I just happened to be in the neighborhood — thought I'd see the kids."

Her face hardened and she stepped out of the house and closed the door behind her.

"I'm late."

"Go on. I'll stick around till you get back. Maybe I can help Sean fix his bike. The front wheel's out of line."

"He's not here. He went to a friend's house."

"Okay. Cathy around?"

Her eyes were cold — a hard, flinty gray.

"She's over at Maude's. It was Trudy's birthday yesterday and she spent the night."

She was blocking him out. He kept the smile on his face, but it was starting to hurt.

"You could phone Maude. She wouldn't mind. It's only a ten-minute drive."

She squared her shoulders and tilted her head sharply to one side.

"No."

Very defensive. He knew all of her mannerisms.

"I'd like to spend the day with my daughter — and my son, if I can drag him away from his friend's house. Is that too much to ask, Claire?"

"Next weekend. That's your time — *next* weekend."

"They gave me two days off — today and tomorrow. I may be on duty next weekend."

She was unmoved. "The court set the rules. I didn't."

"They didn't carve them in stone. We can be a little flexible with the rules." He reached inside his coat and brought out the envelope. "Here . . ."

She took the envelope and stuffed it into her handbag.

"It's more than usual," he said angrily.

There was only contempt in her eyes as she turned away from him and walked quickly toward the garage. He took a rapid step after her and grabbed hold of her arm.

140

"For Christ's sake, Claire!"

She tore free of his grasp, shocked, outraged. "Don't touch me! I'm not one of your whores!"

"Okay . . . okay . . . I'm sorry I touched you. But why can't you be human?"

She stiffened as though slapped in the face. "*Human*? *Human*? What do you know about being human? You were an animal in heat from the day we got married. A dirty, rutting animal. You chased every slut in this city while I sat home and prayed for you. *Prayed*! Well, you can go to hell, James Dempsey. You can go to hell!"

She ran toward the garage and he made no move to go after her. There was no point in it. There would only be more words, another twist of the knife in old wounds. He stood and watched as she swung open the garage doors and backed her car down the drive, burning rubber in her haste to get out of his sight.

It was a long walk back to the station. A long ride back to the city. He rested the side of his head against the window and listened to the song of the wheels.

Gorman's need for sleep robbed him of his appetite — that and the sight of Richard eating a sandwich. The boy lay on his stomach on the living-room floor, reading the paper and gnawing on what looked like a pound of bologna, hot pickles and mustard precariously supported by two pieces of rye bread. Only a fifteen-year-old stomach could handle it and survive.

"Hi, Dad," the boy mumbled.

"Hi. Don't talk with your mouth full," Gorman said.

"Sure." He smiled.

"Where's your mother?"

"Kitchen."

Michael Gorman, Inspector of Police, City of Cleveland,

opened the closet door and began to shed the trappings of his office. He hung his heavy jacket on a hanger and placed it inside a green plastic cover for protection against dust and moths. His gun went on the nail above the door frame and his stiff-billed cap on the shelf beside the other two caps which he owned. When he walked into the kitchen he was just a man in his shirt-sleeves home from the office — finally — at one o'clock in the afternoon.

"That's wet wax."

Her cry came too late. He was a quarter of the way into the kitchen. He backed out carefully, like a dog on ice.

"You ought to put up a sign."

"Who'd read it? Richard's been on it twice."

She stood across the kitchen from him, in the doorway leading to the back porch. They were separated by fifteen feet of glossy linoleum tile.

"You should be in the Traffic Division," he said.

She smiled and brushed a loose strand of hair from her forehead.

"At least you have variety. How would you like the Case of the Dirty Kitchen Floor facing you every day?"

"I'd like it better than some."

"I bet." She knelt down and tested the wax with a fingertip. "Still tacky. I can feed you in about ten minutes."

He shook his head groggily. "I'm going to bed. Wake me up in ten days."

She could hear him going up the stairs, one leaden foot after the other. He worked impossible hours. Their lives had been warped to fit the dictates of his job. Even their vacation plans had to be tentative, the date set with crossed fingers. More than one trip had been postponed and then canceled because the department took precedence. There were times when she resented the badge he wore. She resented it now, hearing him drag himself upstairs to bed while warm spring sunshine sparkled against the windowpanes. She could hear Baxter Anderson clipping the hedge that divided his property from theirs. Baxter was the same age as Michael but he looked younger, his face smooth, unlined. He taught English at a junior college and his life was orderly. She felt a twinge of envy. Janice Anderson never knew the anxiety of watching her husband go off to work with a gun on his belt.

When the floor was dry she touched up the marks his feet had left, then put the lamb's wool in the sink to soak out the wax. The phone rang and the sound startled her. It seemed to shatter the calm like a firebell. *If they want him downtown, I won't let him go*, she thought angrily. There was a yellow wall phone by the breakfast nook, but before she could reach it the ringing had stopped.

"Mom?" Richard poked his head through the doorway. "Don wants me to come over and play some ball. Okay?"

"Be home for dinner."

"What are we having?"

"It doesn't matter what we're having. I want you home."

"Okay," he muttered.

He was fifteen and a half. An awkward age for both of them. He was a head taller than she and he sometimes stretched her authority over his movements. A young man, not a little boy any longer. She wished that Michael could spend more time enforcing the rules at home with his strong presence. One more reason for resentment.

She heard the front door close and she felt very much alone in the silent house. She went into the living room, picked up the scattered pages of the paper and the plate and empty Coke bottle that Richard had left on the floor. She placed the newspaper on an end table and took the plate and bottle into the kitchen. It was ten minutes after one. The electric clock above the stove whirred softly in the silence.

There were things to be done — sewing, laundry. She went upstairs to empty the hamper in the bathroom. Their bedroom door was ajar and she peeped in to make sure he was asleep. He lay on his side, facing the curtained window, propped up on one elbow and smoking a cigarette.

"Can't you sleep?"

"No." He reached over to the nightstand and squashed his cigarette in an ashtray. "I can't stop the wheels."

She came into the room and stood at the foot of the king-sized bed.

"Can I get you a sleeping pill?"

"God, no."

"You're probably hungry. How about a sandwich and a glass of beer?"

He lay on his back and stared at the ceiling. "I need something, Annie, but I don't know what. A new job would do for openers. I was lying here thinking about Pat."

"Pat?" She sat on the edge of the bed and he moved his legs to make room for her.

"Yeah. I was remembering how my mother was always worrying about him, and lecturing him. You know. Why-can't-you-be-like-your-brother? Poor Pat. He never had a job longer than a week. I tried to talk him into joining the force." He reached for another cigarette. "He must bless the day he laughed at the idea."

She reached over and took the cigarette from his hand. "Too much."

"I know it."

"Go to sleep. Pat went his way and you went yours. Would you rather be selling swimming pools in California with him? You're not the type."

"He made fifty thousand dollars last year and he's five years younger than I am."

She smiled at him and touched his bare shoulder. "Paul Newman makes more money than you, and his eyes are bluer. What's the point?"

"No point, I guess. I just have a bad case of middle-age slump. The forty-year itch. I'd like to toss in the badge and run off to sea."

"Richard and I would love that. He could scrape the barnacles and I'd sew your sails." Her fingers traced an aimless pattern across his chest.

"It'd probably be better for both of you."

"We have a lot here. Everything balances out."

He took her hand and pressed it lightly to his lips.

"Where's Richard?"

"We have nine innings of privacy," she said, bending forward and kissing him on the brow. "He went over to Don's house."

The clothes came off her full, warm body in the half-light. She moved away — deliberately — to put her dress, bra and panties neatly on the dressing table chair. There was a delicious, almost illicit quality to daytime love while Baxter Anderson was in his garden, clipping the hedge. She thought it might be something like two people in the city checking into a hotel at lunchtime, stealing an hour or two of "nooners," the better the passion for having stolen the time for it.

"You have a beautiful body."

"I have a beautiful *fat* body."

"Voluptuous is the word — full and fair."

She laughed. "Maybe you should sell swimming pools. I'd buy six."

"I like to think of myself as a smooth seducer of policemen's wives."

She slipped into bed and curled up against his body.

"Not wives, Buster, *wife*. You only get to seduce one."

"That's all I could handle."

She scoffed at the false modesty with a wordless sound.

He turned to her with an intensity that surprised and pleased her and put his mouth to her breasts. She had always responded to urgency, demand. Her arms tightened around his back and she pressed him as closely as she could, feeling the muscles move beneath her fingers.

"Annie," he whispered against her flesh, "Annie . . ."

He had not really been thinking about his kid brother in California or of running off to sea. He had been thinking about things that he did not talk about — Eddy Rinzo and the snap of rifles in the morning air, a Polish mother in a house of the dead, and James Dempsey and nameless fears.

"Annie . . . Annie . . ."

She soothed him with gentle sounds and thrust forward the open cup of her body so that he might both fill it with his love and drink deeply of her own. He went to sleep quickly and she lay holding him for a long time, stroking his back, watching the curtains stir in the breeze from the open window.

"Idiot!" Nikki snarled.

She sat up in bed and rubbed the sleep from her eyes. Her head ached with a dull throb and the sight of Johnny sprawled beside her, his robe pulled away from his body and half under him, in no way helped her condition. She felt rotten, and the drooling, unconscious man on the bed was a symbol of all that was wrong with her life.

She had a talent for picking losers. Some women could climb into bed and come out wearing rubies. Maybe they were smarter than she was, or more cold-blooded. Cutting away all the crap she was still Nelda Courts taking lost cats out of the rain.

"Oh, shit."

It was all too much. Boy Johnny and Super Macho were tearing her apart — with a little assist from Small Dago — pet names for pets she could do without. Tearing her in all directions at the same time, like a body tied to running horses going to all points of the compass.

"Lousyfuckingpricks."

There were cigarettes and loose matches in a silver and leather box on the nightstand and she groped in it with her right hand, flicked a kitchen match with her thumbnail, and lit a Virginia Slim.

"Gotohell."

Morning words at two o'clock in the afternoon. Waking-up-fury words. The anger would fade. It always did.

"Story of my life, baby."

She took a deep drag on her cigarette and then reached over and pulled an edge of the blanket across her husband's nakedness.

She fixed a cup of instant coffee in the tiny kitchen and took it into the living room to drink. She sat on the couch and stared morosely out the window. Clouds were drifting and the lake was the color of slate. The sight deepened her depression. The apartment cost a fortune and all she got was a view of floating shit, a whole lake turned into shit.

Jesus, but she was tired. Her body felt like it had been boiled and her head continued to throb. Anger. That's what it was, but she couldn't pinpoint the reason for her anger, the ultimate source of it. Sam? Well, he was a pain in the ass, but he could be handled. He'd give her anything she asked for with no big strings attached. He just wanted his ups from time to time and he didn't want her to leave Cleveland. She had no intention of leaving, anyway. Her dreams of making it big in New York or Hollywood had died with the first wrinkle. Big fish in a little pond. So okay, Dondero's lounge wasn't the Copa, but the piano and the spotlight were hers for as long as she wanted them. Security. That was Sam. Sam Security, a foul-mouthed little Guinea, but he had never given her a headache and he never would.

Johnny. Poor old Johnny. All body and no balls. She felt a twinge of guilt about him every now and then, but not enough to lose sleep. She enjoyed having him around — when he was sober. It was like having a big dog — *fetch the ball . . . roll over . . . wag your tail . . . beg for mama . . . play dead.* The All-American pussy hound.

The anger was Dempsey. He was a killer, in the sack and out of it. He had her head screwed around and she didn't know how to cope with him. Sam and Johnny were simple. When things got too strained, when she had gone just a little too far with either of them, she could straighten things out between the sheets. She won all of her battles in the bedroom. But not with Dempsey. He was a dirty fighter. He'd touched her emotions. Jesus, she thought, I'm in love with the sonofabitch.

She drained her cup and lit another cigarette. She was in love with him, but he treated her like a fifty-dollar whore. He wasn't just a raunchy cop, he was a complex man; but she couldn't find the key, couldn't find the button that would turn him into the kind of man she could handle. James Dempsey was giving her a headache. If she were smart, she'd tell him to fuck off, but she knew that was impossible. All Dempsey had to do was waggle his finger at her. He could do anything he wanted with her.

She reached impulsively for the turquoise princess phone on the coffee table and dialed a number with swift, angry strokes of her finger.

"Sam?"

"Who is this? Nikki?"

She clenched the instrument tightly and hunched over it, speaking in low tones like someone plotting a murder.

"What does he want?"

"Who?"

"Jimmy. What does he want?"

Dondero chuckled. "Tail. Your soft white ass."

"I'm serious, goddamnit! What the hell is he after?"

Sam hung up on her.

Otto Mengus parked his 1963 Plymouth sedan in front of Gorman's house. There was a manila folder on the seat beside him which he stuck under his arm as he walked up the path to the front door. It was ten minutes after three and Mengus had been up for more hours than he cared to think about. He was on the edge of exhaustion, but the turbulence of his thoughts made sleep impossible. Once he had passed on to a higher authority all of the facts that were contained in the folder, then he would sleep — for a little while. The information in the folder would raise questions and he would be expected to find the answers to them. It would be caffeine tablets and cat-naps for the next few days. A bleak prospect, but he pressed the doorbell.

He had to ring four times before Annie Gorman opened the door. She was wearing a robe and her feet were bare.

"Good afternoon, Mrs. Gorman," Mengus said. She was staring at him blankly. "I'm Otto Mengus, from the crime lab at Central."

She remembered him vaguely. "Oh, yes." She spotted the manila folder under his arm and held a hand toward it. "Did you want to leave that for my husband?"

"Well, no. It's something I have to go over with him in person."

"He's asleep."

Her tone made it clear that she wasn't about to wake him. Mengus nodded in sympathy and understanding.

"I hate to disturb him Mrs. Gorman, but this just can't wait." He flicked the edge of the folder. "It's imperative that I talk with him now.'

Her reluctance was obvious, but she showed him into the living room and then went upstairs to wake her husband. Mengus looked at the couch and thought how pleasant it would be to stretch out. He turned his back on temptation by sitting in a straight-backed chair.

Gorman would not have gotten out of bed if the mayor and the entire City Council had been waiting for him downstairs, but the mention of Otto Mengus brought him instantly awake. He asked his wife to make some coffee, then he struggled into a pair of slacks, slipped on an old sweater and went down to the living room.

"I'm sorry, Mike."

"Forget it." Gorman said, suppressing a yawn. "What's up?"

"Something I wanted you to know about first. Something stinks."

Gorman felt his stomach turn. "Dempsey?"

Mengus nodded as he opened the folder and took out a sheaf of papers, neatly stapled together. "You've got intuition."

"It goes with the job. What did you come up with?"

"A lot of wrong answers. I'll go into detail, Mike, but let me get to the point first before I fall on my face. Jimmy shot Max Godansky all right, but it couldn't have happened the way he said it happened — no way on earth."

Gorman took the papers and flipped through him. There was a lot to read.

"Spell it out, Otto."

Mengus got to his feet and walked to the center of the

room. He took his pipe from his pocket and held it in his right hand like a pistol.

"According to Dempsey's statement, Max Godansky went into a panic when he came into the room. He pulled his gun and started shooting. Jimmy drew his gun and fired back. He hit Godansky with all three of his shots and Godansky missed with all three of his. Right?"

Gorman nodded. "As far as I know. I didn't read the report."

"Well, that's what he said. It was just bang-bang-bang in that little room. Godansky was built like a small truck. It took three slugs to put him out and he went down shooting. Now, the way I visualize the scene, it went something like this." He went into a half-crouch and pointed the stem of his pipe at Gorman's middle. "I'm Max Godansky and I'm scared. A cop has just come into my room and I don't like what he's selling. I fire — bang — one shot. It misses Jimmy and tears a hole through the wall. Jimmy draws and fires back. He doesn't miss. The bullet slams Godansky against a table. Godansky fires again — bang — and misses again — another slug through the wall. Jimmy cuts loose with his second shot and Godansky is lifted over the table onto the floor. He's dying but he's still dangerous. He fires one more time — bang — and misses. That makes three holes in the wall behind Jimmy. Godansky is a rotten shot, but he could get lucky. Jimmy shoots him again and that's all there is to it. Now watch me, Mike . . . keep your eyes on the pipe."

Mengus staggered backward and came to a sudden halt as though a table had blocked him. He faked a cartwheel and went down on his buttocks, still pointing his pipe toward Gorman.

"Did you see that, Mike? I was in three different positions. The angle of my gun in relation to you, or the wall, had to change as I went backward. Bullets are hitting me and I'm being jerked off my feet, firing as I go. The slugs from my gun are all going to hit the wall, but they're going to hit at different angles."

"So?"

"So, they *didn't*." He got to his feet and stuck the pipe in his pocket. "All of Godansky's bullets hit the wall the same way. They had to be fired from exactly the same position. The impact and egress routes are identical. There was no deflection of any of the slugs, and no variation to suggest that the man firing them was being shot three times, or attempting to avoid it."

Mengus looked away from Gorman's stricken face and studied the tips of his shoes. He had seen both anguish and rage in the inspector's eyes and he wondered which emotion would have the greater influence over his reaction.

"Who knows about this?" Gorman asked, his voice flat, calm.

"Just the two of us — and Fisher. I asked George to check me out."

"Okay, but don't let it go any further."

"The DA wants the shooting report tomorrow. He'd like to go before the coroner's jury on Friday."

"I'll stall him," Gorman said. He was pacing the room, hands jammed in his pockets. "This opens a can of worms, Otto. I don't want to jump Dempsey on this — not yet. I want you to go through his file . . . double- and triple-check every shooting report he's made for the last couple of years. There are five that I know of. Check 'em, Otto. Check every goddamn fact and figure."

"I thought you might want something like that done. George and I talked it over. We could speed up the process if you'll authorize the removal of the file from Central. George's cousin is a computer programmer at Case. We could feed all the raw data from the file into a computer and get a reading out by tomorrow afternoon sometime. If certain facts don't add up — then . . . well . . ."

His voice trailed off. He could not utter the unspeakable.

"Get started on it."

"Sure." He gathered up the papers and stuck them back in the folder. "It may . . . you know . . . turn out just fine. You know, crazy things happen when people are shooting at each other like that. It only takes two seconds." His words were hollow beats on an empty drum of hope.

"I hope so," Gorman said. There was not a shred of conviction in his tone.

Sergeant Kelmo yawned loudly. "A dead shift."

No one else in the Communications room bothered to comment. There were quiet nights and busy nights, peaks and valleys of action. Why crime and crisis went in cycles nobody could say, not even Captain Henderson who had spent all of his years on the force monitoring calls. There would be hot summer nights when nothing of consequence came over the air from the cruisers, and bitter winter nights when all hell would break loose. The pattern of the city's violence could not be predicted with any degree of certainty. A full moon did not bring any more nuts onto the streets than would normally be found there at any given time. Murder and mayhem were matters of chance; a roll of the dice, a turn of the wheel. This night was a quiet one — so far — and the men were grateful, even Sergeant Kelmo in his own griping way.

"Like a goddamn graveyard. Anybody want any coffee?"

The routine calls came in, one after the other, as the cruisers moved through the streets like pieces on a checkerboard.

"106 to Central . . . coming downtown . . ."

"109 to Central . . . we checked the premises at 468 Lexington . . . no sign of entry . . ."

"Central to 104 . . . see the man . . . 2512 East Ninety-third Street — fight in progress . . ."

At 12:45 that morning there would be a call from cruiser unit 104 requesting an ambulance at 926 Wade Avenue where a fourteen-year-old girl by the name of Bessie Mae Rogers lay bleeding to death with a wire coat hanger in her uterus. She would die at 1:10 A.M. on the way to Polyclinic Hospital.

At 3:15 A.M., a sixteen-year-old boy would toss a brick through the window of a sporting goods store on Euclid and cut his right wrist to the bone trying to drag a bag of golf clubs through the shattered hole. Cruiser 108 would take that call and they would get the boy to St. Vincent's Hospital so that he would live to try the rock again.

At 4 A.M., Homicide Detectives Gordon and Tripoli would be dispatched to an alley behind an apartment house on Wade Park Avenue. They would find a forty-year-old Negro male dying of stab wounds. The man would die without saying anything except, "Oh, shit! It hurts me . . ." and the case would never be solved.

"Kee-rist, what a night," Sergeant Kelmo mumbled, stifling a yawn. He drained an inch of cold coffee from a paper cup, wadded the cup into a ball, and tossed it toward a wastebasket twenty feet from his desk. It went in as neatly as a dunk shot by Wilt the Stilt.

"How about that?"

chapter five

It was a dark day. Flat, gray clouds moved slowly across the city shutting out the sun. At 6:15 that morning an unemployed black laborer by the name of Albert G. Turner had walked up to the Fifth Division precinct house and hurled a can of red paint at the front door. He had neglected to pry off the lid and the one-gallon can dented but did not spill. Sergeants Riker and Obremski, two Fifth Division homicide detectives, witnessed the act and made the arrest, that is, they grabbed Albert G. Turner by both arms and half-carried him into the precinct house.

"Kill me, pigs!" Albert G. Turner screamed. "Go ahead and kill me!"

"Nobody's going to kill you," Sergeant Obremski said.

"I'm ready to die!" Albert G. Turner yelled. He had been preparing for his act of defiance for the past eight hours.

Sergeant Riker caught the full fury of Albert G. Turner's breath.

"Jee-sus, this fucker's drunk."

"No, I ain't," Albert G. Turner said thickly, then proved

the lie by jerking forward and vomiting half a gallon of sweet tokay over the floor and Sergeant Riker's shoes.

Sergeant Riker glared sourly at the mess. "You know something? This is going to be a great day."

Police Chief Keeley was in his office at seven o'clock. He had slept badly, unable to turn off his thoughts of the previous day. He had not been disturbed by the Rinzo boy's funeral, which he had planned down to the last detail and in which he had taken great pride, but by seven telephone calls from the mayor and at least five lengthy discussions with Inspector Gruebner. The mayor had been fuming about the hijackings and was livid about the death of the prisoner. The mayor was facing his reelection campaign and every mayor in every big city was vulnerable these days to problems facing his police.

It reflects badly on me, Chief. I'm sure you understand that.

The mayor's message had been plain — action or the ax — a housecleaning, a purge. Keeley had been a policeman all of his adult life and he had lived through such hysteria before. He knew a lot of good men who had been brought down because of a little panic at city hall. It wasn't going to happen to him.

"You got that list yet?" he barked.

Sergeant Terry Boyle hurried in from the outer office with a piece of paper in his hand. Sergeant Boyle was the chief's driver, aide, and whipping boy. He was also the chief's nephew, but no one in the department sneered at the nepotism. There wasn't a man on the force who would have changed jobs with Boyle, not for a hundred thousand a year.

"Right here, Chief," Boyle said.

Keeley snatched the paper out of Boyle's hand and glanced at it.

"This all?"

"All the important ones. Lots of people have a truck or two, but these are the big ones."

"Okay. Get hold of Blackman, Dutch and Gorman. Tell 'em to be in here by one o'clock. If Dutch hasn't explained to them, tell him to do it before the meeting."

"Okay, Chief."

Keeley flipped the page onto his desk and looked at Boyle over the rim of his glasses.

"Is there any tea out there?"

"Got the water boiling now, Chief."

Boyle hurried out of the room.

Keeley was a creature of ingrained habit. The ritual of morning tea was part of his heritage, a custom that his father and mother had brought with them from County Wicklow and had passed on to their children with a solemnity that bordered on the religious. When Boyle brought in the steaming mug — three teabags steeped for four minutes, a dollop of milk and two heaping spoonfuls of sugar — Keeley leaned back in his chair to sip it down. When the last dark brown drop had been swallowed he placed the mug on the edge of his desk and reached for the list that Boyle had compiled and the telephone.

Tony Arapata was the first name on the list — Delta Trucking. Keeley had met him many times, a tall, white-haired Italian who ran one of the largest trucking operations in the greater Cleveland area. He was also a major financial backer of the mayor.

"Tony? Chief Keeley . . ." His voice was a warm Irish resonance. It glowed with confidence. "I know what you lads have been saying about us lately — and, frankly, I can't blame you. It looks like we've been sitting up here and not doing a damn thing. You know that is not *my* way. We've been putting our heads together the past few weeks and we've come up with something that's going to solve this hijacking business. I'd like you and all the other operators who've been hurt by this thing to come into my office at one-thirty this afternoon. Is that okay with you, Tony? Okay, one-thirty it is. I'll lay it right on the line for you boys . . . spell it out . . . chapter and verse. Because, Tony, we are going to lick this problem and lick it good."

There were seven names on that list and Chief Keeley made the same speech to every man he called — Roger Presley of Interstate, Stanley Webb of Webb Lines, Al Betko of Red Flag, Sam Wiesenthal of AirHaul, Joe Watkins of Ship-Shore Hauling, and Sam Dondero.

"What the fuck was that about?" Dondero asked the question of the nearly life-sized poster of a naked girl that dangled from his office wall on a nail. "What the shit's he up to?"

Harry Prochak grinned as his boss hung up the phone. "What?"

"Keeley — Fart Keeley."

"Yeah? The chief of police calls you now?"

"Wants me to come to a meeting. He says he's got the hijack problem solved. How about that?"

Prochak touched the bandage across his head. He grinned.

"I hope they get them all."

"Oh, yeah, sure . . . So, okay, you were sayin' . . ."

Prochak rested his elbows on Dondero's desk and leaned forward. "Sam, I'm tellin' you, you've never seen anything like it in your goddamn life. I went out there yesterday, an' the stuff was just comin' in. Well, I asked Joey . . . an' he said — skins."

Dondero tilted back in his chair and swung his feet onto the desk. "Skins?"

"Yeah, mink, chinchilla an' sable skins, from Colorado or someplace like that. They was takin' 'em off the plane in bales."

"I thought you said they were coats."

Prochak shook his head in disgust. "Coats? Only a sucker lifts coats, Sam. Let me tell you about coats. Jew tailors make coats an' they can't make a coat without puttin' their mark all over the fuckin' thing — the lining, the skins, everywhere. It's like a fuckin' neon sign. Skins are clean. They're right off the fuckin' animal. Coats are like a one-way ticket to the cooler. *Skins* are like money in the fuckin' bank."

Dondero raised his right hand and studied a nail. "Can we get the job?"

"Oh, sure, no sweat. Joey's the dispatcher. Just pull in and load 'em up."

"Sounds okay. Keep it on ice 'til I see what Keeley has to say. But call Johnny and Charlie Greene. Tell 'em to get in early."

"Well?" Gruebner asked. "How does it sound, Mike?"

Gorman tapped a plate with a spoon. "It could work — if we're lucky. What do you think, Dave?"

Blackman gazed into space. "It's a crap shoot."

The three men were jammed into a corner booth at the Kozy Korner Kafe on Chester Avenue, two blocks from Central Police Station. It was 12:30 and the small table was littered with the remains of their lunch. Gruebner picked sulkily at a crust of bread.

"If you can think of anything better . . ."

"It's fine," Gorman said. "I can't think of anything that would give us a better shot."

"I can't either," Blackman agreed.

"It's a fishing trip," Gruebner said, "but we might get a few bites — and the Chief's happy. He likes it."

"Okay," Gorman said.

Gorman's bitterness and his moody silence during lunch had not gone unnoticed. While they were paying their bills Gruebner took Blackman aside.

"What's the matter with Mike?" he whispered.

"I don't know. Something's eating him."

"Find out what it is, will you? When we meet those truckers we have to look, and sound, confident. Mike's acting like he just buried his mother."

Gruebner directed a stream of cigar smoke toward the ceiling.

"You're the diplomat, not me."

When Gorman turned away from the cash register Gruebner headed for the restroom at the rear of the café, leaving Gorman alone with Blackman.

"Let's walk," Blackman said. "I need the exercise."

"Shall we wait for Dutch?"

"He'll be out of breath walking back from the can. Come on, let's go."

They walked in silence for a block, heads down to the wind. A traffic light, swinging on its cable above the center of the street, blinked red.

"How did you make out with Godansky's mother?" Blackman asked casually.

"Fine," Gorman said.

"Did she take her son's body?"

"No."

"Why not? Does she still want to see Dempsey?"

"Something like that."

"Did you tell her that she can see him at the inquest?"

Gorman was staring up at the light, waiting for it to change. "When is the inquest, Mike? Wednesday?"

"I'm . . . postponing it."

"Oh? Why?"

"I want to double-check Dempsey and Rich's statements before I turn them over to the DA."

"What's wrong?"

The light turned green but Gorman made no move to step off the curb.

"There may be a few . . . discrepancies," he said slowly. "I'd rather not discuss it just yet, Dave."

Blackman stiffened. "Don't pull that, Mike. If something's wrong, Dutch and I have a right to know. It's your *duty* to let us know."

"Give me a little time, Dave. I can't drag the entire department into this . . . until I'm certain about *all* the facts."

"I won't press you. I'm sure that whatever you do it'll be the right thing."

"God, I hope so," Gorman said as he started across the street. The light turned red and a truck driver had to put on his brakes.

"Jaywalkers," he muttered to himself as the two inspectors ran across the intersection toward the stained sandstone hulk of the police station.

The truck line owners were busy men and when Chief Keeley and the three inspectors walked into the third-floor conference room at 1:30 they were already starting to glance at their watches.

"Good to see that you all got here," Keeley said.

Al Betko shifted his three hundred pounds on a metal folding chair that barely supported him.

"We're here," he growled, "so let's get on with it. I lost

three cargoes last month and the insurance bastards are breathin' down my neck. My rate goes up 20 percent every time it happens. What the hell are you guys doin' about it?"

"What are *you* doing about it?" Keeley shot back. It was a logical moment to launch into his favorite speech and he talked for fifteen minutes, hammering home the fact that fighting crime was a two-way street.

". . . the police can only do so much. It is the responsibility of each citizen to take a few elementary precautions — to lock his doors, lock his car, keep his money in a safe place. The best way to *fight* crime is to *prevent* crime . . ."

A couple of the owners yawned. They had heard the speech many times — at Rotary lunches and other civic functions where Chief of Police Keeley had been the guest speaker.

". . . Citizens must meet the police halfway. The crime rate will go down only when people start making it tough for the criminal to commit a crime — and that brings me right to *your* door. Why haven't you installed foolproof alarm systems on your trucks? Or hired men to ride shotgun when you're hauling expensive merchandise? You could make hijacking very difficult."

"We're experimenting," Tony Arapata said. "But we want to know what you guys are planning to do." There was a chorus of assent.

"Yeah. How about it, Keeley?" Dondero called out. "I've been hurt bad the past few months. I've had six . . . seven trucks knocked off and you guys haven't come up with *one* suspect."

"They won't be getting away with it anymore," Keeley said. "Hijacking is going to be as rare in this city as stagecoach robbery!"

"I'll believe it when I see it, Chief," Dondero said. "We've heard that song before."

"Well, you can believe it now, Sam." Keeley motioned Gruebner to step forward. "Inspector Gruebner will explain the basic concept to you, and then we'll answer any questions you may have."

Gorman stood with his back to the wall and studied the faces of the men as Gruebner told them of the department's plans to form a hijacking squad, a team of detectives whose only function would be to crush what was obviously a well-organized gang. He talked at length, using terms such as "interlocking efforts" and "zones of coordination." Certain "simple electronic devices" would be installed on every truck "at a minor cost" so that the specially equipped cars of the hijack squad could "monitor any cargo break-in, using a checkerboard graph plot for almost instant radio car response."

Gorman suppressed a smile. Gruebner's speech was right out of Dick Tracy, but the truck owners looked impressed. Their expressions were rapt and attentive.

"That's the basic idea," Gruebner concluded. "It's up-to-the-minute police technology and we *know* it'll work."

Al Betko shifted from his uncertain hold on the chair. "I won't say I understand it, Dutch, but it sounds good to me."

"Yeah," Dondero said, "but how long will somethin' like this take?"

Gruebner tugged thoughtfully at his ear. "I'd say . . . ten days."

"Better make that two weeks," Blackman said. "We have to train the men . . . install the equipment."

"It'll be ten days," Keeley said with finality, "even if we have to work around the clock to do it."

"That's the spirit, Chief." Sam Wiesenthal, the owner

of AirHaul Trucking, pushed back his chair and got to his feet. "It's a good feeling to know that the police are on the ball. I, for one, would like to thank you — in advance. Anyone second the motion?"

"Oh, hell, yes," Al Betko said, as he maneuvered his awesome bulk toward the door. "You bust up this gang, I'll give you a medal."

"We don't work for medals," Keeley said piously. "We just do our duty."

The owners moved out of the room and down the hall in a haze of cigar smoke and shoptalk. Keeley and Gruebner escorted them to the elevator and then came back to the conference room where Gorman and Blackman remained waiting.

"Well, Mike?" Keeley said.

Gorman shrugged. "One of them could be a bad apple, but you can't tell by looking. They all seemed happy about the plan . . . or the idea of ten days' grace."

"I have a thousand bucks says that one of 'em is behind it. Every hijacking smelled of an inside job."

"Betko isn't smart enough," Gruebner said. "Arapata is *too* smart, Wiesenthal's son is a rabbi — not the sort of man who'd . . ."

Keeley cut him off with a loud snort. "I don't care if his kid is the pope in Rome. This is a million-dollar-a-year pure profit enterprise, and when there's that kind of money to be made . . ." He let the implication dangle. "How soon can you get rolling, Mike?"

"Tonight, I think. Tomorrow for sure."

"Tonight," Blackman said.

"How many teams do you figure?"

"My original estimate was ten," Gruebner replied. "We talked it over and Mike figures we'll need fifteen for maximum coverage — three, maybe four men to a team."

Keeley slipped an old-fashioned fob watch out of his pocket. "Getting late, boys. Better jump to it if you want to roll tonight."

"I want to bring Dempsey and Rich in on this." Gorman ignored Blackman's quizzical look and kept his eyes on Keeley.

The chief scowled. "They have another twenty-four off. We have enough men without dragging them back."

"We need their experience — especially Jimmy's. I want to head a team in the field and I'd like him with me."

Gorman walked away before any objections could be raised or questions posed. Keeley was startled by the suddenness of his exit.

"What the hell's the matter with him?"

"Nothing," Blackman said. "He's just got a lot on his mind."

Keeley grumbled. "He's actin' funny. The DA's been on my back. Mike didn't turn in that shooting report yet and the DA has to go before the coroner. It's a simple matter, isn't it?"

"I think so," Blackman said evenly.

"Well then, he should have had a report in. You turned yours in fast enough and that was a damn sight more complicated." He placed a fatherly hand on Blackman's shoulder. "A damn fair report too, Dave. If the grand jury has one spark of humanity among the lot of 'em, they'll rule Murphy's act justifiable. What's a man supposed to do if a naked fag jumps on him? It was a natural reaction for a normal man."

"He's a police officer," Blackman said coldly. "He's supposed to be above *natural* actions. He could have pushed the prisoner away."

Keeley withdrew his hand. "I know," he snapped. "I read that, too."

Officer Murphy was not a bad cop, both men knew that. He was just a victim of the times. a man who had cracked under the constant pressure of his job. Now he faced a possible charge of manslaughter to be judged by men and women who knew nothing of the day-to-day pressures that could build up to the point of explosion. Some cops released the tension by getting drunk, or cheating on their wives, or going to football games — Christ, anything. But Murphy had lashed out and a man was dead. There was no escaping. *A man was dead.*

Keeley turned away, his shoulders hunched.

"Get going. You've a lot of organizing to do. I want this to run smooth."

"Like the old oil?" Blackman said.

Keeley grinned. "Yes, Dave, just like the old oil."

Gorman stopped off at the crime lab. George Fisher and a technician were there examining plaster tire-mark casts taken from the scene of an accident.

"Where's Otto?" Gorman asked.

"Getting some sleep," Fisher said. He glanced at the technician and then walked over to Gorman who stood in the doorway. "That computer printout is going to take a little longer than we expected. I just phoned my cousin. He won't have anything for us before noon tomorrow. Sorry, but programming that kind of data isn't easy."

"That's all right," Gorman said. "Did you give him everything?"

"Yes, sir. The complete file."

"Have Otto call me when you hear."

"Of course."

It was frustrating, but there was nothing that Gorman could do about it. He walked off down the hall and turned into the robbery squad offices. Sergeant Daley was behind his desk, elbow deep in a backlog of crime reports. Winshaw was at a typewriter, pecking at the keys with two long, bony fingers.

"How'd the interview go?"

"Terrific." Daley said, not bothering to look up. "She told us the story of her life."

Winshaw gave a mirthless laugh. "Max Godansky weighed nine pounds at birth and was breast-fed until he was a year old."

Gorman leaned against the corner of Daley's desk and stole a cigarette from an open pack.

"Okay . . . what else?"

Daley tilted back in his chair and squinted at the ceiling.

Let's see . . . it all comes back to me like a hazy dream . . . me asking Lewandowski a question in English . . . Lewandowski passing the question on in Polish . . . the old lady talking for half an hour or so . . . and then Lewandowski telling us that Max had a happy childhood. I ask another question, you know, like was Max mixed up with any kind of a gang, and the old lady tells Lewandowski that Max raised pigeons and sang in the choir. It was enough to break your heart. That guy was too good to live."

"What about the man who visited her house when Max was sick?"

"That is the extent of her story," Winshaw said. "A man came to the house a couple of times. Period. He upset her little boy and so she developed a bad case of the hates for him. No, she'd never seen him before and she hasn't seen him since. Just a man in a gray suit."

"Cut the jokes."

"Give us a break," Daley said. "It was a wasted morning."

"You can make up for it by doing something useful this

evening. We're forming a hijack squad. You're both on my team."

Daley looked puzzled. "What kind of a hijack squad?"

Gorman picked up a lighter that Daley had been using as a paperweight. "Truck decoys with a cargo of riot guns. Fifteen teams cruising the streets and freeways. We might get lucky, who knows?"

Daley snorted. "Who dreamed this one up?"

"Dutch — with the Chief's blessing. Don't knock it."

"Heaven forbid. We like gung-ho jobs, don't we, James?"

"Yeah," Winshaw said.

"We get rolling at eight." Gorman started for the door, then paused to look back. "Dempsey's coming along with us."

Daley pursed his lips and said nothing, but Winshaw slapped the side of his typewriter.

"I've never ducked a job since I've been on the force, but goddamn it, I don't want to be around that trigger-happy sonofabitch. I mean it, Mike."

"Cool it," Daley said.

Winshaw glared at his partner. "You feel the same way and you damn well know it. I don't like the idea of being around that bastard when he's got a gun in his hand."

"You take it the way it comes," Gorman said. "It's you, me, Bob and Dempsey. That's the team — and that's final."

Winshaw muttered under his breath and stared bitterly at the typewriter.

"Okay, *Inspector*, but I'm going to sit 'way in the back of the bus."

"Suit yourself," Gorman said as he walked out of the office. He was halfway down the hall when Daley caught up with him.

"Wait a minute, Mike." He placed a firm hand on the inspector's arm and steered him to the wall. "We've

168

been friends for a long time, and we've always played square with each other. What's with Dempsey?"

"Nothing. He's a good cop and I want him along."

The sergeant's face was stone. "I'm not talking about that. I've had a funny feeling since yesterday morning. You know what I mean by a funny feeling?"

"Feelings don't mean much."

"You're wrong. In this business, they mean everything. I've got that tingle, like every nerve was a live wire. Do you want to know what I was thinking while that old lady kept jabbering away this morning? I was thinking about Dempsey. I was wondering if he had ever sat in that room." He let go of Gorman's arm and took a step backward. "Tell me I'm full of shit, Mike, because I hope I am."

Two lawyers came striding down the hall, talking loudly.

"I told him I wasn't God. I told him . . . Larry, they'll go for the plea . . . five years instead of fifteen . . . what the hell do you want?"

"I know, I know . . . shmucks like that . . ."

They wheeled into the restroom, bearing their arrogance to the urinals.

"Well?" Daley asked quietly.

Gorman gave him a hard stare. "Call Lewandowski. Tell him to have Mrs. Godansky over here by seven-thirty. I want her kept out of sight, but someplace where she can see the men lining up for roll call."

Daley's breath came out like a sigh. "Okay . . . Inspector."

"And, Bob — just you and Lewandowski on this. Keep Winshaw out of it. He's good, but he's got too much temper."

"Sure." He walked quickly away. There were questions that he wanted to ask, but he had seen the pain in Gorman's eyes. It stunned him, and when he returned to the office he slumped into his chair and stared bitterly at the stack of crime reports, at the cases that would never be solved.

Winshaw glanced at him in amusement. "What did you run after him for? Trying to beg off?"

"James," he said softly, "shut up — or I'm going to clout you right in the goddamn chops."

chapter six

DAYLIGHT WAS A HAND GRENADE going off in Johnny's head as he lurched out of the bedroom. What time was it? Morning? Noon? One day had been shot to hell, he knew that. He remembered a vague waking — sunset glowing on the windows, a screaming argument with Nikki, some quick drinks, oblivion. Nikki had said she was leaving him, but she was still there, seated on the couch with her hair in curlers.

"Nice of you to get up," she said.

He went into the kitchen. The idea of coffee made his stomach churn. His body craved cold wetness. He longed for a crystal stream, an icy river. He would dive into it, open his mouth and let the swift flowing waters purge body and mind. He found a bottle of club soda in the back of the refrigerator and popped off the cap with his thumbs. That minor accomplishment pleased him. He'd won a hundred bets doing that to beer bottles. Johnny Davis, the strongest thumbs in the Air Force. He took a long pull of soda and took the bottle into the living room.

"What time is it?"

"What do you care?" she snapped. "The bars are open, if you're worried about it."

"Drop dead." He said it without malice.

Nikki tested the dryness of her hair and began to take out the rollers.

"Let's do something."

He sat stiffly on the edge of a chair and nursed at the bottle. "Like what?"

"I don't know — anything. It's my night off from the flea trap. Let's get a breath of fresh air."

He looked toward the windows. Clouds tumbled across the sky.

"We could rent a boat," he said. "Go for a sail."

"Oh, great. That's really my idea of a good time — watching you barf over the rail."

"I never get seasick," he said with great dignity. "I'm a good sailor."

"A good *drunken* sailor."

"I sober fast." He drained the bottle and belched loudly.

"Pig."

"Sorry." He took the bottle into the kitchen and tossed it in the trash bag under the sink. Opening the refrigerator, he took out a quart of milk and drank half of it from the carton. He felt much better.

"Johnny?"

"What?"

"Let's *do* something."

She was combing out her hair when he came back into the living room. It tumbled across her bare shoulders in waves of honey. He noticed for the first time that she was wearing nothing but a bath towel tucked around her like a sarong.

He sat next to her. "Anything you want, Nikki."

She turned to face him, the towel falling away from her thighs.

172

"We could go for a drive. Just follow the lake or maybe down to the Amish country. Anywhere but here. This city stinks so bad it's like living in a big plastic bag of garbage."

He was staring at the smoothness of her legs and shadowy hollow at the joining of her thighs. His throat felt tight.

"Sure," he said. "Just get away."

"Sam told me about a steak place near Sandusky. Is that too far to go for a meal?"

"No . . . not too far."

"Well then, how about it?"

"Sure, Nikki . . . sure." Her flesh drew him downward with the strength of a giant magnet. His lips touched her thigh. She nuzzled his face with her leg. He felt drunk again with the sudden rush of craving to devour her.

"Hey, tiger," she whispered.

"Nikki . . . Nikki . . ." He slid his hands around and beneath her and pulled her closer to his mouth. She gave a little whimper of pleasure and ran her fingers into his hair, directing him, petting him.

The phone rang. He raised his head.

"No," she said. "Let it ring."

He stared at the instrument, hoping it would stop, but the ringing went on and on. He sat up and reached for it.

"Hello," he said, his voice husky.

It was Prochak. "You took long enough."

"I was busy."

"Get your ass down here — Sam says we roll tonight."

"So soon? Is he crazy?"

"Tell *him* that, asshole."

Nikki moved close to him and pulled the robe away from him, teasing him with her fingertips.

"Tell them to go to hell," she whispered into his ear.

"I'm taking the day off," Davis said.

"Bullshit," Prochak said. "Get your ass in here. You been told." He hung up.

"Harry . . . wait a min——" But the phone was already dead.

"Well?" Nikki asked.

"Nikki . . ." he gasped, groping for her. "Nikki . . ."

She let go of him and jumped to her feet. He was still reaching out for her. "Nikki . . . please . . . before I go."

"Go screw!" she said and stalked out to the bedroom.

He stayed there on his knees for a moment. It had almost been right for him.

It began to rain as Dondero headed back to the city. Good, he thought. The rain made it easier. Drivers never saw anything but their own windshield wipers when it rained. They drove staring straight ahead. Fifty people could get murdered on the side of the freeway and not one driver would notice. The rain was beautiful, the day was beautiful.

"Ten days!" he shouted. The cops were beautiful. Ten days was a gift from the gods. After Keeley had passed on the good news, Dondero had driven out to Shaker Heights to tell Guido Franchini. That was a courtesy but he had also wanted someone to take the skins off his hands. He knew how to dispose of booze quickly enough — but *skins*?

Gambini in Toledo. I'll give him a call.

Guido knew everything.

It was a good feeling to be part of an organization that knew how to do business. A few hours after the skins were lifted they'd be in Toledo, and a few hours after that they'd be on their way to half a dozen places across the country to be turned into coats and stoles, expensive and untraceable.

The rain slanted in the wind. The traffic along Shaker

Boulevard was crawling, but Dondero didn't mind. He pushed in the tape and listened to a Sinatra medley, keeping the sound low so that it wouldn't interfere with his telephone calls. He talked to his lawyer, a girlfriend in Lakewood, his tailor, made an appointment with his barber, gave a wholesale butcher hell for overcharging the club on strip sirloins, and checked with Prochak to make sure he had made the calls to Johnny and Charlie Greene. Sinatra sang while the windshield wipers hissed against the glass and the heater purred. He made his calls from the white instrument by his right hand. This was utter comfort. The big Eldorado was his office, his home, his shelter against cold and rain. He felt a twinge of regret when he finally turned into the parking lot of the Dondero Freight and Hauling Company.

They were waiting in his office — Harry Prochak, Charlie Greene, Johnny Davis, Al Summers and Fred Bolen. The crew.

"How's it goin'?"

Fine, they said, just fine, Sam. Only Johnny was silent. He sat slouched in a chair, staring at the floor.

"What's the matter, Johnny?"

"Nothing."

"He wanted the day off," Prochak said.

Davis gave him a hard stare. "I came in, didn't I?"

No love between those two, Dondero was thinking as he sat down at his desk. He knew why. Prochak had a wife who looked like a truck's rear end. It was raw jealousy and Dondero poured a little fuel on the fire just for the hell of it.

"If I had a wife like Nikki I'd take a month off. How about it, Harry, what would you do if you had a fox like that at home?"

Prochak peeled cigarette paper from his bottom lip and

gazed sullenly at the pinup girl on the wall. The girl's drum-taut breasts and plastic smile mocked him. He was married to a dog. He knew it, and so did everyone else.

"Business before pleasure," he said without conviction.

Dondero chuckled. "That's it, Harry. You'll get your nooky in heaven, kid."

Davis chewed his bottom lip in irritation. "Come on, Sam. I get dragged in early, so what's the big deal?"

"A half-million in skins," Dondero said. "Think about it, kid. Figure your share. Tell him, Harry."

"They're pourin' in like a river," Prochak said. "Comin' into the airport from Colorado or Wyomin' . . . mink skins. We can pick up a load tonight for delivery to some Jew firm on Prospect."

"Charlie picks 'em up," Dondero said. "You, Harry, Al and Fred pull the switch on 71 just past the Ridge Road bridge and take the load to Toledo."

Davis shook his head. "It's too dangerous, Sam. Jesus, we ought to cool it for a month."

"Cool it, my ass. We got a ten-day pass from the cops. I figure we can pull one switch on our own truck and maybe knock off two outside. *Then* we'll cool it."

"I dunno," Davis said. "I don't like it, Sam. The cops aren't stupid. Harry gets beaned one night and Charlie two days later . . . I dunno . . . they're going to start adding things up."

"Let 'em add," Dondero scoffed. "They can't prove a fuckin' thing." He turned steely eyes on Charlie Greene. "We're goin' to have to make it look good, Charlie. Really paste you one. Maybe break your arm or somethin'."

The tall black man forced a smile. "Don't break my *right* arm, man. I gotta pitch."

"Okay . . . no breaks . . . tire iron across the head like Harry. Maybe a busted rib or two."

176

Greene winced. "The bread better be good, Sam."

"You'll be the richest jig on Scovill Avenue. Don't worry about it."

"I ain't *worried* about it. But my old lady's goin' to be scared out of her mind if I'm laid up with a busted head."

Dondero raised his hands in exasperation. "Will somebody talk to this clown? Harry, tell him the facts of life, for Christ's sake."

Prochak touched his bandaged head. "I figure it came to six hundred bucks a stitch, not counting my regular slice of the pie."

"Okay," Greene said with vague reluctance. "But anybody hurt my pitchin' arm is goin' to get his ass chopped off."

Dondero shuffled some papers around on his desk. "Okay. Out of here . . . work out the details between you. Just have the load in Toledo before dawn — Gambini Brothers, 257 Morris Avenue. You got that, Johnny?"

"Yeah," Davis muttered. "257 Morris."

The others left, but Davis didn't move. Dondero glanced at him.

"You got somethin' on your mind, Johnny?"

"This job. It's a mistake, Sam."

A nice guy, but low on guts. That was Dondero's opinion of Johnny Davis. Any dumb cunt could kick him around.

"Johnny, you scare easy. It takes heat to make bread. You don't want the bread, don't go near the heat."

Davis glared at his feet. "I need the money. You know, I'm savin' up . . . buy a house for Nikki."

"Yeah?" Dondero kept a straight face. The kid was a panic. "Nikki never told me you were savin' up for a house."

"It'll be a surprise."

"I bet it will."

"I don't mind taking risks — but pulling a second job so soon . . ."

Dondero cut him off. "Let me do the worryin', okay? I wouldn't send you guys out if I didn't think it'd be a piece of cake. Now, go on, get out of here. I got work to do."

Davis stood up. He felt leaden and there was a dull ache in his groin. He thought about telling Dondero, just laying it on the line to him.

Sam, that Nikki is a bitch. She's chewing my nuts off. I'm not worried about the job. It's that bitch, she's twisting my head around.

So what? What the hell could Dondero do about it? Maybe he'd be happy. He started for the door and then hesitated, staring down at Sam's head bent over a pile of invoices. The neck was short, thick, covered with fine black hairs. An ape's neck, but under the black hairs and the muddy skin was the spinal cord. He could snap it with one blow of his palm.

"Sam?"

"What?"

"Sam — did you ever make it with Nikki?"

Dondero felt the hairs tingle all over his body. He sensed the looming bulk of the man behind him, but he did not move his head an inch.

"We . . . had a little thing going — a long, long time ago, kid. Before you two got hitched."

"You come to the apartment a lot," Davis said.

"Oh, yeah, sure. You know, we got a lot to talk over — *business*. I want to . . . open a new place . . . maybe top of one of them new buildings on Euclid . . . a penthouse club . . . give Nikki a brand new act . . . back her up with a little combo . . . that sort of thing. We talk it over, every now and then."

He was starting to sweat a little. There was a 9mm

Luger in the top right-hand drawer of his desk and he thought about reaching for it. Then Davis was no longer behind him. He moved to the front of the desk and stood there, head down, like a sulky kid.

"She won't put out to me, Sam."

Dondero laughed in relief. "Is that all that's buggin' you?"

Davis stared at him with bewildered eyes.

"It isn't funny, Sam."

"Hell, I didn't say it was funny." He leaned back in his chair and clasped his hands behind his head. "Let me tell you something about Nikki, kid. She'll walk all over a guy if he gives her half a chance. You gotta be the boss — and I do mean *the boss*. Look at yourself. Jesus, you're built like a fuckin' truck. You gonna let a little woman like Nikki push you around? I've seen you lift a two-hundred-pound crate. You gonna stand there and tell me you can't lift a goddamn nightgown!"

"I'm sorry, Sam. Forget I said anything. I'll work it out."

"Damn right you will." He leaned forward and shoved the telephone toward the edge of the desk. "Go on, call her. Tell her you're going to Toledo tonight. Tell her I'm givin' her three days off, and that when you get back you're goin' to take her on a little trip. Stop at the first motel you come to and keep her in the sack for three days."

Davis plucked the phone off the hook and dialed his number. It buzzed and buzzed in his ear. Christ, he thought savagely, she had to be home, she *had* to be. He was conscious of Dondero's eyes upon him — black, beady, faintly mocking eyes — the eyes of a man who had never had cause to doubt the power of his prick.

"She . . . must be in the shower."

"Let it ring."

179

Davis clutched the instrument and pressed it tightly against his ear. It buzzed and buzzed and buzzed. She would never answer it. He knew that. Even if she were home she'd let it ring on and on.

"Nikki," he said loudly. "You took long enough . . . where the hell were you? Shower, huh . . . Listen, Nikki . . . I'm goin' away tonight . . . Toledo. When I get back we're goin' away for a couple of days. Don't pack too much . . . you won't need clothes . . ."

Dondero was grinning, whispering "She won't need *any* clothes. Tell her *that*, kid . . . she won't need a fuckin' stitch!"

He felt sick. His body was clammy and his ear ached from the pressure of the instrument against it. The buzzing was so loud it seemed incredible that Dondero didn't hear it.

"Okay . . . so long, baby." He pressed down the button in the cradle before taking the phone from his ear.

"Everything okay, Johnny?"

He nodded, not trusting himself to speak. All he wanted to do was to get out of that office and find a nice, quiet place where he could throw up.

Dempsey didn't really care. He wasn't doing anything, or planning to do anything. He had been lying on the daybed staring at the ceiling when the phone rang. Gorman had been apologetic . . .

"I hate to cut your time short, but we need every available man."

"Carl, too?"

"I'm afraid so. I just called him. Report in by six for a briefing."

Like the Army. Briefing at 1800 hours. It was all a lot of bullshit. He lit a cigarette and lay back on the bed, an ashtray balanced on his stomach, and studied the patterns in the plaster.

It was an interesting ceiling, full of ridges and whorls, craters and jagged lines — a moonscape, or the earth from a thousand miles up. He imagined he could see the Caribbean, the horn of Yucatan jutting into it, a deeper-than-real Gulf of Mexico, a stub that could be Florida, and the islands out there in the Gulf Stream, flakes of plaster islands stretching away to the far end of the room.

The Caribbean. Well, maybe he'd go there. Take a cruise ship from Rio, first cabin all the way. John W. Martin, Esquire, gentleman of leisure. The cigarette scorched his fingers and he lit a fresh one with the smoldering butt.

Jamaica and Barbados, Trinidad and Martinique. Calypso and rum. Most of the women were black — chocolate black — Negro and Spanish with a little Portuguese and Yankee clipper thrown in to make the breed interesting. It was something to look forward to. John W. Martin would have a grand time. But John W. Martin, manufacturer's representative, Youngstown, Ohio, would have to wait a bit. John W. Martin was a smart cookie. He knew how to turn a buck. Given X number of dollars to invest in the booming Brazilian economy, John W. Martin would make out just fine. That X could not be too small. John W. Martin deserved better than that.

"Nothing but the best for you, John."

James Dempsey, police officer, Cleveland, Ohio, sent John W. Martin among the plaster islands on a great white ship. Sapphire seas. Palm-fringed shores. Balmy days and torrid nights. He ignored the patter of rain against the windows. He ignored the ringing of the doorbell until somebody started kicking the door downstairs.

He opened the door with reluctance and Nikki Davis stormed in, wet and furious.

"Shit! You took your time!"

"You're wet," he said.

She tossed rain from her hair and peeled off a wet coat.

"I could have frozen to death in that hall! Why do you live in a dump like this?"

"I like it. It suits my personality."

She moved over to the daybed and sat on the edge of it, bent forward and shook her head. Damp hair flopped across her face in tangled coils.

"When did they build this firetrap?"

"The day I was born," he said.

She looked at him through strands of hair.

"You really are stoned, aren't you?"

"Out of my head."

"Who were you talking to? Little green men?"

He pointed toward the ceiling. "A pal of mine. He lives up there. Very happily, too. Just sails around from mildew to mildew having a ball."

She got a comb from her purse and drew it through her hair.

"You're crazy. I guess that's why I . . . love you."

His smile was thin, a shadow. "You had to think about that, didn't you?"

She took her time answering, putting the comb away, leaning back against the wall.

"No, not really. I just hate one-sided emotions. It's rotten for a girl's ego to tell a guy she loves him and then have him laugh in her face."

"I wasn't laughing."

"But you didn't say that you loved me, either."

"Is it important to you?"

"Maybe."

"Okay."

"Oh, shit! Can I have a drink?"

"Hot tea and whiskey."

"I can skip the tea." Her teeth were chattering. "I'd better get out of this dress . . ."

He motioned toward a closet. "There's a robe."

Dempsey fixed himself a mug of tea, laced it with whiskey, then poured some whiskey into another mug and added boiling water and a slice of lemon.

"I made you a toddy," he said, carrying the mugs into the room. Nikki was on the bed, bundled up in a yellow terrycloth robe.

"Thanks, but I like my drinks straight."

He sat on the edge of the bed. "Drink it and shut up. This'll go right to where it hurts."

"That's what *you* think." She sat up and took the mug from him, grimacing at the strong fumes. "Who's your liquor dealer? Standard Oil?"

"Drink it."

They sat in silence, sipping from the mugs, watching the rain slash at the windows. She finished her drink first, placed the empty mug on the floor and then lay back against the wall.

"I wish you had a fireplace."

"Running up and down the stairs for logs. What a waste."

"A fireplace and a white bearskin rug."

"Is that your sexy noise?"

"Yes," she said quietly.

Billy Price teased his Chevy one-ton truck through the glut of traffic around Chester and Fourteenth Street and cursed the day. If it wasn't the rain it was some other thing, the snow or the heat. Always something to make it miserable. A woman in a bright blue Pinto played Sally Stupid in front of him and he slammed his foot on the air brakes. The truck slid on the wet asphalt, but stopped two inches from the Pinto's shiny and vulnerable rear end. In good weather he would have stuck his head out the window and given the broad hell, but she wasn't worth getting his head wet. He gave her a short blast from the airhorn instead.

"Stupid broads."

Finally, the traffic unglued itself and he made a right turn onto Fourteenth. That was when Malloy pulled him to the curb. Malloy was wearing a bright yellow rain slicker and driving a three-wheeled motorcycle. He looked ridiculous and Billy Price was prepared to tell him so, along with a few other choice remarks.

"What the hell ya stoppin' me for? I was in the right. Did you see what that crazy broad did? Did you see it? You ain't blind, are ya, Malloy? Pulled right into my lane. What the hell am I supposed to do? Get out and kiss her hand?"

Dennis Malloy placed one booted foot on the running board and stared impassively into Billy Price's apoplectic face.

"You finished squawking?"

"Maybe!" Price yelled. "*Maybe* I am."

"Because if you're not, I could write a whole block full of tickets on you, Billy. I could keep the city runnin' for a week on your goddamn fines. Now, you all through leakin' at the mouth?"

Price stared at the beefy, weather-grained face of the traffic cop and silently cursed every line on it.

"Yeah . . . I'm through."

"Good. You got a load in back?"

"No — why?"

"Through for the day, huh?"

"Yeah," Price said, starting to squirm a little. "I'm through for the day. So what?"

"So take your rig over to Central and tell the sergeant that you're number 6 from Malloy."

"What the fu—— *heck* for?"

"Police business. Now, just do as you're told, Billy, or you'll be hauling a load down shit alley for the rest of your life."

"Miserable sonofabitch," Price said after Officer Malloy had walked away. He rolled up his window and put the truck into gear. For a moment he debated about just taking the rig back to the garage, but the *number 6 from Malloy* bothered him.

"He's got me on a list. That crazy sonofabitch has me on a fuckin' list!"

He did as he had been told. He drove down Payne Avenue to the Central Police Station and noticed that the street was lined with trucks — ten or more, nose to tail, double-parked. He pulled up behind the last one and a cop in a rain slicker walked up to him with a clipboard under his arm.

"Which one are you?" the cop shouted.

"Number 6," Price said. "From Malloy."

"Okay," the cop said. "Cut your engine and wait in the cab."

"Why? What's goin' on?"

"Never mind," the cop said, walking away in the rain.

Billy Price punched the steering wheel with his fist and cursed bright blue Pintos, women drivers, Irish cops and the city of Cleveland. When he was through cursing he lit a Chesterfield and slumped back on the seat. He was in for a long wait and there wasn't one damn thing he could do about it.

"Police business," he muttered. "The only business the police got is stealing from the poor and innocent."

It went by the book — or, in this case, by Inspector Gruebner's plan — under the code name of Operation White Sox. There had been a number of taxi robberies a few years back in which passengers sharing rides during the rush-hour madness had fallen victim to young gunmen. The robbers had been dressed in conservative business suits and carried attaché cases. There had been four known members of the gang and they would all take separate cabs in the downtown area in front of major office buildings. Sharing a cab was a common practice in the late afternoon or early evening and the gunmen were heisting four and five businessmen a trip, plus the drivers. They had been smoothly professional and none of the passengers had made any attempt to struggle — until two members of the visiting Chicago White Sox baseball team had taken exception to the lifting of their wallets and had fought back. They had been pistol-whipped into agreement and the police had to move to crush the ring. Operation White Sox had been born. It was not used. An informer turned in the robbers. Now it was a viable plan, relabeled Bluebird, with cabs changed to trucks, but with all other factors the same. One of the decoy ducks on the lake was really a bomb.

"How many trucks are out there?" Gorman asked. He was in the Communications room with Blackman, Gruebner, Captain Henderson and Captain Willy Kosko of the Traffic Department.

"Fifteen," Kosko said. "We can line up more."

"Fifteen is what we need," Gorman said.

Getting the trucks this way had been crucial. One big danger was tipping off the hijackers. So Captain Kosko and the men of his division had been handed the logistical problem. Men like Officer Malloy knew every truck driver in the city and they had stopped only independent truckers, the men who owned and operated their own rigs.

"Do you want the drivers brought in?" Kosko asked.

Gorman nodded. "Take them upstairs and talk to them, Willy. There can't be any leaks on this thing so we'll have to hold them for a few hours, voluntarily, I hope. Send a wagon over to Foster's for five or six cases of beer and rib dinners. Give them a tour of the building."

"Listen," Gruebner offered. "Take 'em down to the basement range and let 'em shoot up a couple dozen boxes of practice shells at the targets."

Kosko grinned. "There won't be any objections."

The independent truckers had to be in the good graces of the police. It was impossible for a driver to move through the city for an entire day and not commit half a dozen minor traffic violations. The traffic cops overlooked a lot of double-parking for unloading when a man was making his living with a truck. If the cops got on a man's back he might just as well take his truck and get out of town. Kosko would have no real problems.

"Okay," Gorman said as Kosko moved quickly out of the room. "What's left, Dutch?"

"Just the broadcast frequencies for the walkie-talkies and the communications relay truck."

"Okay, work that out with Ralph." He glanced at his watch. "Quarter to five. The men'll be in soon. Let's get a cup of coffee, Dave."

"Do you want to change first?" Blackman asked.

"Might as well."

The two men went to Gorman's office. Blackman sat at the desk while Gorman exchanged his uniform for a pair of slacks, blue turtleneck sweater and a Windbreaker. He pinned his badge inside his jacket and adjusted the gun at his waist.

"I'd like to ride with you, Mike."

"Like old times."

Blackman smiled. "Do you remember the Hargrove kidnapping stakeout?"

"Yeah," Gorman said. "Dempsey and that rat."

"It weighed ten pounds."

"Easily."

"Fourteen hours in a sewer should be something a man wants to forget. But those were good times, Mike. No responsibilities, just take orders." Blackman picked a loose thread from the braid on his sleeve. "Dempsey and that rat."

"He outstared it."

"How did he keep from shooting it?"

"He has a way with animals."

Blackman toyed with an ashtray. "Did he give you an argument about coming in tonight?"

"Dempsey? No. He couldn't have cared less. Rich was reluctant, but I can't blame him."

"I'd like Rich with me," Blackman said. "I can use him on the plotting board."

"Okay . . . take whoever you want."

"Winshaw buttonholed me. He wanted my help in getting out of the truck detail."

"Winshaw is a pain in the ass."

"Maybe . . . Maybe he sees a different Dempsey than we do."

Gorman hung his uniform in the closet and closed the door.

"What's that supposed to mean?"

"We remember the old times," Blackman said. "He was a brash, tough, funny man when we were in plainclothes. We went up and he stayed. *We've* changed, for Christ's sake, but we still think of him as being the same. Winshaw doesn't have any memories to cloud his vision. I have the feeling that he sees Dempsey more clearly."

"Winshaw is going on the detail," Gorman said flatly.

Blackman sighed. "I know that. I don't think you understood what I was saying."

Gorman took out his gun and checked it. His eyes were troubled. "Dempsey's had a rough couple of years. You know that, Dave. Claire tried to cut his heart out and eat it. Of course he's changed, but he is still a good cop."

"Until proven otherwise," Blackman said, almost to himself.

"Yes," Gorman said hollowly. "Until proven otherwise."

What were they thinking and how did it feel when you first entered them and they spoke the violation and pleasure of it in a soft cry? What? He bore down a little harder, spreading her legs wider with his thighs. He held her with one arm under her neck and the other down below her waist so that he cupped her moving bottom in one hand.

Her breasts were firm against his chest, firmer than those of most women her age. And she moved them against his chest to give pleasure or take it, and perhaps both.

Maybe they didn't think at all. He did — and wished he didn't. It was great pussy, lubricious and smooth, yet tight and clutching, almost sucking. And made better because it was somebody else's and therefore stolen pussy. But he wished he were not thinking as they pumped and perspired against each other. He wished for the mindless copulation of his twenties. Where had that gone, anyhow?

Would John W. Martin think? Dempsey could hear them groan and cry from Port-au-Prince to the Windward Islands, needing John W. Martin and his magic Roto-Rooter.

"Roll over," he said curtly, pulling out of her and letting go.

She rolled instantly, breasts flattened on the bed, round cheeks raised. He knelt behind her and gripped her hips for guidance and support. Obedient, like dogs. You could tell them to hang naked out the window singing the national anthem and they would do it. Just don't miss a stroke. Women took it as it came, and it came hard. Hard and brutal. There was a joy for them in the subjugation. He dug his fingers into her skin and stared up at the ceiling, rocking back and forth, hearing the squelch of his flesh moving in and out of her body. He felt nothing. He was drifting through nameless places — cities, towns, harbors. Islands and continents. A cloud passing over the earth, never pausing, never staying. A free wanderer. In one place and out the other.

"Ahhh . . ." she cried into the bedcover. "Ahhh . . . Oh my God! Jim!"

He looked down at her, momentarily puzzled. She was convulsive, a writhing torso between his hands, pinned to him. Impaled.

It was an obscene thing that was happening to her, a pornographic display, an erotic demonstration of the sex act by a young married woman and her lover. His detachment ended instantly and the enchantment of voyeuristic participation in this act came down upon the top of his skull like a great squeezing hand. Through a schizoid keyhole, he watched a beautiful girl being fucked, cheating on her husband, degrading and demeaning the act and herself by the position she took without protest.

"Fuck you!" he roared. "Fuck you!" as his own orgasm assaulted and raged at his groin for release. It came in a few bone-jarring thrusts and he pulled her back against it, lifting her off the bed with mad strength, holding her a moment in midair.

Then he let her go and she slumped down in a gangling

sprawl. She breathed noises and sounds. He felt relieved but untouched, an observer who has watched a sports event. He got off the bed and searched for a cigarette. He found a fresh pack in the kitchen and when he came back into the room, she was still lying in the same position. He felt nothing for her, thought nothing about her.

"Cigarette?"

"Please."

He lit one and handed it down to her. She stirred languidly and took it from his fingers. Her eyes were hopeful.

"I may never walk again," she said.

The robe was on the floor and he picked it up and draped it across her shoulders.

"Don't catch cold."

She tilted her head and closed her eyes, waiting for him to bend down and kiss her. He could not. He usually did. But now he could not. He hadn't been making love to her this time. He hadn't been part of it. He turned away and walked into the kitchen, poured himself a drink and carried the glass with him into the bathroom. When he came back she was sitting on the bed with her legs tucked under her.

"Sit down and be friendly," she said.

He opened the closet and took out a suit. "Sorry. No time."

She was surprised and it brought out her capacity for instant indignation. "Why? Where are you going?"

"Out to work."

"I thought you had forty-eight hours off."

"And now I don't. Cop's life is really shit for the pigs, isn't it?"

She watched him put on his clothes, her eyes following every movement.

"You can sure get dressed in a hurry."

"When I have to." He buttoned up his shirt and slipped a tie under his collar.

"Have to, or want to?"

She was irritated, but that was her problem.

"My partner's going to be here in about five minutes."

"And where does that leave me?"

He shrugged. "You either get under the covers and go to sleep or you get up and get your ass out of here. Free country."

"You sound like a husband who can't wait to get out with the boys."

"And you sound like some bitch broad I got rid of five years ago."

His words brought her off the bed. She ran into the bathroom, struggled out of the heavy terrycloth robe and hurled it toward him before slamming the door.

"Bastard!"

He reached the door in four strides and banged on it with his fist.

"Come on out of there!"

She yanked the door open and faced him, naked and defiant.

"Why don't you just kick it in! Or shoot the lock off? You think you're such a big man because you've got a gun in your pants!"

He hit her sharply across the side of the face with the hard, ridged back of his hand. The blow snapped her head to one side.

"Shut up," he hissed. "I don't come with a license to nag — you've got a husband for that. I'm going to work because some brass hat says I have to. I'm a *cop*, not some nine-to-five soda jerk."

There was a livid mark on her pale skin. She touched it gingerly, tears of anger smarting her eyes.

"Some cop! You're a whore — working both sides of the street!"

"Both sides of what street?" He cupped her chin in his right hand, his fingers tight along the jaw. "What street, Nikki?"

There was fear in her eyes. The hand was like an iron claw. It cut her cheeks on the ridges of her teeth.

"Forget it," she whispered.

"No," he said. "*You* forget it. Whatever you know — or think you know — wash right out of your mind. Now and forever."

It would have been so easy to snap her neck. One hard twist and he'd have a very silent woman on his bathroom floor. He let go of her and turned away. He could hear the bleep of a car horn and he knew that Rich was waiting for him.

"Dempsey?" Her tone was plaintive. "Dempsey?"

He glanced back at her as he put on his raincoat.

"Do you — do you want me to wait for you?"

He could not think of a reason for it; there were indications it would best be finished.

"Suit yourself," he said, going out the door.

Carl Rich was waiting for him, gunning the engine of the ancient Plymouth to keep it going. The windshield wipers made a loud clacking sound. Carl was fidgeting nervously with the heater controls. Just keeping busy, Dempsey thought; the heater had not worked in years.

"Getting late," Rich said as Dempsey got into the car.

"So it's getting late. So what?"

"Gorman said six . . . It's six now."

"We'll be a little late. That's all, Carl. Relax."

Dempsey stared out the side window as Rich pulled away from the curb. He could smell the fear. Poor Carl. He wore his fear like dirty underwear. Maybe it was part of growing old. Maybe it came with the gray hairs and the paunch. The fear of stepping on toes, of being too late or too early. The fear going to bed and the fear waking up. Fear of death and fear of life. Maybe a man got used to it. Dempsey didn't know or want to know.

"I wonder why they called us in," Rich said.

"Some bullshit, who knows?"

Rich glanced at him. His face was drawn and there were deep circles under his eyes.

"Mike didn't tell you?"

"No," Dempsey muttered.

"That's funny. He didn't tell me . . . but I thought sure he'd let you know."

"Why? I only work there."

"I didn't hear any talk about special details. Maybe it's something that just came up." It was like a question. But Dempsey had no taste for conversation. Rich was seeking assurances that everything was okay. Who the hell knew? He stared out the window at the rain.

"Della was upset," Rich went on. "You know, my being given forty-eight off and then being called back . . . That and the rain. She hates rain . . . and me being out in it. She says every time she hears an ambulance go by she thinks of me cracking up the car in the rain. I told her that's crazy."

Dempsey reached into his pocket for a cigarette and couldn't find one. Nikki. She had thrown off his routine. He never left the apartment without first checking his pockets for a pack of cigarettes and his Zippo lighter. Well, he had left them on the table and he did not want to add to Carl's panic by having him stop at a drugstore so that he could buy a pack.

"We were going to have a steak," Rich babbled.

Dempsey looked at him. "Will you for Christ's sake relax? What the hell are you so worried about?"

Rich gripped the wheel tightly. A truck was ambling along in front of them and he was trying to screw up his courage to pass on the wet street.

"I don't know, Jim. Lately . . . every little thing . . . just scares the hell out of me. I don't know what's the matter with me. Della, I think. I just . . . get scared about her, Jim. You know . . . what if I were dead? Who the hell would take care of her?"

"Nothing's going to happen to you. You're my partner, Carl. Look up the records. I've never lost a partner yet."

Rich managed his first smile of the day. He envied Dempsey's calm. He didn't resent it, far from it. Dempsey's strength was his lifeline. Without it he was lost. "You're one hell of a guy, Jim."

"Yeah," Dempsey grunted, "I know it. Now pass that truck."

Rich swung out to pass. He drove better when Dempsey was around. What a hell of a guy.

It was fifteen minutes past six when they walked into Central. Sergeant Arnold Dernburgh was at the desk, munching a candy bar.

"They got a posse out for you," Dernburgh said.

"I can smell the horseshit," Dempsey remarked.

"Funny," Dernburgh said. He dislodged a piece of almond from between his front teeth and pointed down the hall. "Briefing in 108 — attendance is required."

"What's going on, Arnie?" Rich asked.

Dernburgh raised one sloping shoulder. "I'm not in the Chief's confidence. But it looks like the battle of Cleveland is about to start any goddamn minute now."

"Who the hell would fight over it?" Dempsey said as they turned toward the corridor.

The room was crowded with men, all in plainclothes except for Inspectors Gruebner and Blackman and Chief Keeley. Riot guns had been issued. At least half of the forty to fifty men in the room were holding the big 12-gauge shotguns, butts down, like infantrymen at parade rest.

Rich eyed the guns uneasily. "What the hell's up, Jim?" he whispered.

Dempsey felt a tingle of exhilaration and excitement at the sight of the firepower. It was a big kill. His hunter's instinct rose instantly to the scent.

"We're going to invade Toledo and steal all their niggers," Dempsey said softly.

Rich was shocked; then he stifled a laugh.

They stood in the back of the room, but Gorman spotted them instantly.

"You are late."

"Traffic," Dempsey said. "It was a bitch."

"Okay. We're in a hurry, so I won't go over this again. Rich . . . I'm assigning you to Inspector Blackman. He'll fill you in on your duties. Dempsey, you'll be going with me."

"Where?"

"For a ride — a ten-dollar tour in a one-ton truck."

So that was it, Dempsey thought. A hijack patrol. He had expected them to come up with something like it sooner or later. So tonight was the night. He smiled to himself. Dondero would have to take his chances if he had anything going.

"Boys," Chief Keeley said in the best Rotary Club manner, "I don't have to tell you how important this operation is. All I want is the best — and I know I'm going to get it. Good luck."

The men began to file out, forming themselves into three- and four-man teams in the hallway. Dempsey waited in the room until Gorman came up to him.

"I haven't been on a job without Carl in eight years, Mike. I hate starting with strangers this late in the game."

"I'm your partner, Jim. Like old times."

"Cut the crap. Why isn't Carl on this?"

Gorman flinched. "You're not the only one who looks out for Carl. We might have to use those guns tonight. I don't want anyone on my team I have to worry about."

"Okay . . . okay. So it's you and me." Dempsey's lips curled in a smile of faint mockery. "Who else do we have? Dave, Dutch and the Chief?"

"Daley and Winshaw, and a driver," he replied curtly. "Get a riot gun from the locker and wait for your name to be called. I'll meet you out front."

Gorman strode out of the room and down the hall to the front of the building. Memory lane. Dempsey's sarcasm was part of those memories.

I have a sharp Irish tongue, Mike. It'll keep the braid off my arm.

Dempsey had said that one night after six beers and three shots of rye at Danny O'Neal's tavern. Over fifteen years ago. Dempsey had been right. He had said more than one thing at the wrong time and rubbed a lot of brass the wrong way. It had held him back — that and a lack of ambition, a contempt for success.

The bigger you get, Mike, the more strings they put on you. They jerk you around. They cut the heart out of you and pluck the brain from your skull. They put a tongue in you that can only say, yes, Mister Mayor . . . of course, Mister Mayor . . . by all means, Mister Mayor . . .

Barroom rhetoric, but Dempsey had believed it. He had always been a good, but maverick, cop.

"The trucks are ready to roll, Mike." Gruebner stood by the Nineteenth Street exit, a clipboard under his arm. "Shall I call out the crews?"

"Yes. Be sure to take them in the order I gave you. Okay?"

Gruebner bristled, his heavy Prussian face turning a pale shade of scarlet.

"How else would I take them?"

Gorman laid a placating hand on the big man's shoulder. "Bear with me, Dutch, but they *have* to be in order — no skipping — and go two minutes between calls — it's important."

Gruebner scanned the taut, anxious face before him. He had known Gorman for a long time and they had been involved in many delicate operations, but he had never seen the man so tight.

"Sure, Mike," he said gently. "I'll follow the list — to the letter."

"Thanks, Dutch. When you get to my team, don't call Daley's name. I . . . I have him on a special assignment."

There was a part of Gruebner that wanted to ask what special assignment Sergeant Daley was on at this time of the evening and under these circumstances, and another part of him that didn't want to know about it. He sensed that something was going on beneath the orderly surface of the operation, something that perhaps only Gorman knew about. He was content to leave it that way.

"Okay, Mike. I'll just call . . ." He plucked the clipboard from under his wing and scanned the typed lines on the top page. "Bluebird 15. You . . . Winshaw . . . Dempsey. Is that right?"

"Yes — in that order. Let's get rolling."

Gruebner stood to one side of the wide doors and barked out names in his parade-ground tone.

"Bluebird 1. Callahan . . . Wilson . . . Maggiore . . ."

The three men whose names had been called walked quickly down the steps to the street where the first of the trucks stood waiting, a policeman in plainclothes behind the wheel. One of the men got in beside the driver and the other two climbed into the back. The truck, bearing the words PETE'S POULTRY — WE DELIVER on the side in peeling letters, moved off with a grinding of gears and another took its place.

"Bluebird 2. Ransko . . . Sebring . . . White . . ."

A police car was parked at the curb, just out of the circle of light cast by the lamps in front of the station door. Sergeant Daley sat in the shadows of the back seat beside Officer Lewandowski and the shawl-bundled figure of Mrs. Godansky.

Daley flipped on a penlight and read from the piece of paper on his lap. "Callahan . . . Wilson . . . Maggiore . . ."

Lewandowski spoke quietly to the old woman beside him. Then, "The names don't mean anything to her, Sergeant, and she doesn't recognize any of the men."

"Okay," Daley said. "Ransko . . . Sebring . . . White . . ."

Dempsey waited in the hall, smoking a cigarette from the package he had taken from Sergeant Dernburgh. It was a menthol filter tip and he blew smoke through his nose with a grimace of distaste. He was standing next to Winshaw, but neither man had said a word to the other until Dempsey noticed that Winshaw was not carrying a shotgun.

"Why am I blessed?" he asked.

Winshaw seemed startled that Dempsey had a voice. "What?"

Dempsey held up the heavy gun. "The cannon. Where's yours?"

"One to a truck," Winshaw said coolly.

"I hate like hell to pull the rank of seniority on you, Winshaw, but you just inherited a genuine American scattergun." He held out the gun until Winshaw, his eyes smoldering with suppressed rage, grabbed it out of his hand. "You'll be happy with it, Winshaw. Like they say in the Marines — a good piece is a man's best friend."

"Fuck you," Winshaw said under his breath.

"Bluebird 15." Gruebner's voice boomed in the now empty hallway. "Gorman . . . Winshaw . . . Dempsey . . ."

Gorman was waiting for them on the sidewalk, holding

the side door of the truck open. It was the one-ton Chevy that was Billy Price's pride and joy — his name and slogan painted across the side in black and orange: BILLY PRICE TRUCKING . . . THE PRICE IS RIGHT.

"Where's Bob?" Winshaw asked, looking around.

"Clearing something up with Blackman. We'll meet you around the side."

Winshaw and Dempsey climbed in and Gorman closed the door and walked around to talk to the driver, a slim, dark-haired young man dressed in blue jeans and a leather jacket.

"I'm Inspector Gorman."

The young man smiled nervously. "Abolofo, sir, Carmen Abolofo, patrolman, Sixteenth District."

"How's the truck, Carmen?"

"Pretty good, sir . . . lots of power . . . not beaten to death like some of those rigs."

"Good. Just pull around the corner and I'll be with you in a minute."

"Yes, sir." The young man eased the truck into gear and rolled forward, leaving Gorman standing in the street. He watched the truck until it turned the corner onto Payne Avenue and then walked toward the police car. Daley was standing on the sidewalk, waiting. His face was grim.

"Well?" Gorman asked.

The sergeant stared woodenly at the list in his hand. "She makes Dempsey for two, maybe three visits with Godansky at her house about a month before the shooting."

There was a tight feeling in Gorman's chest and he took a deep breath. He could see the vague shadow of the old woman in the back seat.

"Could she lie, for revenge? Just pick out a cop and finger him for the hell of it?"

Daley chewed his bottom lip and squinted at the dark

sky. "She had like forty-five men to lie about — but she picked Dempsey."

She wasn't lying. Gorman knew it in his heart and in the coldly efficient recesses of his brain. She was telling the truth, so help her God. Dempsey had lied about not knowing her son.

. . . the name had a familiar ring, but I've never seen him around . . .

A lie, premeditated and deliberate. How many more lies rested in Dempsey's file? The thought sickened him.

"What'll we do with the old lady?" Daley asked.

"Have Lewandowski drive her home. We'll take a statement from her tomorrow. Bring Earl Welch with you and get it down in black and white." He gave Daley a searching look.

"I know," Daley said, "keep my mouth shut. Christ, I wouldn't tell my own mother about this."

"Don't *think* anything, either . . . until *all* the facts are in."

He could not look Daley in the face. Turning sharply on his heels he walked toward the corner and the waiting truck. The rain was easing off, but the streets and the freeways would be wet and slick as ice. He had a mission to perform and he tried to clear his mind of James Dempsey — just for now.

"Who's goin' to hit the dinge?" Prochak asked.

Al Summers laughed. "Charlie wouldn't like to hear you call him that. He's sensitive."

"Bullshit." Prochak lowered the window and tossed the glowing stub of a cigar onto the wet street. "I'm a Polack and proud of it. What the hell's wrong in being a nigger?"

"Not a damn thing," Summers replied.

"So, who's goin' to hit him?"

"I will," Davis said.

"Mister Muscles," Prochak sneered. "Well, okay, you hit him, but don't hit him in the head. Niggers got heads like cannonballs."

"Where the hell is he?" Fred Bolen asked anxiously. "He should have picked up the load by now."

"Keep your pants on," Prochak said. "It's only a quarter after seven. He'll be comin' by in about ten minutes."

They were parked on Riverdale Road, just off the airport freeway. Prochak sat behind the wheel with Davis on the seat beside him. Bolen and Summers were in the back of the truck, standing by the narrow opening that gave the driver access to the rear. It was not one of the Dondero Line trucks, but a big, slab-sided delivery van that Prochak had rented under the name of Harry T. Polanski. Through the big windshield the men could see the freeway traffic and the glow of lights that marked the airport runways directly across the freeway. Every few minutes a big jet lumbered up into the wet sky with shrieking engines.

"Look at that mother," Prochak said. "That's a jumbo."

"The *only* way to fly," Summers said.

Prochak looked at him over his shoulder. "How the hell would you know? You never been out of fuckin' Cleveland."

"So what?" Summers shot back.

"So don't give us that *only*-way-to-fly shit, like you was some fuckin' jet-setter."

"Up your ass, Prochak." Summers stifled a yawn. "Are you *sure* it's only a quarter after?"

Prochak squinted at his watch. "Twenty after. Time flies."

Davis leaned forward. "I think I see him coming. No . . . it's an AirHaul rig."

"He didn't blink his lights. I told you, he'll blink twice."

Prochak settled back in his seat and closed his eyes. "Mink. How about it, Fred? Want mink or sable for the old lady?"

"My old woman wouldn't know a mink if it bit her on the ass," Bolen said.

"Neither would mine," Prochak drawled, "or yours, Al. Now, Johnny here's got a little monkey who really has class. Right, Johnny?"

"Lay off," Davis muttered.

"Lay off? I'm handin' you a compliment and you tell me to lay off. Is that nice? Man, you got a sweet little piece who wears mink to bed. Am I right, Johnny boy?"

"I said lay off."

Prochak sat upright, grinning. Davis was a pushover for the needle. He'd grumble and growl and flex his shoulder muscles, but he had the temper of a fat puppy.

"Yes, sir, if my old lady wore mink nighties I'd tell the fuckin' world about it. But not our Johnny."

Davis stared straight ahead and clenched his fists until the knuckles cracked. "Shut up about my wife."

Prochak winked at the others. "Whatever you say, coach, but you can't stop me thinkin' about it. Oh, boy! A sweet little fox in mink drawers! *That's livin'.*"

Davis had been pushed to the limit and, to Prochak's delight, he slammed a fist against the dashboard.

"Shut up! I mean it, Harry. Shut your goddamn mouth or I'm getting right out of this truck!"

Prochak threw up his hands in mock horror. "An' break up the old team on the last game of the season? No! You wouldn't pull a trick like that. Why, how could we — "

"There he is!" Summers yelped. "I saw the lights blink."

Prochak gunned the idling engine and threw the truck into gear.

"Okay, boys, hold onto your fuckin' hats."

Bluebird 15 moved slowly through the flats, past silent factories and deserted loading docks.

"Nothing much around here, Inspector," Abolofo said. He jerked a thumb toward a complex of dark brick buildings and corrugated iron warehouses. "I used to work for that outfit before I joined the force."

"Driving a truck?" Gorman asked.

"No, loader on the shipping dock. Boy, were we busy. You know, Nam was goin' strong and there were three shifts a day. A guy could get all the overtime he wanted. Now look at the place — nothin'. Dark as a graveyard."

"What did they make?"

"I dunno . . . some kind of chemical that killed trees. Tell you the truth, Inspector, I'm glad they aren't doing so good. I mean, why kill off the trees? Pointless, right?"

"Sure, pointless." Gorman smiled in the darkness. He had come to know Carmen Abolofo pretty well in just thirty minutes; a very talkative, and informative young man. Carmen Abolofo was unmarried, but engaged. His fiancée worked for a CPA and took home ninety-eight dollars and sixty-two cents per week. That, plus his salary as a rookie patrolman, was enough to make the payments on a small house in Seven Hills. (The down payment had been assured during a joint meeting of their respective and future in-laws, in-uncles-aunts-and-cousins. Neither Abolofo nor his bride-to-be had a family — they had a clan.)

"Turn around," Gorman said. He picked up the walkie-talkie on the seat beside him and flicked it on. "This is Bluebird 15 to control . . . we're on Fairfield heading for Scranton Road. Nothing happening around here. We'll take the freeway and go out to the airport." He put down the radio and tapped on the sliding panel behind his head. It slipped open and Winshaw's face appeared in the gap.

"What's happening?"

"Nothing," Gorman said. "We're going out to the airport. Everyone okay back there?"

"We're bouncing around like beans in a bucket. Watch it on the rough spots, okay?"

"I'll try . . . sir," Abolofo said.

"And it stinks back here," Winshaw went on. "The guy must've been hauling manure or something."

"How's Dempsey?"

"I think he's asleep."

It was dark in the back of the truck, evil-smelling and uncomfortable. Other than that, Dempsey had nothing to complain about. He sat cross-legged on the truck bed with his back against the side and tried to cushion his spine against the shocks. He was glad that he had foisted the shotgun off on Winshaw because he didn't know what he would have done with the damn thing, short of tossing it out the back. Winshaw was standing, holding onto a canvas strap that dangled from the ceiling. He had the shotgun in his other hand and the butt kept pounding against the floor every time the truck went over a pothole, which was constantly.

"I hope you've got the safety on, Winshaw."

"I'm not an idiot, Dempsey."

"No? You wouldn't be in this truck with me if we both weren't idiots."

Winshaw sulked. Dempsey chuckled. Fifty men rushing all over the city in the back of trucks hoping to catch a hijacker in the act. It was about as silly an enterprise as diving into the Cuyahoga to pan for gold.

He yawned, loudly. "Christ, what grown men won't do to make a living. Hey, Winshaw."

"What?"

"Have you got a cigarette?"

Winshaw's reply was drowned out by the pounding of

the shotgun and the rattle of the truck as Abolofo gunned across some railroad tracks at forty miles an hour.

Carl Rich stood in front of a giant wall map of the city of Cleveland and adjacent suburbs. He had a handful of plastic pins with tiny paper flags attached and he felt like a kid in nursery school as he pinned the little flags to the map, following the directions of the dispatcher over the intercom.

"Bluebird 9 to Harvard Avenue and . . . about One hundred-seventeenth Street. Bluebird 7 . . . Shaker at Woodhill. Bluebird 15 . . . heading for airport on Seventy-one. Bluebird 3 and 5 — stationary — junction Pearl Road and Broadview . . ."

It was a tedious job and he performed it mechanically. He knew the city so well that he could pinpoint the most remote intersection of spidery lines with hardly a glance at the place names on the map.

"Bluebird 6 . . . south on Seventy-first to Woodland."

"How does it look, Carl?" Blackman stood beside him, austere in his gold braid, hands clasped behind his back. He looked like an admiral surveying the progress of some vast battle at sea.

"Placement looks fine," Rich said. "Most of the major truck routes seem to be covered."

"Nothing on the Willow Freeway yet. Get me control, will you, Carl?"

"Yes, sir."

Rich stepped over to a desk and called down to the Communications room on the intercom.

"Ask Dutch who's scheduled for Willow."

"Yes, sir," Rich said. He passed on the question to the dispatcher. There was a minute of silence, then:

"Inspector Gruebner says that Bluebird 4 and Bluebird

11 and 13 are on Willow now . . . going south . . . quarter-mile intervals."

"That takes care of them all," Blackman said. "A nice net — now all we need are some fish to swim into it."

Rich cracked a half-smile. "We might get lucky."

"Yes," Blackman mused. "We might at that, Carl."

Rich had always admired Blackman. He was the type of policeman that he wished he had been — cold without being rigid, firm but fair — a man who walked with surety and pride. A commander with great dignity and unquestionable courage.

"Want some coffee, Inspector?"

"No thank you, Carl, but get yourself a cup. Give your eyes a ten-minute break."

"Would it be okay if I called my wife? You see, she . . ."

Blackman was aware of Della Rich's condition. "Of course, Carl. You don't have to ask."

Rich nodded his thanks and went to one of the desks in a far corner of the office. He had a moment of panic when the phone rang six times and Della didn't pick it up, but finally she did and he gave an audible sigh of relief.

"You worried me. What took you so long?"

"I was in the kitchen."

"Mrs. Markel come over and get your dinner?"

"Oh, yes . . . and we had a nice chat. Are you all right, Carl?"

"Sure, baby, sure . . . working in the office with Inspector Blackman."

"It's starting to rain again."

"Not in here."

The intercom crackled. "Bluebird 8 has spotted two parked trucks . . . Kinsman and One hundred-seventeenth Street . . . investigating. Bluebird 2 going to new location . . . Clair and Marquette . . ."

"Look, baby," Rich said, "I'd better get back to work. You go on to bed and don't worry your head about me. I'm safe, dry and putting in overtime. Okay?"

"Okay," she said. Her voice was wistful. It sounded a thousand miles away.

"Goodnight, hon . . . don't wait up for me." He hung up gently and walked back to the board. Blackman had a small box of pins in his hand and he was peering at the map.

"I'll do it, Inspector."

Blackman handed over the box. "I must be going blind. I can't find Kinsman and One hundred-seventeenth."

"It's right down here, sir . . . flanking Woodland Hills Park." He took a pin from the box and stuck it in the proper location.

Blackman watched him for a moment and then said, matter-of-factly, "Tell me, Carl, how did the sequence go?"

Rich looked at him in puzzlement. "What sequence?"

"The shots Dempsey and Godansky fired — how did they go? Three and three, one and one, two and three and then one? The pattern. What was it?"

The blood drained from Rich's face and the box fell from his hands. A hundred blue and white pins rolled crazily across the floor.

"That mother's a weird driver," Prochak said. "I've never seen a dinge yet who could drive ten feet in a straight line. Look at that crazy coon . . . all over the fuckin' highway."

"Maybe he doesn't know we're behind him," Bolen said.

Prochak hunched over the wheel. "Don't be stupid, man. He slowed down, didn't he? The fucker saw us. He's just showin' off so we'll think he's Mario Andretti or somebody. Johnny, he's your buddy, tell him what the white lines are for. All we need now is a highway patrolman with a new book of tickets. Jesus, look at that spade go."

They were traveling east on the freeway in moderate traffic, following the weaving light of Charlie Greene's truck. Prochak anticipated Greene's maneuvering from one lane to the other, pulled around a struggling 1962 Falcon sedan and settled in behind him. Greene stuck his arm out the window and made the "okay" sign with thumb and index finger.

"What a moron!" Prochak yelled. "How long before Ridge Road?"

"Four miles," Davis said.

"Okay, kiddies, settle back for a nice ride."

Bluebird 15 pulled onto the freeway at the Wade Avenue cloverleaf and headed west toward the airport. The rain came in intermittent bursts, large drops slashing against the windshield like shrapnel. Abolofo never eased his foot on the gas pedal. He was a good and fearless driver. His only reaction to a near-sideswiping by a U.S. mail truck was a vigorous chewing of his bottom lip. Gorman sat stiffly beside him, legs braced against the floorboards. There was no seat belt on the passenger side and Gorman had a vision of himself being catapulted through the tall windshield like a stone from a slingshot if Abolofo hit the air brakes too hard. He tried to take his mind off the dangers of hurtling along a freeway in the rain by thinking about the operation. It had one serious drawback. There was no provision for more than one observer. Two good men in the back of the truck, blind as bats, a driver concentrating on the road and only the man next to the driver doing the watching. He spotted the two trucks as they passed the Ridge Road cutoff — a

Dondero Line truck turning off the freeway, closely followed by another, unmarked truck.

"Let's get off, Carmen," he snapped. "Double back to Ridge Road." He picked up the walkie-talkie and called Central. "This is Bluebird 15 . . . leaving freeway . . . will follow two trucks . . . Ridge Road bridge . . . lead truck has Dondero markings . . ."

Carl Rich was falling apart before his eyes. Blackman studied him without a flicker of relief.

"How did those shots go, Carl?"

Rich ran a sweating hand across his pale lips. "I . . . I'm not sure — I — have to think a min—— "

"*Think?*" Blackman said sharply. "You've been a cop for twenty-two years, Carl. I ask you a simple question and I expect you to give me an answer without having to *think* about it."

The report from Bluebird 15 was coming over the intercom but neither man made a move toward the board. Rich felt his legs giving way and he sat down in a chair and stared at his shoes.

"I . . . was right outside . . . I . . ."

Blackman shook his head. "I read the shooting reports this afternoon in Gorman's office. I think you lied, Carl. I don't think you were in that hall backing up your partner. Where were you, Carl? Where were you when the shooting started?"

Rich buried his face in his hands. "I've got a sick wife. If anything ever happened to me . . ."

"Pull yourself together. You were out in the car, weren't you?"

"Yes." His voice was a sob.

"That's where you heard the first shots. Am I right?" Rich didn't have to answer. Blackman could visualize the scene — Rich waiting in the car while Dempsey went into the building, hearing the shots and then getting out of the car.

"Did you go into the place at all?"

"Went . . . down . . . the hall — yes."

"That's a little bit different from your written version, isn't it?" Blackman's tone was ice. "So, you went down the hall — or into the hall — and three shots came through the wall."

"Yes . . . three . . ."

"Several seconds — perhaps even half a minute — after the first group of shots."

"Something . . . like that . . ." Rich looked up. His face was the color of putty and his eyes were haunted. "I'm sorry — but I just — couldn't go into places anymore — couldn't risk it, risk myself — not with Della the way she is. You've seen her, Dave . . . you know . . ."

"Sure," Blackman said. He looked away. He could pity the man, but he couldn't let his pity interfere with what had to be done — what should have been done long, long before this night.

"I'm placing you on the sick list, Carl. I want you to go home and to stay there until we call you in. We've got falsified reports to straighten out."

"I'm sorry . . . sorry . . ."

"We don't need apologies, we need answers. Mike will want to talk to you, so stay available."

Rich got heavily to his feet. He looked like a dying man.

"Shall I . . . go home now?"

"Yes — and I want you to leave your gun here."

Rich took the .38 Detective Special out of the holster at his waist and set it carefully on the desk. He had one gun and one badge, not much to show for twenty-two years on the force. He could walk out the door and no one would even know he had gone. No one — except Dempsey.

"Jimmy's going to ask questions," he said hollowly. "What do I tell him?"

Blackman picked up the gun, flipped open the cylinder, and let the cartridges fall into his palm. "Nothing. You tell him *nothing*, Carl."

Rich nodded, too filled with misery to say anything further. He walked slowly toward the door as the voice of the dispatcher filled the room . . .

"Bluebird 15 has regained contact with two trucks . . . Ridge Road between Russell and Clinton . . . investigating."

Rich hesitated in the doorway, then stepped over to the board, picked a pin off the floor and stuck it in the map.

Gorman felt that they had something the moment he caught sight of the two trucks moving slowly north on Ridge Road past the dark expanse of West Park Cemetery — a nice, quiet spot to heist a cargo. He tapped on the partition and Winshaw peered out at him.

"A possible," Gorman said. "Two trucks, one of them from the Dondero fleet. Crack the back door a fraction and see what they do after we pass them." He slid down on the seat so that his head was below the window. "Pass them, Carmen. Go flat out, like you're in a hurry to get somewhere."

"Yes, sir."

"Make a left turn on Clinton Road and cut your lights."

"Okay."

The truck rocked gently as Abolofo pressed down on the gas.

"Oh, mama, this baby has *guts*. Love this truck."

"You missed your calling," Gorman said.

"Maybe I did at that . . . and when you think what

teamsters get an hour . . . Mama, I should turn in the badge."

"Wait an hour."

"No way, Inspector . . . turn in the badge, I mean. Give me ten years an' I'll have more gold braid than Eisenhower."

A cocky kid. Gorman hoped he would make it. They would be passing the two trucks any minute at the speed they were going and he closed his eyes, trying to visualize the map. They were on Ridge Road, going north, big cemetery to the left, another to the right. The only turnoff would be Clinton Road. Ridge continued due north to Denison, dogleg to the left into West Seventy-third Street. Three patrol cars could seal off the entire area with no trouble at all.

"Passing 'em, Inspector."

The truck swayed slightly to the left and then straightened up.

"What were they doing?"

Abolofo took one hand off the wheel and held it palm up.

"Nothing. Moseying along, nose to tail." He glanced into the rearview mirror. "Still doing it . . . Hey! Wait a minute . . ."

Winshaw's shout came at the same instant. "Lead truck turned off its lights . . . pulling to the side of the road."

Gorman sat up. "Keep moving, Carmen . . . don't slow down until you make the turn on Clinton."

There was no sign of a side street, just cemetery. Tombstones in the rain.

"Where the hell's the street?" Abolofo said anxiously.

"Half a minute . . . keep your eyes open." He flipped on the radio. "This is Bluebird 15. I think we have a good bet here. Send cruisers to block off Ridge Road . . . north and south . . . and another on Clinton from West Boulevard . . . have them stay well back unless I call."

"Clinton!" Abolofo shouted.

It was a narrow, rutted road flanked by dumps and the rusting outskirts of the Penn Central marshaling yards, a bleak place to be on a dark and rainy night. Abolofo switched off the lights and braked to a stop.

Gorman knelt on the seat and looked through the open port into the rear of the truck.

"We're going to give them five minutes, then go back down the road."

"It's probably a Good Humor man," Dempsey called out. "Moonlighting."

"I hope you're right, but if it's a rip-off we're going to hit hard and fast — so be ready."

"I'm ready," Dempsey said. "I'd walk through fire to get out of this truck. How about you, Winshaw?"

"If it'd get me away from you!"

"Just stay in front of me with that elephant gun, boy. That's all I ask."

"Knock it off," Gorman said. It really was like old times.

Prochak didn't give the big Chevy a second thought as it roared past. Ridge Road ran into Lorain via Seventy-third Street, and Lorain cut through the heart of the industrial flats, so the road was well known to truckers. When Charlie Greene pulled over to the side and cut his lights, Prochak did the same. He looked into the rearview mirror and then glanced at the road ahead. Nothing, just the rapidly diminishing taillights of the Chevy.

"Okay . . . everybody out. Who's got the rope?"

"I do," Bolen said.

"Bolt cutters?"

"In my hand," Summers replied.

It was Prochak's plan and he enjoyed the feeling of being in command and handing out the orders. He fancied himself as a leader of men, an organizer of smoothly functioning jobs. Davis might have the body, but he had the brains.

"You got a tire iron, Johnny?"

"No, I'll use my fists."

"You'll bust your hands like fuckin' glass, man. That nigger has an iron jaw."

"Let me worry about that, Prochak."

"Suit your fuckin' self. No skin off my ass." He opened the door and climbed down out of the cab. "Okay, let's *move!*"

Charlie Greene stood at the rear of his truck, shoulders hunched against the rain. He watched the four men walk toward him, took a final drag on a cigarette and then flipped it toward the road. The glowing tip fizzled out before it hit the ground.

"Right on schedule," he said. His voice was strained. He knew he was going to get hit in about one minute and the thought bothered him. He didn't trust the Polack. If Prochak came at him he'd bust him first. Fuck it. He wasn't going to get worked over by that honky sonofabitch.

"Who's gonna bust me?"

"I am," Davis said.

Greene smiled lazily, relaxed. "Okay, coach. Hit the man who's gonna get *you* the league cup."

Davis feinted with his left, whipping it in toward Greene's stomach, pulling the punch at the last second.

"Two for flinching!"

Greene laughed, his teeth flashing white in the gloom. "Shee-it, man. I didn't flinch. I always jerk that way."

"You're blockin' the fuckin' doors," Prochak said. "Fred,

give Johnny the rope . . . Al, get on that lock. Let's go go go."

Greene and Davis stepped out of the way as Al Summers moved to the doors with the bolt cutter, a monster pincer with fifteen-inch handles. He raised the heavy tool and cut the combination lock that sealed the doors as easily as a man slicing butter with a hot knife. Prochak pulled the doors open, then noticed Davis and Greene watching.

"What the hell ya doin'? This ain't no goddamn circus. Get that guy tied up, for Christ's sake."

The two men walked slowly to the front of the truck.

"I hate that bastard's guts," Greene muttered.

"He's not a bad guy, just uptight all the time."

Greene turned his back on Davis and clasped his hands behind him. Davis took a piece of rope and wrapped it around the black man's wrists. "Too loose, man. Can't you tie a knot?"

"I don't want to cut off the blood."

"You want it to look good, don't you? Pull on the mother."

Davis retied it, grunting with each tug of the line. Greene winced as the thin manila rope cut into his flesh. He'd have marks for months, Davis was thinking, but if that was the way he wanted it . . .

"Don't cut me up," Greene said. "You know, I don't want no fuckin' money for stitches. Just belt me in the ribs."

"Wherever you want it."

Davis struggled to make a firm knot. He could hear the men inside the truck, moving around, their feet clattering on the steel floor. Then he heard the fur bales — thump, thump, thump — dropping like bodies onto the wet ground.

216

Gorman watched the luminous hand on his watch sweep up to twelve.

"Let's go."

He unzipped his jacket and pulled out his gun. The chrome gleamed in the light from the dash. The gun seemed too ornate a weapon for such a dark moment. Okay, he thought as he pulled back the recoil action, moving a bullet into the chamber, the gun was fancy, but it was still a .38 Colt automatic. So it was shiny and had ivory grips. So it would still kill.

Abolofo backed the truck onto Ridge Road. "Lights on or off, Inspector?"

"On. We're just another truck coming down the highway. Pass them, than make a sharp U-turn and pull alongside." He tapped the partition. "Get ready back there, and brace yourselves for a spinout."

"Let's go, Carmen."

Abolofo threw the truck into gear and hit the gas. Gorman tightened his grip on the gun, feeling a surge of adrenaline. He had once tried to explain to his wife what it felt like to move toward the unknown with a gun. Her reaction had been horror, and fear. In a way, that was his own reaction now as he watched the dark road sweeping toward them and Abolofo pressed hard on the accelerator. His stomach tightened in anticipation.

It's like your first roller-coaster ride . . .

You're crazy . . . really crazy . . .

All cops are crazy, Annie.

The excitement was almost unbearable.

"Comin' up fast, Inspector."

Gorman could see the oblong shapes of the trucks by the side of the road about fifty yards ahead. He thought that he could see two men standing by the cab of the lead truck but he was not certain. They whipped past and he strained to see what was taking place at the rear of the truck. The doors were wide open and there were objects on the ground, but he could not see any men.

"Now!"

Abolofo hit the brakes and spun the wheel at the same time. The big truck went into a spin, the rear tires smoking on the pavement. It was a dangerous maneuver on a rain-slick highway, but Abolofo performed it perfectly. He slammed into low gear and the truck lurched forward, still rocking from side to side after the snap U-turn.

Gorman opened the door and was halfway out of the cab, using the big door as a shield, before the Chevy came to a stop alongside the two trucks. He could see the shadows of men in the back of the Dondero truck as their headlights swept across it.

"Police!" he shouted. "Freeze!"

The light caught Prochak in the eyes. He dropped a bale of furs and dove for the open doorway, yanking a .45 Colt automatic from the waistband of his pants.

"Shit! Cops!" He started firing as he went, slamming shots at the cab of the truck before leaping out into the darkness. He heard glass shatter and the screech of bullet-torn metal.

Carmen Abolofo died with his foot on the brake. The bullet came through the windshield and hit him above the bridge of the nose, blowing his brains out the back of his skull. He was dead before his body slumped against the wheel. Gorman did not see him die. Prochak's second shot tore out the window of the open door before Gorman had a chance to fire. A spray of busted glass peppered the side of his face like birdshot and one large piece sliced a furrow above his left eyebrow, blinding him with a rush of hot blood.

"Oh, motherfucker!" Charlie Greene yelped as he saw

218

the truck bear down on them and come screeching to a halt. He tried to run away, but Davis didn't panic. They were shielded from direct view by the body of the truck. Davis pushed Greene against the door of the cab and hit him flush on the point of the chin with a short left hook. The black man went down just as the first shots exploded and for a moment Davis thought Greene had been hit. Davis dropped down on the gravel and pressed himself against the front tire. The shit had hit the fan. *Cops.* Maybe he could crawl away into the blackness, but, oh, Jesus, there might be a hundred men out there moving in with shotguns. Charlie was in the clear. He was unconscious and his hands were tied — a victim. Davis looked around in a panic, spotted the sharp edge of the fender a foot from his head, closed his eyes and lunged toward it. Lightning slashed across his eyes and then it was all darkness.

Dempsey hit the rear door with his shoulder and jumped out the way a paratrooper would jump from a plane. He landed in a half-crouch, gun in hand, raced around the side of the truck, and almost stumbled over Gorman who was kneeling on the ground, trying to wipe the blood out of his eye.

"Mike! You okay?"

Gorman nodded, waving his gun in the general direction of the Dondero truck.

"Back . . . of the truck . . . watch it."

Dempsey ducked behind the right front fender and squeezed off four shots, aiming for the dark cavern of the truck body.

Al Summers caught a bullet in the chest and spun backwards, dying with his face against a bale of furs. Fred Bolen fell flat on his stomach and began to crawl toward the doorway, pushing a bundle of furs ahead of him as bullets cracked over his head. He managed to worm a short-barreled Smith & Wesson .38 from his back pocket and thumbed back the hammer. He knew what it was like to serve time and he was determined never to see the inside of a jail cell again.

A bullet thudded against the bale but did not penetrate it. He had almost reached the doors when he spotted the form of a man coming around the back of the police truck. He aimed carefully . . .

Winshaw moved cautiously. It was his plan to cut behind the rear truck and catch the hijackers in a cross-fire. Bolen broke up the play with his first shot. He saw a man spin and fall, dropping what looked like a rifle or a shotgun. The other man dove headfirst for the ground.

"Pricks!" Fred Bolen rose to his knees, holding his gun with both hands, aiming for the dark shadow of the man . . .

Winshaw groaned and tried to get up. Rain washed against his face, the drops spinning in at crazy angles. The black sky seemed to be moving around him, bearing down. He wanted to sit up and get out of the rain, but he felt paralyzed. Bolen's slug had shattered his collarbone and exited through the scapula, leaving a hole as round, and as big, as a golf ball. He was going into shock but was dimly aware of someone yelling.

I'm going to get shot again . . . I'm going to die . . .

He could feel the cold metal of the shotgun under his right hand but he knew that he would never be able to lift it.

Dempsey snapped off two shots at the man kneeling in the truck and saw him jerk backward with a hoarse scream. He pressed the trigger again and the hammer slapped down on an empty chamber.

"Shit."

He cursed himself for not having slipped another gun

into his pocket. It sure as hell wasn't the time or the place to start fumbling with loose cartridges.

"Mike! Your gun — quick." He reached back toward the still-kneeling form and Gorman chucked him the shiny automatic. Dempsey grabbed it, grinning. "Fancy!"

Prochak lay flat on the ground, face pressed against a clump of wet weeds. It was suddenly very quiet. He'd heard Bolen scream. Or was it Summers? It didn't matter. Somebody had bought the last ticket. He couldn't think straight, couldn't put all the pieces together. He was Harry Prochak and this was *his* job. The cops were on the other side of the two trucks. He could get into his own truck, but that would mean having to back onto the road and then go forward. Shit, they'd have fifty slugs in him before he got out of reverse. Greene's rig . . . Had the nigger left the keys in the ignition?

Prochak raised his head and stared at Greene's truck. It was less than twenty feet away and pointing in the right direction. He could crawl through the weeds and slip in through the passenger side, keeping his head low — low all the way, baby, crawl like a fuckin' snake — start the truck and drag the hell out of it.

Maybe.

Okay. Maybe, but it was the only maybe he had. He started to crawl. Where the hell was everybody?

Gorman leaned against the side of the truck behind Dempsey.

"We get them?"

Dempsey took a slow step away from the comforting bulk of the fender. There was no way of knowing who they'd got. He'd seen one man go down, but there had been at least two, maybe three. He gripped the unfamiliar gun, not knowing how much squeeze the trigger wanted for firing. There was only one way to find out. He pulled stead-

221

ily until the gun bucked in his hand, the slug smacking into the truck's side, right through an o in DONDERO.

"Okay," he yelled. "Come out with your hands behind your head."

Silence. The drum of the rain. Then an engine roared into life . . . tires spun, spraying gravel and mud . . . the truck moved forward with a gear-wrenching jerk that sent a bale of furs and the body of Fred Bolen tumbling out the back. The rear wheels rolled over Charlie Greene's right foot and missed Johnny Davis's head by an inch.

Dempsey was shooting, but he'd never stop a truck that size with a .38. Not when the target was getting smaller by the second. They might as well spit after it. Dempsey spun toward the door of the Chevy and leaped into the cab. The seat was grainy with pulverized glass and wet blood.

"Holy Mother!"

He touched the slumped body, feeling for the vein in the neck. Then he saw the shattered bones of the skull and he knew that there was no point in trying to find a pulse. He opened the door and pushed Carmen Abolofo's body out onto the road. He put the automatic in his lap as he sat behind the wheel and fumbled for the switch and the gearshift lever. He started the engine and shifted into low almost at the same instant and the truck jumped forward like an iron toad.

"Christ! Don't stall it!" Gorman shouted as he flung himself onto the front seat.

Gorman picked up the walkie-talkie from the floor and was pressing the button as Dempsey pulled away, careening onto the highway.

"Bluebird 15 to Central . . ."

"What the hell . . . !" Dempsey looked at the windshield for the first time and could see nothing but a spider-web of lines radiating from a neatly drilled hole that was in direct line with his head. He grabbed the gun off his lap, held it by the barrel and swung the butt at the glass, chopping at it, spilling broken glass all over the dashboard. Wind and black rain thrashed his face, but at least he could see the road as he pressed the gas pedal to the floor.

"We are in pursuit of GMC truck — Dondero Freight Lines — license negative — proceeding north on Ridge Road toward Denison — intercept — all cars . . . and send ambulance . . . previous location . . . imperative. Repeat . . . imperative."

Prochak clutched the wheel of the rocketing truck with his left hand and fumbled through his pockets with his right. Nothing. Not a cigar or a cigarette. There was an ashtray under the dash and he pulled it out, his hand shaking. He was like a drunk hoping to find a quart of booze in the glove compartment. The ashtray was clean. Charlie hadn't smoked or he'd popped his butts out the window.

"Asshole!"

One butt, one tiny drag of smoke, that was all he wanted, and he wasn't going to get it. He was going to get shit if he didn't get off this road in a hurry. He had the gas pedal floored and was hitting seventy, but the road never seemed to end, it went on and on — and there were headlights behind him now, a long way back, but *there*.

He saw the police cruiser as he neared Denison Avenue, parked across the road at a forty-five degree angle, red light blinking on and off. Prochak sucked in his breath and kept his foot firmly pressed on the gas. There was a gap in the left hand lane that was *almost* wide enough for the truck to get through if he hit it just right. It would mean losing his right front fender and he prayed that he wouldn't blow the tire at the same time. The cops were out of their car, waving flashlights in his face and running around like a couple of crazed ants as he bore down on them, the engine screaming like a jet. He cut the wheel sharply to the left and then to the right, the truck lurching from side to side. He braced himself for the shock as he hit the front side of the police car. His fender spun the police car off to the side of the road, one tire exploding and the hood flying upward as the front end caved in.

"This is Bluebird 15 . . . Bluebird 15 . . . suspect's vehicle has passed roadblock . . . Ridge to Denison . . . he's turned right on Denison and we have him in sight . . ."

Gorman squinted in the wind. There was no way he could instruct Central to set up new roadblocks. There were any number of streets the truck could take now. He might head for the freeway, but that was too much to hope for. Gorman gave him credit for being smarter than that, whoever he was. No, he would turn left on Denison, up Sixty-fifth or Sixtieth and into the maze of streets that lay between Lorain and Storer avenues. If they lost sight of his lights for a second they would lose him.

"Keep on his tail!" Gorman shouted, the wind tearing his words to shreds.

Dempsey could hear only the words *keep* and *tail*, but he knew what Gorman was saying to him.

"What the hell do you think I'm doing?" he screamed. He was driving like a lunatic and pushing the Chevy as it had never been pushed before. He was tearing the guts out of Billy Price's most precious possession, stripping gears and burning brakes. He took the corner of Denison in a long, sliding skid that drove a terrified Volkswagen owner onto the sidewalk and into hysteria.

Far ahead of them . . . weaving red lights . . . cars scattering to the sides of the highway. The red lights wavered . . . were lost to view. Gorman spotted the reflection of light on the side of the truck as it turned left.

"Turning!" he bellowed, pointing. "Sixtieth."

Dempsey nodded. He'd spotted the turn, and he knew the area. A tangle . . . a warren . . . they'd blown it.

The street was dark and narrow. Cars parked on both sides. Small frame houses, leafless trees. Everything rushed past him in a jumble of images. Harry Prochak stared straight ahead — *thinking, thinking*, Storer Avenue up ahead . . . barrel across . . . keep on to Clark . . . right on Clark to the sprawling wilderness of the Baltimore and Ohio railroad yards . . . ditch the truck . . . lose himself in the endless rows of parked freight cars . . .

Think . . . think . . . think . . .

He never saw the big concrete mixing truck until it was too late. It was the last street in the city he would have expected to come across a monster truck like that. The driver lived there. He drove it home at night so he could be out before dawn to pick up a load. Now it was turning onto Sixtieth Street, blocking the entire road. Prochak slammed his foot on the brake and the wheels locked. Gray streaks of burning rubber streamed behind him like the vapor trails of a squadron of planes. He swung hard to the right, between two slender trees and a parked car. Trash cans piled on the sidewalk hurtled into the street like mortar shells. The impact tore the wheel from Prochak's hands. He fought for control again, grabbing the spinning wheel and throwing his weight to the left. The careening truck sideswiped a parked car, snapped a tree off at the roots, and then was back on the street, skidding past the tail end of the huge concrete trailer. But Prochak could feel the truck tilting dangerously, the right wheels off the ground, spinning air. He ducked toward the floorboards as the truck went over, hanging for a second before crashing down and going into a long, metal-shriek-ing slide.

Dempsey swerved to avoid a trash can rolling down the center of the street and pulled up in front of the cement truck. The driver, white-faced and shaking, stood on the running board of his cab, staring over the top of it to the overturned wreck.

"Burning!" the man yelled. "Jesus Christ!" He ducked back into his cab for a fire extinguisher.

Gorman was out of the truck before Dempsey came to a complete stop. He scrambled under the cement truck on hands and knees and ran down the street to where the wreck lay on its side, wheels turning lazily and a thin river of fire snaking out from under the front end. There was a raw stench of gasoline and he could see the dark red fluid bubbling out from the gas tank and flowing in an ever-widening pool toward the flames. The sight stopped him. In a matter of seconds the fumes would reach the fire and the truck would go up like a goddamn bomb. There was a man in that cab.

Harry Prochak clawed his way up with the big .45 in his hand. He used the gun to smash out the glass on the passenger side window and then he pulled himself half-way through the opening. Flames were eating into the cab from the burning engine and thick, black smoke billowed up around him.

"Throw the gun down!" Gorman yelled.

Harry Prochak shook his head groggily and made a motion with his gun hand, the automatic swinging toward Gorman's head.

Dempsey came out from under the tanker firing. The slugs ripped the life out of Harry Prochak just as the flames erupted beneath him and he dropped from sight.

Dempsey reeled back from the flames and found refuge from the searing heat behind the cement truck. Gorman stood with him in silence, watching the truck burn, sparks whipping toward the sky. They could hear the scream of sirens coming down Storer Avenue. Gorman closed his eyes. He thought of the man in the truck — burning. He wondered if they could have got him out.

Gorman couldn't believe it was only ten o'clock. It seemed like years . . .

"Don't move your head," the young intern said firmly.

"Sorry," Gorman mumbled.

"Glass . . . is . . . hard . . ."

Gorman gritted his teeth as the intern picked at his face with a pair of needlenosed tweezers. The intern whistled softly to himself as he worked. After ten months at Charity Hospital he had seen just about everything that could happen to the human body. This was nothing.

"You're lucky. You know that, Inspector? Real lucky."

He stopped whistling and began to hum as he picked away.

Dempsey strolled down the corridor smoking a cigarette. There were No Smoking signs painted on the dingy green walls and a hatchet-faced nurse gave him a hard stare as he walked past the desk and into the emergency wing, but he stared right back at her, the cigarette dangling from his lips.

"Where's Inspector Gorman?"

"B dispensary — please put out that cigarette. This is a no smoking area."

Dempsey blew smoke through his nose and kept on walking.

The intern was painting the side of Gorman's face with Merthiolate when Dempsey stepped into the room. The cut above the eye had been stitched and taped.

"You look like the loser in a saloon brawl," he said.

"Yeah . . . maybe I can catch Annie before she faints." He pressed the edges of the tape with a fingertip. "How's Winshaw?"

"He'll live. Fracture of the collarbone and a hole in his shoulder blade. In and out as neat as a drill."

Gorman let out a sigh that came from his ankles. "Abolofo, Jim. He . . . was behind the wheel when you got in, wasn't he?"

"Yeah . . . he was there. He never knew what hit him — if that's any comfort to his family."

Somebody cried out in agony and an orderly ran down the hall. The intern stepped away from Gorman.

"Have you had a tetanus booster?" Gorman nodded. "Okay, you can go."

The intern ambled out, following the trail of the scream. It came again, filled with horror and fear.

"Let's get the hell out of here," Dempsey said.

It had stopped raining. A few stars could be seen through torn patches of dirty gray cloud. Dempsey took a deep breath of the rain-washed air.

"Life is sweet."

Gorman said nothing. There were a couple of police cars parked in front of the hospital, but he made no move to walk to one. The thought of going back to the office, of starting on the reports, was unbearable. But it had to be done. Men had died tonight, one of them a policeman. There would be questions that needed answers. He stood on the wet sidewalk in an agony of indecision. All that he really wanted to do at that moment was to walk off into the night. Walk and walk and walk until there was nothing above his head but blue skies, nothing around him but sun-drenched fields.

"You know where we are, don't you?" Dempsey said.

Gorman stared at him as though from a great distance. "What did you say?"

"I said, do you know where we are?"

"Charity Hospital."

"No. We are exactly two short blocks from O'Neal's emporium of forgetfulness, eighty-six-proof lotus land. How about a drink, Mike?"

The police cars were waiting. They would always be waiting. Gorman turned his back on them and started walking, Dempsey keeping silent pace beside him, along Scovill Avenue to Thirty-third Street and the smoky interior of Danny O'Neal's.

"I don't believe it," O'Neal said. He ducked out from behind the bar and met them halfway across the room, a towering wreck of a man, ruined by his own product. Photographs lined the cheaply paneled walls, fading 8 x 10 glossies of Danny O'Neal, the Cleveland Flash, the most promising heavyweight of 1938. The flash had faded by 1941, reduced to punching bag status for better, younger fighters. A smart wife and a little capital had put him in business. He had done just fine over the years and his girth showed it. He raised bearlike arms in welcome.

"The old James I see, but you, Mike. God bless my eyes. Where have you been keepin' yourself?"

"He drinks in better places," Dempsey said. "You know how it is, Danny. When a man wears the braid he starts drinking martinis, and Scotch whiskey."

"God forbid," O'Neal roared, then clasped Gorman around the shoulders. "Still . . . you're forgiven. What the hell, it's a free country. Come on, belly up. First round on the house, and you buy a second or I'll set the dog on ya."

There had always been a dog at the end of the bar, in defiance of all known health laws, a fat, wheezy pug lying on a scrap of carpet.

"Is that . . ." Gorman searched his memory. "Jip?"

O'Neal scratched his head, scowling. "Well . . . it's *a* Jip. You know, Mike, I call 'em by the same name, but I don't think it's the Jip you knew. No . . . this is maybe the *third* Jip since those days. Bit ya, if memory serves."

Gorman scowled at the day.

"I never did blame Jip," O'Neal said. "That dog showed good taste."

Gorman rested his elbows on the varnished bar. The room was full of memories. He could almost hear scraps of long-forgotten conversations and the bright laughter of girls. It had been the best joint in the city. He looked around. The place hadn't changed at all, but the girls were no longer there — just a few elderly men sipping beers and watching the color TV. There had been no TV in the old days, no jukebox either, just young people — Catholic men and Catholic girls, predominantly Irish, the men starting in their careers and the girls, a year of two out of school, working as secretaries or salesgirls or nurses, earning money, learning about life, doing their best to forget the harsh moral codes the nuns had taught them. Ahhh, how great those girls had been. He wondered what had happened to them all. Married, he supposed, like Annie — grown a little thick around the waist, rearing sons and daughters, worrying about their husbands. Getting old.

"Not the same crowd," he said, almost to himself.

O'Neal grunted as he ducked under the bar. "Nothin' stays the same, Mike — 'cept you and Jimmy there. You lads still a team?"

"No," Gorman said, a little too quickly. Dempsey caught the overtone and covered it with a false cheerfulness.

"Pour the drinks, man. We've got the rain in our bones. What the hell kind of *English* pub is this?"

"I'll give you English," O'Neal said, playing the Irishman. He placed a bottle of Bushmills on the bar and reached for two thick shot glasses, then paused, laughing. "Tell you the truth . . . this place is old Warsaw, an' that's a fact. Warsaw and Tel Aviv. Nothin' but Poles and Jews. You know, nice old gaffers . . . very polite drinkers. Got sons and daughters livin' out in Shaker Heights and Lyndhurst. They all got a bit of money from the Social Security and from their kids . . . spend their days in here playin' clabber and talkin' a blue streak." He opened two bottles of Carling's and set them on the bar beside the bottle of whiskey and the shot glasses. "Like a senior citizens' home — not like the old days an' that's for sure."

"Where have all the flowers gone?" Dempsey said wryly. He scooped up bottles and glasses. "Let's get a table, Mike."

They sat in the front, facing a dusty window streaked with rain.

"Here's mud in your eye," Dempsey said, pouring the whiskey.

Gorman looked at the pale amber fluid and turned the glass slowly between thumb and forefinger. "You didn't have to shoot the driver, Jim."

"No," Dempsey said wearily. "I could have let him finish the job on you and there'd be one less pain in the ass on this job."

"He was going to throw down that gun. I could see it in his eyes."

Dempsey downed his drink and poured another. "So you're a mind reader now. So what? I read it different. I saw a punk with a .45 in his hand — and nothing to lose." He drummed the side of the glass with his finger. "What the hell's eating you? That little chip of glass get to your brain?"

231

Gorman took a sip of his drink, then placed the glass on the table and looked Dempsey square in the eye.

"A lot of things are eating at me, Jim — reports that don't add up . . . a worn-out cop whose statement just parrots your own . . . a killing tonight that might have been avoided."

Dempsey's lips twisted like a crooked pin. "Christ, you sound like a nervous rookie with his first purse snatching."

"No, Jim, I'm an old cop and all my instincts are jumping like the needle on a lie detector — and every time it jumps, it points to you."

Dempsey took a drink of whiskey and washed it down with a beer. "To hell with your *instincts*. You're dropping little green turds, and for what? Because I wiped out a two-bit hood who drew on me? For trying to protect a tired old man until he can get his pension? Or for saving your ass? Tell me, *Inspector*. Let's cut through all the bullshit. I don't expect you to pin any medals on me, but you're not going to pin anything else, either."

Gorman pushed away from the table and got to his feet. "You're going to bury yourself with your mouth one day. Just dig a hole and disappear."

"I can't wait — it'd get me away from all this fucking static."

The inspector's face set like a concrete mask.

"You're getting damn close to being suspended for insubordination, Dempsey."

Dempsey tilted back in his chair and pulled the leather flap that enclosed his badge from his shirt pocket. He tossed it on the table with contempt.

"You want it, buddy? Take it and stick it."

"I'll let you know when I want it," Gorman said coldly. "Put it back in your pocket. You're on tomorrow's duty roster." He walked toward the door.

"Mike — " Dempsey said.

Gorman paused in the doorway and looked back. "What?"

"You turned out to be a real bastard."

"Yes — and don't you ever forget it."

And then he was gone. Dempsey watched his shadow pass the window.

"Where's your buddy goin'?" O'Neal called out.

Dempsey reached for the bottle. "Lookin' for a hole. He wants to bury a guy."

Inspector Gruebner jumped up from his desk as Gorman came into the office.

"Jesus! Why aren't you in the hospital?"

"They kicked me out. I'm walking wounded." He sat down at his own desk and stared numbly at the papers piled in the basket. Gruebner walked over to him, his face grave.

"Can I get you anything, Mike?"

Gorman touched the side of his face and smiled ruefully.

"Yes — ten inches of new skin . . . and a cup of coffee."

"Sure, Mike . . . sure." Gruebner bustled out of the office like a Dutch bride. When he was gone, Gorman slumped forward against the desk and buried his face in his hands. An almost crippling depression overwhelmed him. His mind was blank. There was so much to be done and he didn't know where to start. The men were drifting back from the patrol; he could hear loud voices and bursts of laughter in the hall. There was the clatter of shotguns being turned back into the armory and the backfiring of trucks in the street outside his window. Each team had to make a report, each report had to be read and initialed. Shooting reports had to be filed with the DA's men. Christ . . . where did he start?

233

"Come on, drink this — hot and black."

He looked up into Gruebner's concerned face. "I'm so goddamn tired, Dutch."

"Get the hell out. Come back tomorrow. The world won't end."

Gorman took the plastic cup of coffee and sipped at it. It was strong and good. He felt a warmth coming back, creeping down his spine.

"I'll be okay. Fill me in."

Gruebner stepped over to his desk and picked up a notebook. "Let's see . . . fire department pulled the corpse out of that truck — burned beyond recognition. The coroner's making some dental casts. There were three DOAs at the scene . . . Patrolman Abolofo . . ."

"Has his family been notified yet?"

"Yes. Dave went over to St. Alexis Hospital. The priest called the family in."

Gorman felt grateful that Blackman had handled that bitter task. "Who was the other man?"

"A guy by the name of Fred Bolen . . . freight handler for Dondero. He had a record. Served time for robbery a few years back. No ID on the other one yet." He flipped a page. "Now then . . . what else . . . the driver of the quote hijacked truck unquote is named Charlie Greene. He's in Charity with a crushed foot. The man with him also works for Dondero, John Davis. He's at Charity having his scalp sewn up."

"You get statements from them yet?"

"Welch is over there now. It should be interesting — if you like to read fairy tales."

Gorman took another sip of coffee. "You think they set themselves up for a knockover?"

"What do you think?"

"It'll be tough to prove."

Gruebner made a fist. "Ten minutes in a locked room. That's all, ten minutes." He turned another page. "Dave sent Rich home . . . put him on the sick list. He said he'd tell you why tomorrow. And Otto has something important to show you, but he wouldn't tell me what it was." He tossed the notebook down on the desk in exasperation. "Goddamnit, Mike. What the hell's going on around here? Everybody's whispering behind my back — you and Dave . . . and Otto. I'm getting the feeling that no one trusts me."

"You want the straight dope?"

"Damn right I do!"

"I think Dempsey lied about Max Godansky. No, let me take that back. I *know* he lied. It's become a question of *why*."

"Well, I'll be goddamned." He placed both hands on the desk, bracing himself. "I can't believe it. Dempsey?"

Gorman kept his eyes on the coffee in his hand. Gruebner had always been fond of Dempsey. One tough cop's respect for another.

"Godansky's mother claims that Dempsey came out to her house a couple of times to talk to Max — a month before the shooting. Jimmy says he never saw Max before in his life until the other night. Somebody's a liar, Dutch."

The big inspector straightened up, sucking in his gut. He looked enormous in the small room.

"Jesus . . . some old lady . . ."

"No, Dutch, not *some old lady*. If she'd wanted to put the finger on a cop just for the hell of it, I gave her plenty to choose from. She saw forty, fifty men walk out of this building tonight. She only pointed at one."

Gruebner turned away and squinted up at the light bulbs. "What are you doing about it?"

"What would you do about it?" He finished his coffee

and wadded the cup in his hand. "You don't have to answer, Dutch. You'd do what I'm doing — investigate. Welch will get a statement from Mrs. Godansky tomorrow morning. I'll have some data from Otto and then I'll go to the Chief. He can take it from there."

"I hope . . ." He stopped, choking the words back.

"I know," Gorman said, standing up. "We all feel the same way."

Dempsey walked home — four miles — the bottle of Bushmills in a paper sack. He stopped every few blocks and took a pull. A few people looked at him with pity, others with disdain — just another rummy. The streets were full of them. But Dempsey wasn't drunk. He could have been drinking water for all the effect it had on him. When he reached his apartment house he tossed the bottle in the gutter and heard it smash. He thought of the windshield smashing down on the dashboard. He thought of Patrolman Abolofo's smashed head. That was life — one damn thing after another falling apart.

She was waiting for him, seated in a chair by the window. She stood up when he walked in, her robed body silhouetted against the light from the street.

"I paid the electric bill," he said. "You don't have to sit in the dark."

"I like the dark," Nikki said. "It hides all the crap."

"A philosopher. That's what I need tonight — a fucking philosopher."

He walked into the kitchen without turning on the light. A bottle of bourbon was on the sideboard and he poured three fingers into a water glass. He would feel this drink — here — in the quiet of his own place.

"You had a bad night, didn't you?" She had followed him into the kitchen, her bare feet making no sound.

"Just routine."

He drank slowly, savoring the harshness. The Irish had been too smooth — too refined.

"I killed a couple of guys, Nikki." He chuckled softly. "Isn't that a bitch?"

She drew in her breath sharply and rested her head against his back, her hands drifting silkily around his waist, under his coat.

"Want to talk about it?"

"Sure. Why not? I was doing a job for the city. You're a citizen. You have a right to know where your taxes go. I blew a buck and a half on bullets. Write a letter to your councilman."

"Oh, Jim . . . Jim . . ."

He set the glass down on the sideboard and turned to face her, pressing her body tightly against him. Her hands were at his waist, tugging expertly at his belt.

"Let's go to bed, Jim . . . let's go to bed."

He moved with her into the other room, sat on the bed, and let her undress him.

"It's the easiest thing in the world, Nikki. One little squeeze of the finger and a man dies. A kid could do it. Some do."

"Quiet," she murmured, kneeling before him, brushing her lips against his thigh. "Don't talk."

He reached out to touch her hair. He leaned back on his elbows, stared up at the chain of Paradise Islands mottled against the ceiling, and felt the warmth envelop his body.

Gorman knew that Otto Mengus was in the lab because he could smell his tobacco halfway down the hall. He pushed open the door to find him bent over a spectroscope, pipe in mouth, the room a blue haze of burley.

"What have you got for me, Otto?"

Mengus stepped away from the instrument. When he

saw Gorman's face he plucked the pipe from his mouth and took a step backward.

"What the hell happened to you? Fighting a wildcat?"

"Something like that. Did the computer man come through?"

"On three of the shootings. We'll get the balance first thing tomorrow morning."

They looked at one another, neither man making a move.

"Well?" Gorman finally asked.

"It looks bad — for Jimmy."

"How bad?" Gorman's tone was hollow.

"There are eighteen discrepancies in those three shootings alone." He gestured with his pipe toward his desk. "The cards and printouts are there, Mike. The Joey Crespi, Adolph Myers and Carlo Tedeschi deaths."

Gorman walked over to the desk and looked down at neat stacks of computer cards and wide rolls of paper that had been spewed out of a high-speed printer. The single-spaced lines were a blur of letters.

"George's cousin gave us a couple thousand dollars' worth of free computer time," Mengus said. "He thinks he'll get a free ride on his parking tickets."

"What made him think that?"

The technician shrugged. "I guess I made a promise. He kept telling me how much it cost to run those machines. I got the feeling he would have been happy if I took out my checkbook. I did the next best thing. Everybody wants something, Mike."

"Sure." He picked up one of the read-out sheets and stared at it uncomprehendingly. It could have been written in Greek.

"They're difficult to read." Mengus said. "It's a new language — computerese. I'll be happy to translate."

"Please."

"It's pretty late. Do you want to go over this in the morning? Mike, you look like a man who could use eleven hours' sleep."

"I'll settle for two." He looked at the wall clock. 12:30. "What shift are you on, Otto?"

"Who knows? I've been sleeping like a cat lately. I just curl up in any convenient chair. I'll be here 'til George comes in at eight."

"Okay. I'm going up to the Chief's office and stretch out on the couch. Wake me in two hours."

"Will do." Mengus had already decided to wake him in four.

Gorman sat on the couch in the chief's outer office and took off his shoes. Before lying down he picked up the phone on Sergeant Boyle's desk and called Gruebner.

"Dutch, do me a favor. See if you can find Claire Dempsey's address. I think she lives out in Shaker Heights . . . or maybe Warrensville. I'm taking ten up in the Chief's office. If Dave calls in tell him I'd like to have a meeting around seven."

"I take it I'm invited?"

"Sure, Dutch, sure." He hung up and then stepped over to the couch and flopped down on it. The leather felt cool against his raw face. He fell asleep instantly, but was plagued by dreams. He kept seeing Dempsey sinking in a black pit. He tried to save him by holding out a stick, but the stick kept dissolving into reams of paper and stacks of cards. It fell away in Dempsey's outstretched hands and he sank deeper and deeper — and then he was gone.

Dempsey waited for the dawn. If whiskey and women didn't throw the switch and close you down, then you waited. Nikki was warm against his back. He listened to the

239

slow rhythm of her breath and the gentle swish of an occasional car passing along the wet street. The small Westclox on the table by the bed hummed and whirred. He could measure time's passing by the thud of his pulse while the world turned slowly, heartbeat by heartbeat, bringing the day closer.

He stirred and flicked ash on the carpet. There was nothing he could do except wait, and think.

What was Gorman onto?

"Nothing," he whispered. There was nothing Gorman could know — for certain. There had been no witnesses. Just Max Godansky. Something about the shooting hit Gorman the wrong way — a little flack from Daley and Winshaw, probably, griping at having their prize pigeon shot on the wing. They would dig into the shooting a little deeper just to satisfy the boys from robbery. To hell with them. He would come up clean. Maybe they would slap his knuckles for carrying Carl, but so what? No one would blame him for that. They might transfer Carl to a desk job and give him a new partner, a young hotshot out to make a name for himself, some clown who would arrest his own grandmother for a good rap record. But there was the cop's intuition. Gorman had it. That was more of a threat than any fact or small discrepancy.

"Fuck it."

It was getting time to move. He eased out of bed, inching away from Nikki carefully, and walked over to the window. The sky was a pale mauve and the edges of the dark clouds were tinged with gold. It was going to be a nice day.

He shaved and dressed, fixed a cup of coffee, and stood at the stove to drink it. Money. It all came down to that. Any way he cut it, there would not be as much as he had hoped. John W. Martin would have to tighten his belt a little, but there would be enough to get started. Cities like Rio . . . São Paulo . . . Buenos Aires . . . Caracas . . . Mexico City were full of opportunity. He had skills that found a steady market anywhere, in any language.

He sipped his coffee slowly and watched an ant wander haphazardly across the top of the stove, searching for grains of sugar or spots of grease. Dempsey reached out with his free hand and crushed it with a finger.

Ten thousand dollars in an envelope under his shirts.

Thirty-five thousand dollars in the bank under the name of John W. Martin.

He had just given Claire five. Another five would do her until he could send more from South America.

That wouldn't leave him with much. What he needed right now were two or three more jobs.

. . . *my instincts are jumping like the needle on a lie detector* . . .

What the hell did he mean by that? Gorman was a smart cop.

"Sore," he said quietly. "Getting the needle." Daley and Winshaw, screaming to the Chief about all the time they put in setting Max up as a stoolie. Then the Chief jumping Gorman's ass . . .

"*If Dempsey had a lead on the Higbee thefts he should have checked with Daley before moving in. Jesus, Mike, let's get things organized and integrated around here.*"

Dempsey smiled at the thought. He could almost hear Keeley saying it, laying the stress on his favorite words, *organize* and *integrate*. That's why Gorman's nose was out of joint.

He walked into the other room. Nikki was still asleep, curled into a soft ball under the blanket. He had the feeling that she was moving in. The thought bothered him. What the hell would she do all day? Wash the floor? Look

241

through his drawers for dirty shirts? He stepped over to the bureau and pulled out the top drawer, carefully, so that it didn't squeak. Two envelopes were taped to the bottom of the drawer. He peeled them loose and stuck them in the inside pocket of his suit jacket. One envelope held ten thousand dollars in hundred-dollar bills, the other, John W. Martin's passport. The papers to get that passport had cost him one thousand dollars, but they had been worth every cent.

"Jim?" She peeked at him from under the blanket, squinting against the first rays of the sun. "So soon?"

He nodded. "I have an early shift."

"What time will you be back?"

"Four . . . maybe later. I'll give you a ring."

She turned on her back and stretched one long, naked leg out of the covers. Her skin was a golden rose in the morning light.

"Do you have to rush, baby?"

He sat on the edge of the bed and ran a hand under the blanket. Her flesh was warm. She took hold of his hand and moved it down across her body.

"I'm going to stay here till you get back," she said.

"There's better places."

"I like it here."

He nodded, stood up, and walked to the door. She was moving in on him.

"So long," he said.

Sergeant Earl Welch went to 957½ Bridge Street at five A.M. A crazy hour, but that was when Lewandowski had asked him to be there. He got out of the car with his portable typewriter and walked toward the front door, thinking that it was a shabby neighborhood of small frame houses, paint-peeled and listing. Patches of blistered green that had once been gardens struggled for life amid concrete and soot. It had probably been a pleasant place between the two world wars, a place where immigrant Poles had proudly built their homes, raised kids and chickens. Only the old were left, clinging to the houses and their God while the factories crept in on them. The factories would win.

Lewandowski opened the front door before Welch had a chance to ring the bell.

"Sergeant Welch?"

"Yeah," Welch grunted. "The old broad got insomnia, or something?"

"Mrs. Godansky wouldn't make a statement unless her priest was here." He stole a quick glance at his watch. "Father Brosta has mass at six, so you'd better hurry."

"I'm hurrying," the sergeant growled as he took a slow step inside.

The house bothered Welch. It was like stepping into a shrine. The small, dark room smelled of furniture polish and burnt tallow. Faded oleographs of St. Stanislas and the Virgin Mary hung from the walls and black crepe paper festooned a small framed portrait of a child set in the center of the mantelpiece. Max Godansky, he assumed, aged five, a fat kid with a balloon head and demented eyes.

"This is Mrs. Godansky," Lewandowski said, "and Father Brosta."

Welch looked at the other occupants of the room for the first time. Mrs. Godansky stood by the fireplace next to the picture of her dead son. Her face was sallow and her eyes were filled with suspicion and distaste. Welch wondered why she was staring at him and then it dawned on him that he was probably the first black man to ever set foot in her house. The priest stood beside her, a very old man with eyeglasses as thick as the bottoms of Coke bottles. His hands were fulded in front of him, the fingers waxy and limp, like entwined candles.

The priest peered myopically at Welch for a second and then spoke softly in Polish. Patrolman Lewandowski cleared his throat and looked at the floor.

"What did he say?" Welch asked.

Lewandowski coughed discreetly. "He . . . wants to know if you're . . . Polish, too, and understand."

Welch suppressed a laugh. He had been feeling uncomfortable, now he felt loose.

"Tell him I'm Irish — a black Irishman." He moved farther into the room, looking for a table to set his typewriter on. "Let's get on with this, man. Whatever she has to say, tell her to start talking."

Welch placed the machine on a small dining table covered with oilcloth and opened the case. A single sheet of paper was already wound through the roller. It was a printed form headed Crime Report — Statement of Witness. Welch centered the page before pulling up a chair and seating himself. Mrs. Godansky and the priest watched in silence.

"Okay," Welch said. "How do we handle this, Lewandowski?"

"She's going to make a statement and I'll translate. You write it down as I give it to you and Father Brosta will witness it."

"Does he speak and read English?"

"Sure — when he wants to."

Welch sighed and typed in the date with two fingers. "Okay — let's have it."

Lewandowski said a few words in Polish and then Mrs. Godansky began to speak, her voice rising in passion. At one point in her tirade she began to beat her breast with gnarled hands and Father Brosta placed an arm about her shoulder until she calmed down. Her torrent of words ended in dry, gasping sobs.

Welch took out a stick of gum and chewed on it methodically.

"Is that it?"

"Yes," Lewandowski said.

Welch frowned at the typewriter. "I hope I have enough space."

"A lot of what she said is irrelevant. I'll just give you what's important. Ready?"

"Yeah — ready . . . but take it slow . . . one word at a time."

"Okay. First, the name of the witness is Mrs. Valerie Godansky . . ."

"*My name* is Mrs. Valerie Godansky . . ." Welch emphasized as he began typing. "Keep it in the first person."

"Sorry . . . My name is Mrs. Valerie Godansky and I live at number 957½ Bridge Street, Cleveland, Ohio. I am the mother of Max Godansky who was shot and killed by a Cleveland police officer by the name of James Dempsey. On or about the third day of March of this year, one month before my son was killed, Officer James Dempsey came to this house to visit my son who was ill at the time . . ." Lewandowski hesitated. "You aren't typing."

"No," Welch said thickly. "Is this shit on the level?"

"Yes," the patrolman said. "I'm afraid it is."

"Well . . . I'll be a sonofabitch." He resumed typing, fingers stabbing angrily at the keys. ". . . Officer James Dempsey came to this house . . ."

Sergeant Lester Cole was at the desk. He was on the midnight-to-eight shift and nothing much had happened since four A.M. when Officers Lucas and Grodin had brought in a would-be rapist, bloodied and bowed, his intended victim, a statuesque blond who worked in a Chester Avenue Go-Go bar, trailing him down the hall, still screaming and still swinging a leather, brassbound purse that weighed ten pounds if it weighed an ounce. He had spent the past two hours doodling on a pad and day-dreaming about the blond. Sergeant Cole was not married and he had not only calmed the blond down and brought her a cup of coffee, he had gotten her telephone number as well. It might just come to something, he was thinking. He hoped so. The blond had a pair of knockers that were —

"Morning, Les . . . how's it going?"

Sergeant Cole snapped out of his reverie in time to see Dempsey going down the hall. He leaned out over the desk.

"Hey . . ."

Dempsey ambled back.

"What are you doing in so early? I hear the shootout was a bitch."

"It was," Dempsey said.

Cole rested his elbows on the desk and settled in for some shoptalk.

"That Abolofo kid. Nineteenth District, I understand."

"I wouldn't know."

"Yeah . . . Nineteenth District. How's Winshaw doing?"

Dempsey shrugged. "Okay — I think."

The sergeant leaned forward conspiratorily. "What happened to Carl?"

Dempsey looked blank. "Rich?"

"Yeah . . . I notice he's on the sick roster. Dernburgh told me he saw Carl walk out of here last night . . . about seven, seven-thirty. He sick or something?"

"Yes," Dempsey said, walking away. "Sick and tired of all the bullshit around here."

. . . a worn-out cop whose statement just parrots your own . . .

So they got to Carl, Dempsey thought as he went up the stairs. They leaned and Carl snapped like a plastic spoon. It was to be expected. Dempsey paused before stepping into the second-floor hallway, hearing the voices of Blackman and Gruebner.

"It's a quarter to seven now," Gruebner said.

"Fine . . . let's get started. Where's Otto?"

Dempsey could not hear Gruebner's reply. There was the sound of footsteps going off down the hall and then the closing of a door.

Dempsey waited for a moment and then entered the hall and walked quickly to the records section. Officer Schlom was dozing in his little cubbyhole. Dempsey slapped the desk with his palm and Schlom woke up with a start.

Dempsey smiled thinly. "That's a good way to get a job walking up and down Scovill Avenue in the snow."

"Just closed my eyes for a second."

He held his hand out. "I need the key to the hijacking files."

Schlom, still blinking sleep out of his eyes, fumbled in the top drawer of his desk, took out a ring of keys, and began to sort through them.

"I know the one," Dempsey snapped. "I'm in a rush."

Schlom tossed the keys. "Do you need any help?"

"No . . ."

Dempsey walked past the desk and into the file room, down a narrow passageway between tall cabinets. The hijacking files were near the front, as were all the current crime files. He unlocked the case and began to sort through the cards. Schlom was watching him and

Dempsey took his time, reading each card from top to bottom.

"Hey, Schlom . . . how about a cup of coffee?"

"Okay," Schlom said, getting out of his chair. "What do you take?"

"Black."

When the man was gone, Dempsey hurried to the far end of the room where the active personnel files filled a corner. He pulled out the drawer labeled DEMP THRU DENA and he knew what he was going to find even before his fingers located the manila folder marked DEMPSEY, JAMES. The folder was empty, a penciled note attached to it with a paper clip: *See Insp. M. Gorman re contents file.*

"The sonofabitch," Dempsey murmured, almost in admiration. But he felt the fear working, too. Gorman knew.

Dave Blackman gazed at the computer cards and read-out sheets that Otto Mengus had placed neatly on the conference room table.

"Very impressive," he said softly, then slapped his hand down on the edge of the table. "Damn it, how could that many discrepancies be overlooked? How the hell is it possible?"

Otto Mengus turned his back on the three inspectors and stared out the window, puffing gently on his pipe. He had presented the facts to them. That was the extent of his job, and his involvement in the problem. He felt rotten enough about Dempsey. He didn't want to add his voice to the discussion of Dempsey's fate. He was a laboratory technician, a forensic scientist, not a judge, a jury, or a cop.

Gorman pushed back his chair and began to pace

slowly up and down the room, past the furious Blackman and the silently brooding Gruebner.

"It happened, Dave, because we're human beings, not machines."

"I know that," Blackman sputtered, "but goddamn it to hell, Mike . . . how many errors were there . . . eighteen? Twenty?"

"Eighteen — in the first three shootings," Gruebner said, eyes fixed on a notebook in front of him. "Crespi, Myers, and Carlo Tedeschi. The Jacoby shooting came through clean — is that right, Otto?"

"Yes," Mengus said, not turning around.

"And Karl Neale and Godansky?"

An attractive girl with bright red hair was waiting at the bus stop across the street. Mengus kept his eyes on her. He wished he was down there. "I'm sorry, Dutch . . . I didn't hear the question."

"Neale and Godansky — how many?"

"I just got those reports in a half-hour ago, with Jacoby's. Jacoby was clean. There seemed to be a couple of minor, perhaps *debatable*, errors in the Neale shooting and, of course, a whole flock in Godansky's."

"Nothing *debatable* about Max Godansky's, is there?" Blackman asked acidly.

"No, very cut and dried." A bus pulled to a stop, blocking the redhead from view. When the bus pulled out, the girl was gone. Mengus sighed and walked back to the table. "If you care to wait for half an hour I'll cross-check the Godansky read-outs with Dempsey and Rich's statements. Offhand, I would say that there are six or seven discrepancies."

"Never mind," Gruebner said. "I think we all get the message."

"No!" Blackman said. His voice was loud. It was almost

touched with hysteria. "I'm damned if I do. We have one of the best police departments in the country and yet we let something like this slip right on by us — eighteen, maybe twenty-five glaring faults and we didn't catch one of them, not *one*!"

Gruebner made a low sound in his throat, like a bear growling. "That isn't what I meant. Sure, there were errors, and I think we all know how we overlooked them." He tapped the table for emphasis with the point of one thick finger. "We weren't looking for anything, Dave. It's as simple as that — we-weren't-looking-for-anything-wrong. Goddamn, we are talking about Dempsey, one of the best detectives on this force. *James Dempsey*, not John Dillinger. There was no reason to be suspicious. Look at those names . . . Joey Crespi — Mafia hatchetman, some-times armed, always dangerous. Adolph Myers — an enforcer, worked for the Cohen mob in Miami. Carlo Tedeschi — well, I remember *that* shooting. I was on duty that night. Dempsey typed up his report in my office. Carlo Tedeschi, a *capo* from Toledo . . . biggest dope dealer in Ohio . . . hooked on his own product, a morphine addict, tried to shoot Dempsey."

"Only he didn't," Blackman cut in. "The computer tells a different story."

Gruebner turned livid. "I know what the goddamn computer said! We talk about the machine like it was human. Well, it isn't! But *we* are, and a man we know . . . a man we've worked with for a long, long time was involved in those killings during the regular performance of his duty. I happen to be very happy that those three bastards are dead — and so are you. There was never any reason to doubt the word of . . . of . . ."

"One of our own?" Gorman asked quietly.

Gruebner nodded, his face purple. "Yes . . . one of our

own. Okay, I admit it . . . we *all* admit it. If anyone but a police officer of Dempsey's caliber had been involved we would have gone over the scene with a fine-tooth comb and we'd have come up with exactly the same discrepancies — angle of shots, position of spent shells, the whole miserable ball of wax." He got a bent cigar from his pocket, tore it in two and jammed the longer section into his mouth.

Gorman continued his slow pacing. "All right. Let's stop beating our backs with thorns. Dempsey came up against some rotten characters and killed them under *questionable* circumstances. They were killers. Dempsey says they tried to kill him. We have no proof that they were shot down without cause — none whatsoever. But *supposing* they were. That poses one hell of a question. Why? Why in God's name would Dempsey burn those men? For kicks? Some warped sense of dealing out justice to men who have laughed at the law for years? We don't have an answer. It's something the computer doesn't know, but we have to find out."

"How?" Blackman asked.

Gorman paused in his pacing at the end of the table and riffled through a stack of cards. "The way we find out everything in this business — we dig for it. These cards represent six men. What did they have in common, I wonder? Godansky, Jacoby, Neale — smalltime punks — but Crespi, Tedeschi, Myers — they were big shots. The Mob, Mafia, the Organization. They weren't in Cleveland to see the view. They were here to do business — or to rip off somebody else's business. Any particular name come to mind who might have had an interest in what those men were up to?"

"Guido," Blackman said. "Guido Franchini."

Gorman nodded. "Papa Guido. Let's dig out the intelligence files, make a list of every man ever suspected of playing footsie with that bastard. Let's see if anything clicks." He started for the door.

"Where are we going?" Gruebner asked.

"Legwork, Dutch . . . legwork."

Gruebner listened to the hard clicking of Gorman's heels going off down the hall, then he stood up with a sigh of great weariness.

"Okay . . . let's get started. Something tells me we're taking a wild shot at the moon. How many people do you figure Guido has toyed around with over the years — in one way or another?"

Blackman's smile was bitter. "How big is the phone book?"

Gorman needed a shave, but a razor wouldn't have done much for his appearance. The Merthiolate was a rosy splash across one side of his face, and the cut eyebrow was puffy and tinged with blue. There wasn't anything he could do about it, but when he had changed back into his uniform he at least looked like an inspector of police — from the neck down. He was adjusting his tie when Sergeant Welch came into the office after a perfunctory knock on the door. He grunted a good-morning and placed a manila envelope on Gorman's desk.

"What's that?" Gorman asked.

"Witness report . . . Mrs. Godansky."

Gorman caught a quick glance of the sergeant's face as he turned to leave.

"What's the matter with you, Earl?"

Welch scowled. "I didn't like the duty this morning, Inspector. I don't like the sound of it."

Gorman studied his image in the narrow mirror that dangled from the door of his locker. "How did it sound to you?"

Welch stared resentfully at Gorman's back. "Like we're out for somebody's scalp. That's all. I . . . I don't like to shoot my mouth off, Inspector, but you asked me."

"Fair enough — but what's wrong?"

"You know what I mean. Jesus . . . Dempsey's a cop."

"And Max Godansky?"

The sergeant ground a fist into his palm and cracked his knuckles. "A two-bit jerk with an arrest sheet as long as my arm. Trouble."

Gorman closed the closet door. The morning sun poured through the tall windows and he walked through its rays to the desk.

"Let me tell you something about Max Godansky, Earl. He was the victim of a shooting. It's our job to find out how and why he died. And until we do, I'm on his side." He picked up the envelope and held it out for Welch to take. "So are you. That's the way the law works and you get paid to know it. Wipe that look off your face and give this to Inspector Blackman. You'll find him upstairs. Okay?"

Welch took the envelope, bitterness lurking on his face like a dark shadow.

"Yes, sir . . . but . . . damn it . . ."

"Just take it up," Gorman said sharply. "If you have any comments to make, make them on your own time."

Everybody was falling apart. Gorman watched the sergeant plunge out of the office with the envelope in his hand, holding it by the edge as though the very paper was contaminated. He thought of Blackman's stricken face — and Gruebner's smoldering rage. One of their own had crossed over the line. One of the best apples might be rotten and the barrel was in a panic. Tough. There wasn't anything he could do about that either. He couldn't shave a raw face and he couldn't put Dempsey's image back together just to please everybody. Wheels had turned.

Those wheels had turned other wheels. There was no way he could stop them. No way he could turn back the clock. He strode out of his office and down the hall to the garage.

Dempsey pulled out in an unmarked Plymouth Fury and headed west on Payne Avenue to Superior. He was on his own. No partner. MacLendon, the civilian chief of the motor pool, had made his comment.

"Talking to yourself today, Jim?"

"Yeah, Carl's got a bellyache."

He drove through the city, south on Ninth Street and then over to Woodland, bucking the morning rush hour, his hand heavy on the horn. The traffic eased as he continued along Woodland past the Kinsman Avenue junction. Shops and small office buildings gave way to a neighborhood of two-story frame houses. He turned down a side street and parked in front of one of them.

"Jim."

Carl's face was ashen and there were deep shadows under his eyes. He was wearing a ratty gray sweater and beat-up slippers. He looked two hundred and ten. The front door was only partly open, held by a stout brass chain. Dempsey gave the door a slight kick.

"Open up, this is a raid. We know you've got women in there."

Rich's smile was the smile on a corpse. "You're crazy, Jim."

"Sure . . . what the hell. Life's a circus. Now, will you please open the door and let me in? I haven't had breakfast yet and I smell . . ." He sniffed loudly. "I smell nothing. What do you eat in the morning, Carl? Cornflakes and skimmed milk?"

Rich closed the door and Dempsey could hear the chain being slipped out of the slot. Pathetic, he thought, a sad way to live. Rich was a prisoner, locked up for the night with his own fears. The door opened wide and Dempsey stepped into the gloomy living room.

"Open the curtains," Dempsey said. "Let the sun shine in."

Rich closed the door, a thin, gray ghost. "Later . . . when I bring Della in."

"How is she, Carl?"

"Oh . . . you know . . ." It was difficult to speak. Words caught in his throat and his mouth was beginning to twitch. He placed a hand against his jaw to hide the twitching from Dempsey's sight.

"I'll go back and see her — if she's awake."

"Sure, Jim . . . sure. She's up. Go ahead. I . . . I'll make some coffee."

It was a relief to see Dempsey walk off down the hall. It gave him a chance to pull himself together. He struggled to take a deep breath, squared his shoulders, and went into the kitchen. There was a bottle of Seagram's on the sideboard, next to a jar of instant coffee and the sugar bowl. He unscrewed the cap and took a quick drink from the bottle, a double-gulping swallow to calm his nerves. He made a wry face, choked the stuff down. Carl Rich's elixir at the start of a new day.

Dempsey leaned in the doorway and watched Della struggle upward, her thin hands hooked to the metal ring like the claws of a fallen bird.

"How ya doin', doll?"

She managed to squeeze a smile from the depths of her pain. "Hello, Jimmy . . . it's . . . so good to see you."

Pretty, Dempsey thought. Chestnut hair and green eyes. Silver in the hair now, and the eyes had lost their sparkle, the body its flesh, but he could still see the woman she had been.

"Carl treating you all right, sweetheart?"

"Like a queen — but I worry about him, Jim. He's so tired all the time."

"Don't worry about it. Papa fix. I . . . I've got plans for your boy. It's about time something nice happened to you people, starting right now, but I have to warn you of your constitutional rights first — I'm not only staying for breakfast, I'm going to cook it. If you don't like it, call your lawyer."

Dempsey strolled into the kitchen, startling Rich, who still had a hand on the whiskey bottle.

"Beats orange juice, eh, Carl? Come on, pour us both a belt." He opened the refrigerator and took out a carton of eggs and a pound of bacon.

Rich leaned back against the sideboard, his body rigid, a nerve twitching in his cheek. "I told them, Jimmy. I told them that my nerve was shot . . . that I stayed in the car."

Dempsey whistled softly as he searched for a frying pan. "So you told them, so what?"

"That's what you wanted to know, isn't it? You didn't come out here because you like to fry eggs."

"I came out because I like you, Carl. You and Della. Two nice people who never had one half-assed break in your lives. I don't give a shit what you told Gorman or any of those pricks downtown. Just pour the whiskey and shut up."

It was a good breakfast — eggs, lightly basted, crisp bacon, toast, jam and coffee. Rich brought Della's into her on a tray. The two men had theirs in the kitchen. Eating eggs, drinking whiskey.

"You should get Della out of this climate," Dempsey said. "Take her where she can see the sun more than five days a fucking year."

"Sure," Rich said bitterly. "How about the south of France?"

Dempsey sliced into an egg and watched it bleed yellow all over the plate. "Lots of people go to Mexico . . . place like Guadalajara. Live like a king down there on a couple of hundred a month. Rum a dollar a gallon, a maid for five bucks a week. Think about it."

Rich's laugh was like a dry cough. "Oh, sure, think about it. I think about it all the time. But how would we get there? Hitchhike? Or maybe I could sell my other two shirts and the car. A blind man with an oil well might buy that pile of crap. Ah, bullshit. Why talk about it?"

"You could take what pension you got coming, Carl . . . take it and go . . . tomorrow if you wanted to. You don't even need a passport." He pushed the plate to one side and laid the envelope in its place, the thick envelope with no writing on it.

"This will get you started."

Rich stared at it. "What's that?"

"Ten thousand," Dempsey said quietly.

Rich blinked hard, trying to focus his eyes. The whiskey was heavy on his chest.

"Ten thousand what? S and H green stamps?"

"Open it, Carl."

Rich opened it with sweaty hands, tearing off one corner, opening it just enough to see the neat pile of green inside.

"Where did you get it, Jim?" His voice was hollow. It seemed to come from the bottom of his toes.

"It's clean."

"Sure — clean." He dropped the envelope back onto the table and pushed it toward Dempsey with a stiff finger.

"Think about it, Carl. You and Della in the sunshine. You just put in your papers and screw this stinking town.

257

You don't answer any more stupid questions and you don't sign any more lousy reports. I'm giving you a break, Carl — the only one you'll ever get."

Rich got slowly to his feet, his eyes glazed, starting to fill with tears.

"Get out of my house, Jim. Go on, get out of here. It's a dump, right? A real dump, but get out of it." He shook his head like a blind dog. "You don't have ten thousand — you never had any more than me. Oh, you sonofabitch. You dirty sonofabitch. You *took*! You were taking from somebody all the time we worked together. Get out!"

He snatched up the envelope and slapped Dempsey across the face with it — once, twice — before dropping it on the floor. "You took!" he roared.

Dempsey picked up the envelope, put it back into his pocket and rose to his feet.

"So long, Carl," he said.

Rich turned away. His shoulders rose in spasmodic heaves of the dry sobs tearing at him.

"Oh, Christ!" he moaned, shuffling away.

A better neighborhood than he could afford, Gorman thought as he parked in front of Claire Dempsey's house. He made a rough appraisal as he walked to the front door. Forty-eight, fifty-eight thousand, at least. The lawn was manicured, the trees and shrubs pruned. Probably had a gardener . . . another fifty dollars or so a month. Gorman was impressed. He pushed the doorbell and heard chimes ring deep inside the house. She took a long time answering, and when she did open the door she made no move to step aside so that he could enter.

"Hello, Claire."

"Michael."

"It's been a long time."

258

"Yes." She was looking at him warily. "What do you want?"

Gorman removed his hat and took a tentative step toward the threshold, but the tall, beautifully austere woman didn't back up an inch.

"I'd like to talk to you for a few minutes, Claire. *Inside*, if you don't mind."

She did mind. He could see anger, resentment and a trace of fear in her eyes. But there was no way she could refuse his request.

"I'm in a hurry."

"Five minutes, Claire," Gorman said as he stepped inside the house.

The living room was finely furnished, but it had a cold, unlived-in quality, as though it were more for display than comfort. Beautiful, but unused — like Claire.

"What do you want to talk about, Michael?"

Gorman made an all-encompassing gesture with his right hand.

"This . . . A lovely house, Claire. I'd like to know what it costs."

She turned her back on him. "That's none of your business."

"I'm making it my business. I don't want to, but I must. You lived with a policeman for ten years, Claire — you know I'll find out whether you tell me or not."

She whirled toward him, her face contorted. "Go ahead — find out. You're all alike. Men with guns and badges, but no heart, no feelings."

"Five or six men," Gorman said stonily, "going to every house in the neighborhood . . . every store . . . every real estate office . . . asking questions. I can do that, Claire, and you know it."

"Don't you dare!" she hissed. "If you do that to me and my family I'll . . . I'll call the Chief . . . I'll get a lawyer."

"That won't help. The only one who can stop me from doing it is you. How much does all this cost, Claire?"

The telephone rang, a soft purring sound. She let it ring, her eyes searching Gorman's face. She saw no pity there. The phone rang six times and then was silent.

"The house cost fifty-nine five," she whispered.

"Do you sent the kids to parochial schools?"

"Yes."

"How much does that cost? Two, three thousand a year?"

"Yes . . . about that."

"And how does he give it to you? Cash or check?" He watched the color drain from her face. She seemed to be aging, drying up. She shook her head.

"I want to know how much money he gave you over a period of, say, two years."

"I don't know. I didn't keep track."

He was incredulous, cynical. "Didn't keep track? How could you *not* keep track?"

"He just . . . just gave me my money."

"Goddamn, Claire — cash or check?"

"Cash," she said.

Gorman could not hide the revulsion he felt. She saw it, sensed it, and met it with a hatred of her own.

"You bastard," she hissed, taking a step toward him. "Don't you understand? He *has* to pay for what he did to me. It's his duty to pay for his sins! And *you* . . . you make me sound as filthy as all those whores of his!"

He walked away from her burgeoning rage, out of the living room and down the hall toward the front door. She trailed him, screaming . . .

260

"Whores . . . dirty whores . . . *his* sin, Michael! Don't you understand? He had to pay for his sin . . . !"

The sunshine was warm and the air sweet. Gorman walked across the grass to the sidewalk, closing his ears to the woman's shrieks. He was thinking about money and six dead men.

chapter seven

GORMAN SAW THE WHITE CADILLAC as he came down Payne Avenue. It was parked in front of the building, virtually in the middle of the street. He had to admire the man's gall. Only Sam Dondero would double-park in front of a police station.

Sergeant Cole was on the phone when Gorman entered the building, but he took the receiver away from his ear and placed a hand over the mouthpiece.

"Inspector . . . Room 308. Inspector Blackman and Gruebner are waiting for you."

Gorman nodded his thanks and went up to the third-floor conference room. The place was a shambles, paper all over the table and spread out on the floor. The blackboard was crawling with names written in chalk. Gruebner, coat off and sleeves rolled up, was squeezing one more name on the board in tiny, barely legible script. Blackman sat at the long oak table, brooding over a mug of cold coffee.

"Well?" Gorman asked, closing the door behind him. "What have you come up with?"

Gruebner stepped away from the blackboard, dusting chalk from his fingers. "Plenty."

Blackman drained his coffee and made a sour face. "I think we have a pattern, Mike."

Gorman studied the board. "A lot of familiar names."

"We went through every scrap of information that Intelligence has on Guido and his activities," Gruebner said. "These names repeated consistently. A few are friends, but most seem to be enemies or business associates — unwilling associates, most of the time."

"A lot of arms out — like an octopus."

"No, Mike, a shark." Gruebner gestured at the board. "Look at some of those names . . . liquor dealers, food wholesalers, restaurant owners . . . small businessmen. Intelligence believes Guido has the bite on every one of them. Some kind of protection racket, but they can't prove it. Nobody complains. Death is so permanent."

"I see Dondero made the list."

"Yeah," Gruebner said. "So did Al Betko and Tony Arapata, but that doesn't mean too much. Maybe they pay protection to Guido to keep their trucks running, and maybe they don't. There's one name on the list that *is* interesting. Albert Jacoby."

"One of the men Dempsey wasted," Blackman said.

Gorman looked puzzled. "Jacoby? How does he fit with Franchini?"

"Explain the connection, Dutch." Blackman stood up and walked to the window, hands clasped behind his back; a rigid figure, tight-lipped and grim.

Gruebner cleared his throat. "Okay, this is how we figure it, Mike. Jacoby was a runner for Guido, oh, fifteen, twenty years ago. A bagman in the numbers — a smart, ambitious kid. He was smart enough to get away with it. No record, even minor. Jacoby works for Franchini for a couple of years and then drops out of sight for a long time. Then, lo and behold, five years ago he goes to work for Sam Dondero. Not with the trucking line. He's an accountant now. He apparently dropped out to go to school. That's new. And Dondero puts him in charge of an import company he owns. Everything goes along smoothly for a year or two and then Jacoby winds up with one of Dempsey's slugs in his head. Jimmy gets a tip that there's a burglary in progress at the import firm. He investigates . . . finds Jacoby drilling the safe. Jacoby pulls a gun and Dempsey kills him. The computer ruled it a clean shooting, but Dave and I think it stinks. A setup. The link is there, Mike. Jacoby to Guido to Dondero. We think Dondero is a big-timer in the Mob . . . maybe bigger now than Guido, who is getting old . . . and we think Dempsey's his enforcer . . . a hired gun."

The pulse in Gorman's neck began to throb. When he spoke, his voice seemed to be coming from far away.

"I just had a talk with Claire. Dempsey's given her sixty, maybe seventy thousand dollars in cash since they split."

Gruebner seemed to sag, as though someone had just punched him in the belly, but Blackman was icy calm.

"That does it, then." He turned from the window and fixed Gruebner with a hawk's stare. "We have enough for the district attorney to go before the grand jury."

Gruebner shook his head like a dying bull. "Enough for the DA? Dave, we have enough to blow this city into the goddamn lake!" He took a step toward Blackman, his heavy fists curled by his side. "Jesus Christ, don't you understand what we have here? We have a *killer cop* . . . a cash-on-the-line gunman for the Mob! Haul Dempsey before a grand jury and every cop in this town will be suspect. Kids'll write it on the walls in red paint — *pigs kill*. Goddamn it, we're hanging on with our fingernails as it is. We're a very thin blue line, Dave, and that line is getting thinner every day."

"Don't give me a speech," Blackman said angrily. "I know what our position is. I've got eyes."

"Then use them!" Gruebner bellowed. "And use your brain while you're at it."

"That's enough," Gorman snapped. "Let's talk this over reasonably or not at all. Can we *prove* Dempsey shot those men for money?"

Gruebner snorted. "He didn't find seventy thousand dollars in a box of Cracker Jacks."

"*Prove* that he didn't," Gorman shot back. "Or *prove* that he didn't win it at Thistledown."

Gruebner's face turned scarlet. "Six men, Mike! Six men shot by Dempsey. We could dig through the backgrounds of those men and, by God, I *know* we could come up with connections. Max Godansky . . . dies with a gun in his hand before he can tell Daley and Winshaw what he knows about the hijacking scheme. Joey Crespi dies with a gun in his hand, and I'll bet my balls that Crespi came to Cleveland to try and muscle in on the action. So, okay, maybe we can't prove without a shadow of doubt that Dempsey shot those men in cold blood and fixed up the scene to make it look justifiable. But you get the picture. Do I have to draw a diagram, Mike?"

Blackman made a move toward the door. "Goddamnit, it's not our job to try Dempsey."

"Isn't it?" Gruebner moved to the door and leaned back against it. "I want to say something before you go screaming for the district attorney. Open this can of worms in front of the grand jury and you can kiss what's left of the law in this town good-bye. There won't be a cop in this city who could walk down a street without somebody spitting at him. Think about it, Dave. You're the guy with the district that's going to be the first to blow."

It was suddenly very quiet in the room. Somebody laughed down the hall and a door slammed. The sounds seemed amplified, exaggerated.

"What do you suggest, Dutch?"

"Yes," Blackman said, the words barely audible, a hissing sound through thin lips. "What do you suggest — a medal? A desk job? Exactly what kind of whitewashing do you have in mind? We're here to enforce the *law*. The *law*, goddamnit, not the social apparatus."

No one was leaving and Gruebner knew it. He walked away from the door and sat down at the table. His eyes had a distant look, as though he were seeing things far beyond the narrow confines of the room. He took a cigar from his shirt pocket and rolled it between blunt fingers.

"It may seem funny, but I was a country boy. That's right. Born and bred on a Fairfield County farm. My old man raised pigs, corn, a few chickens. You know, nothing grand, a truck farm, but we were self-sufficient."

"What the hell is this?" Blackman fumed.

"It's important," Gruebner said abstractedly. "Well, we did all right . . . we survived . . . depression, you know, lots of people starving in those days. I had a dog — a big, black Labrador named Gypsy. A great dog, but she learned a bad habit. She learned to kill chickens — our chickens."

A nerve popped along Gorman's jaw, tugging the corner of his lips upward in a spastic snarl.

"I thought Gypsy would change," Gruebner went on in a soft, tired voice, "but my old man said no, the dog had the taste of blood. There was a wild streak in that dog, he said, it would just keep on killing the hens . . . and the hens meant eggs . . . and the eggs meant the mortgage money. I thought I could train old Gypsy, break her of the

266

habit, but it wasn't any use. She went on killing — every night a dead hen. One day, when I was at school, my old man took Gypsy for a run in the woods and blew her head off with a shotgun. The old man didn't put it that way, but he was enforcing the law by which we survived as a family, the social order of survival. It broke my heart and damn near broke his, I imagine, but he did what had to be done."

Blackman coughed delicately and stared at the ceiling. "Dutch," he asked softly, "are you planning to take Dempsey for a run in the woods?"

Gruebner found a kitchen match in the deepest recesses of his pants pocket and struck it on the edge of the chair. He held the flame to the tip of his cigar, toasting it slightly before shoving it in his mouth and lighting it.

"If I was in a position to do it, I would," he said flatly. "Yes. Without a twinge of conscience. On a job — a raid — an operation like last night. Yes. I would do it . . . and so would you, Dave, so would you. It would be a mercy, for everyone."

Only they would never have the opportunity to do it, Gorman was thinking. They were too tied in with administration — desk men, planners. It had been a long time since either one of them had been in the field. He could sense their eyes on him, but Gruebner was scowling at his cigar and Blackman was studying the woodwork. It had been an illusion, a feeling. They were watching him not with their eyes, but with their thoughts.

"He's clever," Gorman said. It was difficult to speak properly. His tongue was dry, sticking to the roof of his mouth. "Very thorough in his work. A man like that isn't . . . taken easily."

Gruebner nodded. "I never said it would be easy — only necessary."

They were waiting. Gorman knew that he could walk

out of the room and they wouldn't blame him for it. But to walk out would solve nothing. A decision had to be made — now. The fuse was getting short.

"A smart cop. But sooner or later he'll make a wrong move. He's made mistakes enough to lead to this."

Gruebner removed the cigar from his mouth and examined the smoldering tip. "Yes, Mike. A move — right or wrong. And when he does, you have to be there."

Dondero liked cops. He beamed at every one he saw in the halls, and he knew his way around Central. He didn't need Keeley to guide him, but it pleased him to be seen with the chief of police.

"Hi there, boys," he called out as they passed the robbery division ready room. "Hell of a job you guys did last night. Hell of a job. Anytime you're in my club . . . drinks on the house." He grinned at Keeley. "Or is that okay?"

"It's okay, Sam," the Chief said as they continued on.

Keeley was looking for Gorman and finally found him on the third floor, talking quietly to Gruebner in the hall.

"Mike," Keeley said, "you know Sam Dondero, don't you?"

"Sure," Gorman said, holding out his hand. "How are you, Sam?"

"Great," Dondero replied. "After what you boys did last night I'm feeling on top of the world. Thanks to you, this business is a lot cleaner today." His face fell and he shook his head sadly. "But a couple of things hurt . . . knowin' some of my own people were involved. Guys I trusted, worked with and tried to help. This is a tough business and, Jesus, you learn to take your lumps, but I thought everybody was honest . . . like Charlie Greene and Davis — two good boys — risked their lives tryin' to save that cargo."

"Heroic," Gorman said dryly.

"Damn right. Greene with a busted foot, Davis with a cut on his head you wouldn't believe."

"We lost a good man doing it," Gruebner said angrily.

"Yeah," Dondero sighed. He took a handkerchief from his back pocket and wiped his nose. "Damn shame. A young kid like that. I was just talkin' to the Chief about it. I'd like to make a little donation to the widow."

"He wasn't married."

Dondero ignored Gorman's interjection. "A coupla thousand bucks . . . in appreciation . . . not a hell of a lot for what he did . . . but every little bit helps."

"We're grateful," Keeley said.

Dondero blew his nose loudly and jammed the handkerchief in his pocket. "Well, I gotta get back to the grind. See you fellas around."

They watched him swagger off down the hall toward the elevator.

"Quite a character," Keeley said. "How do you read him on the hijacking operations, Mike?"

"Guilty as sin."

"Can we nail him?"

"Sooner or later. I'm going to put a man on his tail — full-time."

"Who?"

"James Dempsey."

He went through the motions, putting in his time. He used his lack of a partner as an excuse to stay in the office and catch up on his paperwork. He tried to gauge the atmosphere without being obvious about it. Gorman had called him downstairs before noon to give him the Dondero assignment.

It's a job you can do, Jimmy . . . better than anyone I

*can think of. I want him kept under surveillance, but for
Christ's sake don't be obvious about it. If he thinks we're
scanning his operations he'll lay low . . . he'll be clean as
a saint until we get tired of watching him.*

Dempsey had studied Gorman's face carefully. All he
had seen was a tired man carrying too much of a load.

*I'm going home — finally. Start on this detail first thing
tomorrow, Jim. Spend the day doing your homework.
We're going to bust this hijacking business once and for
all.*

Sure, Dempsey had said, *Sure.*

Dempsey quit at six, just like any other civil servant in
the city. Being on special assignment, he was entitled to
an unmarked police car. He picked one that the narcs had
been using for undercover work, a nondescript green
Chevy.

"She's got more guts than a mule, Jimmy," MacLendon
said. "I had her rebored — dual carbs — there's plenty of
the old moxie under the hood, don't let the body fool ya."

He drove out grinning, but the smile faded quickly.
Angus MacLendon was an old fool, but Gorman wasn't. He
drove slowly toward his apartment, checking the rearview mirror carefully for tails. Two blocks from his place
he made a hard right turn and doubled back to the center
of town — checking, always checking. He was clean. But
he knew. He had the intuition, too, the cop's radar. The
whole thing was falling apart, caving in.

He parked the car on Superior and ate in a Chinese
restaurant of the Tasteless Dynasty. He couldn't have cared
less. He ate mechanically, the way a horse eats, and after
he had paid for the meal he sat for half an hour sipping
tea. It was ten minutes after eight when he walked into
the club on Short Vincent Street and stood at the packed
bar.

270

Nikki was playing her first set of the night for the supper crowd and she spotted him through the smoke. She did her act, singing her love songs, giving fresh meaning to banal words in a throaty voice that promised so much to every man in the room. When she was finished, the pale mauve spotlight went out and she moved to the bar, her body shimmering in skintight sequins.

"I thought you'd phone." There was an edge to her voice. She took one of his cigarettes and he lighted it for her.

"I was busy. A real busy day."

"One lousy call — just to say hello."

"That's how it goes."

She snapped her finger at the bartender and he poured her a martini.

"You have a rotten place, Dempsey. A truly miserable place to sit in all day waiting for a phone call."

"I'll get it cleaned and pressed."

She touched the back of his hand, stroking the fine black hairs that spread down from his wrist.

"Let me find you a new place. Okay? I mean it. Let me pick out a place. I've got good taste."

"Your husband can drive you around while you look."

She scowled, but not enough to crack her makeup. "I made a decision today, Jimmy. It's no good. I'm going to tell Johnny tonight. I'm going to really level with him. It's been a rotten marriage — I know it and he knows it. He'll find some dumb little bunny who goes bananas over biceps and live happily ever after."

Dempsey smiled into his glass and sucked a piece of ice.

"Got it all figured out, Nikki?"

Her martini came and she popped the olive between her teeth.

"Yes. I know what I want."

"Why me?"

She made a low, purring noise. A happy cat sound.

Dempsey signaled for another drink and cast an idle glance at the room. He spotted Dondero talking to a man at one of the center tables. Their eyes met for only a second.

"I'll be back," Dempsey said.

He threaded his way past the tables and down the short passage that led to the men's room. A man was having his shoes shined and another man stood at a urinal. Dempsey recognized both of them as local businessmen. Two honest johns. He crossed to a urinal.

He was washing his hands when Dondero came in.

"How's it goin'?"

"Just fine, Sam."

He took Dempsey's place at the washbasin and dunked his hands under the flowing faucet. "Try the strip steak tonight. It'll melt in your mouth."

"I'm not very hungry. What I need is fresh air."

"Yeah," Dondero said, reaching for a towel. "Nothin' like fresh air to work up an appetite. Take me, I gotta be around here all the fuckin' night in the smoke. When I get off I go for a drive . . . three in the morning . . . up around Wade Park. I walk a bit . . . breathe a bit . . . then I go someplace and eat a horse. I mean it, eat a fuckin' horse."

"Sounds like a good idea," Dempsey said, starting for the door. "Maybe I'll try it myself one night."

"Do that," Dondero said, taking a comb from his pocket.

Dempsey walked back to the bar just as the spotlights flicked on again. Nikki put a hand on his shoulder and gave it a quick squeeze.

"Stick around."

He shook his head. "No. I'm out on my feet."

"Should I come by later?"

"No. Tomorrow."

"Bright and early," she said, blowing him a kiss.

He watched her move to the piano, lights darting off the sequins. They were all alike, he thought, always after something, always putting on the pressure. They thought they paid for the privilege with bed games.

Dempsey's apartment was a miserable place. She was right about that. A hole. Dempsey lay on the bed, fully clothed, watching the reflected lights of passing cars move slowly across the dark ceiling. He tried to visualize the type of apartment John W. Martin would live in when he got to Rio — or Caracas, or Mexico City — but he couldn't focus on it. His thoughts kept slipping away from John W. Martin to Officer James Dempsey — and Inspector Gorman — and Sam Dondero. He tried to think of the future, but what was happening *now* kept crowding the thoughts out of his head. He sat up after a while and paced the room, watching the clock. It seemed to take forever for the hour hand to reach three. When it did, the telephone rang twice and then was silent. He was out the door before the sound had faded.

It took him fifteen minutes to get to Wade Park. He passed the dark, mist-shrouded buildings of the university and parked on a dead-end street that had a fine view of the city. It was a lovers lane in the summertime, but the only car that was there tonight was a white Eldorado. He waited until he heard a car door slam, then he got out, lit a cigarette and flicked the match into the bushes.

"Funny you should come in tonight," Dondero said. He stood in the road behind Dempsey, his squat body encased in a camel's hair overcoat. "I was hopin' you would."

"Vibrations," Dempsey said. "Maybe we're on the same wavelength."

"Yeah. What've they got you doin' these days, Jimmy?"

"Trucks. They want the guy who runs the trucks off the road."

Dondero laughed softly. "Interesting. You got any clues?"

"Sure. We're on a hot trail."

"Is that so? I feel sorry for the guy. You know, when a trail's hot a guy gotta be pretty smart to cover his tracks. Now, if I was that guy I'd be plenty worried." He walked up to Dempsey and stood beside him, hands thrust into his pockets. "Yeah . . . plenty worried. You know, like I'd worry about the people around me. I wouldn't want nobody with me that maybe could get bent. You know what I mean?"

"Sure," Dempsey said. "One weak link and it's twenty to life for the man we're after."

Dondero whistled through his teeth. "You know, Johnny Davis is a good kid. Jesus, I love him like a brother — but he's soft, Jimmy. A real softie under all that muscle. He's a kid who'd be putty in the wrong hands."

"That's too bad."

"Yeah. It's a shame. A cryin' shame. I wish you'd talk to him before the wrong people get to him and make him sweat."

Dempsey took a deep breath. The air was cold, the mist going into his lungs like needles. "I'd be happy to do that for you, Sam, but I'm going to retire. I thought I might go to South America. I'll need some traveling money."

"Oh, sure, a trip like that ain't cheap. How much do you figure you'll need?"

"Twenty-five big ones. Say half now, the rest when I talk to your friend."

Dondero stirred some gravel with the toe of his shoe.

His shoes were black and pointy, out of style, but they suited Dondero.

"Tell you what, Jimmy. You gotta have this little talk right away. I mean, it can't wait too long. He'll be on the docks tomorrow night. Nice and quiet out on that dock around two, three in the morning. Know what I mean? Well, for a favor like that I don't fuck around. I got twenty on me right now. You take it an' I'll owe you five."

"Forget the five," Dempsey said. "Give it to your favorite charity."

"Yeah . . . why not? Make some orphans happy." He drew his right hand out of his pocket as he walked away. A thick envelope fell at Dempsey's feet, but he didn't stoop to pick it up until he heard the door of the Eldorado slam and Dondero drive away.

Between the hours of three and six that morning, Inspector Gorman slept fitfully, tossing and turning as he struggled in and out of dreams, none of which he could remember when he woke up every twenty minutes or so. His wife lay beside him, unable to help him, but sharing his anxieties — whatever they were.

"Are you all right, Mike?" she asked when he bolted upright.

"Sure," he said. "Just a bad dream."

"Are you worried about something?"

"Sure, everybody's worried about something. Go to sleep."

He'd go under again until the dreams woke him. He gave up the struggle at dawn, put on his robe and went down to the kitchen. Annie thought of going down too, but she had been through episodes of tension and worry with him and she knew that if he wanted her company he would ask for it. She rolled over, grateful that he was out of the bed, and fell into a deep, untroubled sleep.

Sam Dondero sat in the kitchen of an Italian restaurant in Cleveland Heights sharing a huge platter of *spaghetti alla Fiorentina* with Guido Franchini. The restaurant was one of seven that Franchini had a piece of in the Cleveland area, Dondero owning a few pieces of his own.

"It's a problem, you know," Dondero said in between mouthfuls. "His wanting to take off really threw me."

"Let him go," Franchini said, winding the pasta delicately on his fork. "Wish him a good trip."

Dondero frowned as he chewed. "I dunno. Out of sight . . . who knows what a man will do . . . right, Guido? The whole thing about somebody crazy as he is, you never know where he is, what he's doing."

"I could get you a soldier. He is in Detroit and I could have him here by noon. A very good man, Sam."

Dondero thought about it. He took another helping of spaghetti and continued to think about it. He could picture Dempsey coming along the deserted platform toward the little office where Johnny Davis would be seated. He could picture Dempsey shooting Davis in the head and he could picture the soldier, whatever he looked like, stepping out of the shadows and giving it to Dempsey in the back.

"Not a bad idea, Guido. I think you're right about this. I need a soldier. I need a real good man."

Guido Franchini reached across the steaming platter and picked up a wicker-covered bottle of Chianti. "You will get a good one, Sam. You will get the best."

Dempsey counted his money, neat piles of one-hundred-dollar bills spread out across the table. Cash on hand

— thirty thousand dollars. A lot of money. A large, leather suitcase was on the bed. He had slit the lining with a razor blade and now he carried the money over and laid it in the bottom of the case. When it had all been packed in and the lining replaced there was no noticeable bulge at all. It was a neat job. He smoked and drank a cup of tea before starting the ticklish job of gluing the lining back in place with rubber cement, making sure that the join was invisible to the naked eye. It was his new safe deposit box, he thought. When he had finished, he went into the bathroom and took a shower. The alternating blasts of hot and cold water invigorated him like a good night's sleep. He had to be on his toes. There was a lot to be done — the bank at ten, the travel agency, pack, get out to the airport — a great many things to do. By this time the following morning he would be . . . where? Mexico City? Rio? It didn't matter. All that mattered was that he would be long, long gone.

Somewhere in the apartment house an alarm clock clanged hysteria and a hand groped to shut it off. It was six o'clock in the morning. A new day. He wondered if he would make it all the way through.

There had been no argument from Johnny. Nikki had told him bluntly that she was leaving him and he had done nothing except stare at her. He hadn't said a word — no tears, no pleading — he had simply gone into the living room and drunk himself into oblivion. He was still there, sprawled out on the couch, when Nikki left the apartment at seven-fifteen. She took nothing with her. There was nothing she wanted to take. It was a quarter to eight when she rang Dempsey's bell.

"I told you I'd be early," she said.

Dempsey blocked the doorway. The suitcase lay open on the bed, partially filled with clothes.

"I was just going out," he said casually. "I'll buy you a cup of coffee." He closed the door gently in her face, put on his suit jacket and a light tan raincoat, then joined her in the hall. She was shocked and angry.

"What the hell was that for? Do you have another woman in there?"

He smiled at her. "The room's a mess."

"It's always a mess."

His moods again. What did this one mean?

He didn't answer. They had reached the first-floor hallway and he ushered her along it and out into the street.

She shivered slightly and pressed closer to him. "Where do you dine in this part of the world?"

"Two blocks over and one block down. Produce market . . . smell of fresh vegetables in the air . . . and coffee and donuts."

"I told Johnny," she said. "It's all over." She looked for a response from him. There was none.

Gorman watched them cross the street. He had been parked one block down from the apartment house since seven o'clock. He was driving his own car, a 1970 Pontiac, and wore a dark blue suit that gave him middle-class anonymity. He put down the newspaper that he had been holding rather than reading and started the car.

"What do you see in this place?" Nikki said, crinkling her nose.

"I see tomatoes . . . potatoes . . . green beans . . ."

"It's enough to put you off food for life."

It was a commercial market and it was the tag end of the day for the produce wholesalers. The jobbers and the small market owners had been there at four in the morning, loading their trucks, haggling over prices, and now

278

thrifty housewives sought the bargains of wholesale prices.

Dempsey got a container of coffee and a cruller from a little mobile stand. She declined. He started walking, looking at the food.

A fat little man wearing three sweaters and a dirty yellow ski cap hawked lettuce, holding a bright green head in each hand.

"Let-tuce, ladies . . . fresh let-tuce . . . fresh this morning . . . let-tuce . . . let-tuce . . ."

"How about it?" Dempsey said.

Nikki stared at him, uncomprehending. "How about what?"

"Lettuce. You can't beat that."

"What would I do with it?"

Dempsey stepped over to the man and handed him a five-dollar bill.

"Two heads, and a big shopping bag — with handles."

"Sure," the man said. "I got tomatoes too, nice, fat tomatoes."

"Give me half a dozen." He waited patiently while the man stuffed lettuce and tomatoes in a large brown bag.

"What *is* this?" Nikki was confused as Dempsey handed her the bag.

"Tomatoes and lettuce. How about some apples?"

She was uneasy. Dempsey was doing ordinary, sensible things that made no sense at all and it was unnerving. The bottom of the bag rubbed against her hand and the smell of the market, the pushing, jostling crowd of women, depressed her. Dempsey held onto her arm and steered her to another stall where giant stalks of celery lay stacked like cordwood.

"You like celery, don't you?"

Dempsey faced her, cupping her chin in his hand. "I'm sending you home."

She pulled violently away from him, clutching the bag to her breast the way a woman would clasp a child to protect it from harm.

"Are you out of your mind?"

"No, baby . . . you're going home. You recognized that it was a mistake. So you went shopping just to make up for the things you said . . . went to the market when everything was nice and fresh. You want to fix him a nice salad and make him happy . . ."

She wanted to scream. He was doing this crazy thing to her.

"Insane . . . you must be insane . . ." she said.

". . . and he says — that's swell, baby, because you were a real bitch last night."

"Oh, my God, what are you doing to me?" Her voice was a wail.

He stared at her a moment and smiled. "Nikki, this is where the bus stops, and this is how you get off."

She grabbed him before he could walk away. The bag tilted under her arm, spilling tomatoes on the ground.

"What happened?" she sobbed. "Jesus . . . everything was all right with — "

"I'll tell you what happened," he said coldly. "Somebody changed the rules of the game. In fact, it's a different game. The new rules will be distributed shortly."

"Game?" she shrieked. "I don't know about your god-damn game! I love you, Jimmy . . . and you're killing me!"

A few shoppers paused to stare, but not for long. She was probably torn up about the price of tomatoes. Who wasn't?

He gave her a distant smile. "No, baby, I'm not killing you. I just turned out to be a fireman after all — in and out of the burning house. Go home, Nikki. Go home."

And then he was gone, swallowed up by the crowd. She stared blankly into a prism of tears and let the bag fall at her feet.

At ten minutes after ten o'clock, Dempsey walked into a branch of the Cleveland Trust on Woodland Avenue and withdrew thirty-five thousand dollars in cash from the savings account of John W. Martin. The teller packed the money, all of it in one-hundred-dollar bills, into a stout manila envelope.

"Be careful with all this cash, Mr. Martin."

Dempsey assured the young woman that he would be very careful. He walked out of the bank with the envelope under his arm and did not notice the tall man in the blue suit two blocks away on the other side of the street.

So he had money stashed away, Gorman thought. He was not surprised. He assumed that it was under a different name. It would be simple to find out — that could wait. The only important thing at the moment was keeping Demsey in view . . . both by car and on foot.

10:30 A.M. D. into Acme cleaners . . . picked up suit.

11:10 A.M. D. bought suit bag . . . Jackson Bros., Euclid.

12:30 P.M. D. stopped for lunch . . . McDonald's.

1:10 P.M. D. into Wilson Bros. Travel Agency, Prospect Ave. Stayed one half-hour. No observable transaction.

2:30 P.M. D. entered his apt. house.

It was now 3:30 P.M. and Dempsey had not left his apartment. Gorman got out of his car and walked to a police call box one block from the apartment house. He leaned close to the telephone pole, almost hiding behind it, and put in a call to Blackman.

"Dave? He's getting ready to skip. I want the man in the Wilson Brothers Travel Agency over on Prospect interviewed right away. Dempsey talked to him for half an hour."

"Okay, Mike."

"And check with the Cleveland Trust — Woodland and Fortieth branch. He made a transaction this morning. Teller's a short, plump blond with a beehive hairdo. I doubt if he used his own name."

"I'll get on it right away. Anything else?"

"Yes. I want an unmarked car with a radio. I'm at call box number 5736. Have the driver honk when he passes me, park around the corner, and leave the keys on the vizor."

"Will do."

Blackman hung up. Gorman stood by the pole for twenty minutes. No one entered or left Dempsey's place. When a cream-colored Ford honked and turned the corner, Gorman stepped away from the call box and walked slowly after it.

It was a narcotics surveillance car, the radio hidden under the front seat, the aerial built into the trunk so that no whiplash antenna gave the car away. Gorman drove the car around the block and parked down the street from Dempsey's green Chevy.

"Gorman calling Central . . . get me Inspector Blackman . . ."

The radio crackled with routine calls — and then Blackman came on, speaking quickly and cryptically.

"Name is Martin, John W., amount thirty-five thousand. Discussions centered on flights to South America tonight. Varig flight 40, departure 5:15, to Rio. TWA to Mexico City, departure 8 P.M., flight 302. Inquired if tickets could be bought at airport. Negative on Varig."

"Thanks, Dave."

So it was eight o'clock to Mexico City, unless Dempsey went out soon and bought a ticket for Rio. Gorman slouched down on the seat, folded his arms across his chest and waited, thinking about James Dempsey — and Martin, John W. If Dempsey tried to leave the country they would have to stop him. Could the thirty-five thousand dollars be traced? No way. Not cash. But what was a cop doing with that bundle? Blood money. The wages of death.

"Martin," he said quietly. "John W. Martin . . . John W. Martin." He tried to drive the name into his consciousness and force James Dempsey out. It would make it a lot easier if he could think of him that way.

Dempsey finished packing his suitcase and placed it by the door. He then sat on the bed and, using a razor blade, slit the leather lining on the bottom of the garment bag he had purchased that morning. He laid one hundred and fifty one-hundred-dollar bills inside the flap and then glued the leather back into place. He hung three suits and two sport coats in the bag and draped it over the suitcase. There was a question nagging at him. It was not clear, but it was something to do with this. He almost had it: why was he bothering? And then it faded away and he could not remember it.

"That's that," he said, then wandered through the apartment. He was leaving some old shirts and slacks, a worn-out suit with a cigarette burn in the lapel, and other odds and ends. He tossed his holster and gun-cleaning equipment into a wastebasket along with two boxes of .38 cartridges and shoved the Colt Python into the pocket of his raincoat. He'd toss it into the river on the way to the airport. He kept his badge, taking it off the leather flap and slipping the heavy gold shield inside his breast pocket. When he was through checking the place he sat down in the kitchen and went through the balance of the money he had drawn from the bank. He counted out five thousand dollars, wrapped them in a sheet of plain white paper, and stuffed them into an envelope. He did the same with another five thousand. One envelope he addressed to Claire, the other to Mrs. Della Rich; he estimated the weight and placed stamps on them.

Done. Nothing left to do but wait — and make certain he would get to the airport without any trouble. He had no illusions. Gorman had someone out there or he wasn't the cop he knew him to be. He waited until six-thirty and then picked up the phone and dialed Central.

"This is Dempsey. Who's got the duty?"

"Inspector Gruebner."

"Get him for me." He carried the phone over to the window. A cream-colored Ford was parked three lengths ahead of his own. A narc squad car, Dempsey mused. Why didn't they just paint a big sign on it, Unmarked Police Vehicle.

"Gruebner speaking."

Dempsey looked away. "Hi, Dutch . . . Dempsey."

There was a pause. Then, "Where've you been all day, Jimmy?"

"Home. Making a lot of phone calls. Listen, Dutch . . . I've come up with something on the hijackings. I've got to talk to Mike right away."

"I'll try and get hold of him, Jimmy. Any message?"

"Yeah. I've got a guy on the hook who'll play ball . . . a freight loader out at the airport. I'm going out there now to pick him up. Now write this down, Dutch . . . it's very important. I'm going to drive the guy to Metropolitan Park Drive and Brookway. Have Mike meet us there in, say, an hour and a half."

Dempsey hung up and waited. It took ten minutes. Then the Ford pulled away from the curb and he stood watching it until its taillights were lost in the traffic.

284

Gorman drove ten blocks then parked at a call box and phoned Gruebner.

"We'll have to stay off the radio, Dutch. He's got a set in his car."

"I take it you don't buy what he's selling."

"No. But I don't want to crowd him, so stay clear."

"Are you sure you can handle this by yourself, Mike?"

"Yes — my way. I'm going to the airport now. I want to get there ahead of him."

"Okay," Gruebner sighed, "but if he gives you any trouble . . . damn it, Mike . . . I still can't think of Jimmy that way. Giving trouble, I mean. This whole thing . . . it's like a rotten dream."

"I know," Gorman said. "But it isn't a dream. We all have to wake up and face it. God knows, it's real enough to *him*."

Dempsey kept the gun. He made that decision before driving across the bridge that spanned the dark and fetid waters of the Cuyahoga. There had been menace in the lights behind him. He didn't think that he was being followed, but there was no way he could be certain. The gun was his only friend now. There were things to do before he said good-bye to it. Only he had trouble remembering them. What was happening to his memory?

The airport was jammed, and he was grateful for that. He parked the car and joined the throng, just another businessman leaving town with a suitcase in his hand and a garment bag draped over one shoulder. He walked to the international carriers section, showed his passport and health certificate, and bought his ticket.

"Have a nice trip, Mr. Martin," the ticket agent said with mechanical politeness.

"Thanks." He watched his bags being tagged and

waited until he saw them glide out of sight on the rubber conveyor system.

"How much time do I have?"

The agent looked up at the clocks that showed the time in all parts of the world. "They'll be boarding in fifteen minutes, Gate 12."

Dempsey nodded his thanks and started to walk down the causeway, toward the whine and roar of the big jets. Then he saw Gorman. He stopped, letting a flow of excited people pass by him. Gorman seated in one of the lounges up ahead. Dempsey saw only a tall man in a chair, a newspaper held up to his face, but he had known this man for too many years. He knew how he sat — how he crossed one leg over the other, how he scratched an ankle from time to time. He *knew* him. Gorman! And when he saw Gorman, Dempsey remembered what he had to do.

Come on, Gorman thought. Keep moving . . . take ten more steps. Dempsey took a sharp turn in the crowd, right, into a restroom.

Gorman tossed the paper aside and pushed his way against the stream of happy travelers. A voice echoed over the PA system.

"United Airlines flight number 625 for Los Angeles and Honolulu now boarding at Gate 11."

The press grew stronger. A small child tugged excitedly at Gorman's leg, almost tripping him. He disengaged the child's hands as gently as possible and then raced into the restroom, drawing his gun as he went.

Dempsey wasn't there. Gorman knew it the moment he went through the door with the gun in his hand. He could tell by the shocked look in the eyes of a young sailor shaving at one of the washbasins. The sailor had a razor poised near his cheek and his round, frightened eyes went from the gun to the back window, open to the night breeze.

Gorman shoved the gun into his holster and darted back into the corridor.

"TWA flight number 302 for Mexico City and Bogatá now boarding at Gate 12."

Gorman leaned against the wall and watched the crowd. Dempsey could have gone out of the window and then doubled back. He could move with the crowd and get on the plane, but the idea seemed unlikely. He was a man on the run now and he knew it. Dempsey had caught too many men in his life who had done stupid things at the last minute. He would never join the ranks of the foolish. Gorman started to run down the long corridor toward the parking lot. An elderly man in a loud sport coat put out a hand and tried vainly to slow him down.

"Hey!" the man shouted. "Where the hell's the Sunshine Tour?"

Dempsey drove back toward the city, holding the car to the speed of the traffic. As he drove he thought of his bags moving slowly off into the bowels of the building, into the belly of the plane. The thought amused him. All that money . . . all that time . . . the sweat and the blood . . . all for nothing. He turned on the radio. He had to keep track of the calls. Nothing yet . . . all routine. A robbery in progress at a store on West Twenty-fifth. A request for an ambulance and tow truck on the Willow Freeway . . . car 705 signing off . . . coming downtown . . . car 603 responding to a prowler call on Mayfield Road. Sounds of the night.

"APB all cars . . . be on lookout for dark green Chevrolet model sedan 1969, license M Mary, J Jasper 6910. This is an unmarked police vehicle. Do not detain . . . repeat . . . do not detain. Report position only and keep under surveillance."

287

Dempsey stared ahead. He would stick to the freeways and hope a cruiser or a motorcycle cop didn't get lucky and pull in behind him. He would be okay if the traffic stayed heavy. And then what? He had no plans . . . he had nowhere to go.

"This is Inspector Gorman calling . . . come on in, Jim. Do you read me, Dempsey? *Come on in.*"

Dempsey reached for the mike under the dash and pressed the button.

"Fuck off!" he said. He turned off the set. The man you want, he thought, is on his way to Mexico City. I saw him off at the airport fifteen minutes ago. If you want Martin, grab a plane and go after him, but don't take up *my* time. I'm working on a case, remember?

John W. Martin was far out in space, riding a golden bird to the land of the sun. He had a smile on his lips and fifty thousand dollars within reach of his hand. All that Officer James Dempsey had was a gun — and a job.

"I'm the best man you've got, Inspector." He clenched the wheel until his knuckles turned white.

He parked the car in a deserted factory yard a quarter-mile down the road from the Dondero Lines terminal. He took the Python out of his raincoat pocket and checked it. The cylinder was full and there was one empty chamber under the hammer. He had the spare cartridge in his pocket and dropped it in. Six bullets — six men. Well, he thought, there might not be six men there. The only one he wanted was Sam Dondero. One bullet — one man. One man — one shot. It paid to be thrifty. He got out of the car, pushed the gun into the waistband of his pants, then took off his raincoat and tossed it onto the front seat. He didn't want a coat flapping around him while he was doing what had to be done. He could see the lights on the Dondero loading dock, a long way across a dark expanse of factory yards and empty parking lots, and he walked toward them — quickly, the way a man walks when he has something important to do.

Johnny Davis was angry. He sat in his little office on the loading dock and stared out at the night. He had a long shift ahead of him and nothing to look forward to at the end of it. Nothing but a crazy wife — a wife who had walked out on him and then had come back — hysterical, screaming, out of her skull. Maybe she'd kill herself, but he didn't think she was the type. Their marriage had committed suicide. She had done nothing all day but moan the bastard's name. Dempsey . . . James Dempsey . . . He sat stiffly in his chair and thought about Dempsey, picturing him in his mind — tall, dark-haired sonofabitch. He'd seen the bastard plenty of times, nosing around the docks, looking for stolen cargo. A gumshoe, a nothing. He spat between his feet and tried to get his mind off Nikki and Dempsey, but it was hard to do. He kept seeing them together, fucking on *his* bed . . . wadding *his* pillow to put under her ass . . .

"Bastard."

He heard Dondero laughing in the back. Talking to some creep who had shown up that evening, a sallow-faced man with eyes like glass beads. Dondero had introduced him as a Mr. Karbo from New York. The man had smiled slightly when Dondero had said that. The man had thought it was funny. *Mr. Karbo — from New York.* Very funny. A private joke. Mr. Karbo carried a small, black bag and Dondero had said that Mr. Karbo was in the plant protection business and wanted to know if they kept a gun in the loading dock office. Davis had opened the desk drawer and brought out the old Ruger's Blackhawk .44 and had shown it to him. Karbo had smiled at the gun.

"Bastard."

Davis swiveled his chair around and took the gun out of the drawer. It was old and heavy, but he liked it. He stuck it inside his belt when he made rounds early in the morning, especially in the winter when bums crept into the empty trailers to keep from freezing to dea . All that he had to do was to show the gun and the bums ran off. It was a frightening-looking piece, big as a cannon.

Davis had the gun in his hand when he heard the footsteps coming up the wooden stairs onto the dock. They were slow steps . . . one careful foot after the other . . . the footsteps of a creeper. He thumbed back the hammer and moved quickly out of his chair and through the open doorway of the office, and there, not ten feet away, was James Dempsey . . . Officer James Dempsey . . . wife-screwer James Dempsey. And he was smiling.

"Hello, Davis."

Davis fired. He didn't aim, or even raise the gun very much — he just pulled the trigger. The big revolver bucked in his hand and the slug tore a six-foot splinter out of the platform and went howling away toward Lake Erie. He never fired another. Dempsey's right hand came up from his side in a blur of movement — black gun in a big white fist, leveling dead center. The bullet slammed into Davis at the joining of the ribs and kicked him backward to the scarred planking.

"One," Dempsey said. He moved cautiously past the body and then ran into the warehouse, past a ten-foot pyramid of new tires and a wall of paint cans, toward the glass-walled offices in the back.

Mr. Karbo came out of Dondero's office five seconds after the first shot with a Walther P-38 in his right hand and a .45 Colt in his left. He crouched in the shadows of a fork-lift truck and started shooting when Dempsey was ten feet inside the warehouse. He pressed the triggers of both guns and watched a paint can burst apart and saw the man he was shooting at stagger and fall to one knee. He stepped away from the shadows to finish the job — it was a bad mistake. Dempsey put two shots in his belly. Mr. Karbo dropped his guns and sat down, pressing his long, thin hands against the two holes in his gray suit. He was still sitting there, dying without a murmur, when Dempsey limped past him and lurched into Dondero's office to fire two bullets into a cringing, whimpering creature hiding under a desk.

Gorman took the freeway at eighty miles an hour and burned out the tires braking to a stop in front of the Dondero Freight Company warehouses. As he climbed out of his car he could hear the dull thud of a gun being fired somewhere in back of the dark buildings.

"Oh, Christ," he said, running. He could hear more shots.

He saw the sprawled body of Johnny Davis. Gorman kicked the big Ruger when he ran onto the dock. The blue-gray revolver skittered away from him and he stopped quickly to pick it up as he continued running toward the open warehouse doors. The firing had stopped, but thin tendrils of smoke drifted lazily toward banks of fluorescent lights dangling from the ceiling. Dempsey was coming toward him, one slow step after the other, blood spurting from his left thigh. A gun was in his hand, dangling from one crooked finger.

"Mike . . ." he said sadly. "Mike . . . I . . ." . .

Gorman raised the revolver with both hands, aimed carefully for Dempsey's heart, and pulled the trigger.

He didn't watch him die. He heard him fall and he knew that he had not missed. He walked slowly back along the dock and looked down at the body there, the arms outflung, the dead eyes staring at the black sky. He wiped the handle of the Ruger clean on his pants and then knelt beside Davis and pressed the gun into his right hand, molding the still-warm fingers around the butt and through the trigger guard. When he was done, he continued to kneel there. He was still kneeling when car 704 arrived to investigate the sound of shots in the area. A routine call.

They buried him without fanfare. It was the type of funeral that he would have wanted, Gorman thought. No one at the gravesite but the people who had known him well. His wife and his children. Chief Keeley. Gruebner. Blackman. Carl Rich and himself. No banners and no bugles. Just a few words for a tired man being laid to his rest.

When it was over, when the plain wood coffin had sunk from sight, Gorman walked slowly across the grass toward the road. Carl Rich kept step beside him.

"I should have been with him that night," Rich said.

Gorman shook his head. "No, Carl. He had to do it his way. It was something he had to do alone."

"Shot in the line of duty," Rich said quietly. "I guess it makes up for — a lot."

"It helps, Carl. It helps." He quickened his pace and left Rich behind. Tears stabbed at his eyes and he walked faster, fighting them back. There was no time for tears. It was over and done. His car was waiting and there would be calls coming in. There would be things to do. He found himself running down the hill toward the road while far above him clouds drifted in over the brooding trees.

the end